Windswept

Windswept

A DIGGER DOYLE MYSTERY

Rosalie Rayburn

Book design by Sara DeHaan, DeHaanArts.com

Cover photos: Istock.com/bojanstory; Istock.com/GoergioMagini; Wikimedia Commons. Title page illustration: detail, George Elbert Burr, Desert Sentinels, Apache Trail, Arizona, c. 1930, NGA 169510.jpg; Wikimedia Commons

Publisher's Cataloging-in-Publication Data

Names: Rayburn, Rosalie, author.
Title: Windswept : a Digger Doyle Mystery 2024 / Rosalie Rayburn.
Description: Albuquerque, NM: Rayburn Publications, 2024.
Identifiers: Library of Congress Control Number: 2024921642
    ISBN: 979-8-9892110-2-9 (paperback) | ISBN: 979-8-9892110-3-6 (ebook)
    Subjects: LCSH Hispanic Americans—Fiction. | Lesbians—Fiction. |
    Wind power—Fiction. | New Mexico—Fiction. | Political fiction. |
    Mystery fiction. | BISAC FICTION / Mystery & Detective / Women Sleuths |
    FICTION / Political | FICTION / Romance / LGBTQ+ / Lesbian
    Classification: LCC PS3618 .A93 S86 2024 | DDC 813.6—dc24

To my mother

Chapter 1

Donna Mendez closed her eyes, her heart pounded like a hammer in her chest. Years had gone by but she knew the day would come. She had done everything to stay safe but the fear never went away. Now and then, the dream returned and she relived that hot afternoon, the picnic beside the vast expanse of volcanic rock, the laughter, and then the fight. Watching them disappear among those twisted shapes of stone, and then the sickening anxiety as they searched for her, calling her name over and over again. He said she ran away, but how long do you keep silent, feeling the knowledge corrode your heart?

She kept in touch with the others. They emailed, sometimes a phone call, occasionally an in-person meeting. For a few years she felt almost normal; marrying Alfredo, the birth of her two girls, and her job at the hair salon.

Then Sylvia died.

She used to envy Sylvia's confidence. But after that day she changed. They all changed. Sometimes when she talked to Sylvia on the phone, her friend became weepy. Gradually Sylvia became desperate. Then there was the day when she said, "I can't do this anymore, Donna. I've got to talk to someone!"

"Does your husband know?"

"No, of course not. It would kill him. I need a therapist or something!"

Two weeks later Sylvia's husband called with news that she had died of a heart attack. Donna was pretty sure Sylvia had no history of heart disease. The fear returned. She called Carmen.

"What do you think happened to her?" Donna asked her friend.

Carmen, the calm one, reassured her. "I don't know. I haven't heard from him in a while. I've blocked him on my phone. You should too."

The dreams receded, and the fear subsided. A few more years went by. Her girls grew up and graduated. Carmen called to congratulate them. They talked for an hour. Then, just at the end of their conversation, Carmen said quietly, "I think it's time I talked."

Donna knew what she meant. All at once the fear came flooding back.

Chapter 2

A full moon hung huge and golden above the serrated crest of the mountains. Some people called it a Harvest Moon but in the old Native American tradition, it was the Corn Moon, a sign of plenty and promise. It glowed over the distant foothills and gave the evening a magical air, a good omen for Maria's thirtieth birthday.

The birthday girl emerged from the bathroom dressed in a white silky blouse that showed off her olive skin and a midnight blue skirt that swirled below her knees. They'd spent the day celebrating with family and now it was time to go out for the evening.

Digger looked at her wife, smiling to see the silver choker she'd given Maria gleaming at her neck. She marveled for the umpteenth time at how lucky she was to find this woman and this family after losing her parents.

"You're not dressed yet!" Maria threw up her hands in surprise.

Digger surveyed her black jeans and scuffed cowboy boots. "I thought this was good enough for Frankie's."

Smiling, Maria shook her head. "What about the shirt I got you last week? And maybe those earrings I gave you last Christmas."

Digger put on her newest jeans and the shirt Maria suggested. She peered into the bathroom mirror and ran her fingers through the blond hair that flopped over one eye. Next, she picked up one of the silver earrings.

She was inserting it in her left ear when Maria said, "Oh, I meant to tell you, I invited Carmen to meet us at the bar."

Carmen Lawlor was a state representative from Santa Fe who helped guide Maria during her first week at the Roundhouse where the New Mexico legislature convened.

"What?" Digger spun around and dropped the earring. "It's your birthday! I thought we could have a night like we used to!"

It seemed like they'd hardly had any time together since Maria's election. When she wasn't at work, Maria was talking to constituents or rushing to meetings in Santa Fe. Digger's new job had her working late most evenings too. Her editor always had questions.

"I know," Maria said. "But Carmen *really* wants to meet you. She's planning to make a big announcement soon and hopes you could cover it for the paper."

Maria's words didn't make Digger any happier about the prospect of Carmen joining them. Sure, she was a bright star at the legislature, one of those up-and-coming faces making a name for herself in the climate debate. Ordinarily, Digger would have jumped at the opportunity to have an exclusive interview with her, but tonight?

On Maria's birthday?

At the bar where they met?

She put on her pout face. "We could have gotten together at a straight bar somewhere. Frankie's is special."

Maria came up behind her and wrapped her arms around Digger. Their eyes met in the mirror—Maria's black as olives, Digger's sparkling blue like her Irish grandmother's.

Maria gave *the* smile. "I knew you'd bring me to Frankie's because you're sentimental."

Maria was right. She was sentimental but she hated to admit it.

Half an hour later, Digger pulled her Subaru into the parking lot in front of the scruffy strip mall. Frankie's, the funky little women's bar had been there since the 1990s, somehow managing to cling to life unchanged while everything around it moved on.

Digger had told her friend Lexi, Frankie's owner, that it was Maria's birthday and she was happy to see a rainbow of crepe-paper flowers festooning the archway at the entrance. Party music blared from inside. She shot a glance at Maria.

"You ready for this?" Digger squeezed her hand.

Maria nodded. "Let's go."

They walked into the bar arm in arm, waving to a crowd of familiar faces. Lexi spotted them and signaled the DJ to switch Shania Twain for a rock rendition of 'Happy Birthday'. A chorus of voices joined in. Maria stared around, open-mouthed, eyes shining with tears. She turned and kissed Digger.

For Digger, it was one of those moments where she wanted time to stop. She'd had a lot of those moments lately as she felt the old dread, the inexplicable fear that a radical change was lurking, ready to pounce. Maybe it was the article, another shooting, another close escape. Maria didn't seem concerned, but *she* was. She closed her eyes and yielded to the kiss until the singing subsided and the country music returned.

Lexi beckoned them over to the bar. "First one's on me. The usual?"

Lexi's spiked hair had streaks of blue tonight, and she wore a tank top that showed off the Celtic tattoos on her shoulders. She slid two bottles of Corona across the bar, flashing a smile at Maria. "Hey, birthday girl, you're looking good. How's it feel to be a big important politician up in Santa Fe?"

Maria laughed. "Thanks. I'm still an art teacher. Politics is supposed to be a part-time gig, but it keeps me busy."

Lexi leaned her ample chest over the bar, hunched close to them. "Is that sleaze-bag developer Danny Murphy still hassling you?"

Maria shot Digger a look before she answered. "He's still pissed that he lost to me, but I won and I've moved on."

Lexi eyed Digger. "I heard about your new job too. You back to being a reporter again, huh? You gonna keep an eye on Murphy?"

Digger shrugged. "Maybe. It's a small online operation and we're stretched pretty thin. I cover a little of everything; business, politics, environment, crime. Whatever my editor throws at me."

Lexi grinned. "I know you love it."

Lexi was right. She did love it. After a year at a state job with a manipulative boss who was now being investigated for fraud, being a reporter again felt like slipping into a familiar old coat. You knew the feel of the collar on your neck, the way your hands slid comfortably into the pockets, and the reassuring warmth it provides.

"Oh, hey, look! It's Francie and Joan." Maria pointed at a couple of women waving at them from across the bar.

Digger waved back. "Why don't you go say hi to them and get us a table? I'll be over in a minute with the beers."

Maria kissed her on the cheek and rushed to greet their friends.

As soon as she was out of earshot Lexi moved out from behind the bar to stand next to Digger, watching Maria. "You hear about that county commissioner that nearly got shot at last week? The guy pulled up right outside her house?"

Digger knew where this was going. "Yeah. I read about it."

"Stuff like that make you worry about Maria?"

She nodded. "Sure, it does." She didn't want Lexi to know how much she worried. You lose your parents in a car crash and your world changes. There's always the fear it could happen again.

Lexi patted her shoulder. "Just know I'm always here for you. Now go enjoy her birthday."

She thanked Lexi, grabbed the beers, and headed toward the table next to the far wall.

Maria was looking at her phone. As Digger sat, she said, "Carmen messaged. She should be here any minute."

Digger scowled, still resenting the intrusion. "I wish we could have met somewhere else. Women come here to dance, not talk shop."

Maria waved a hand dismissively. "Oh, come on! Don't be a spoilsport. Carmen said she's fine with it. She thought it would be fun!"

Digger took a sip of her beer and glanced toward the entrance. Moments later she noticed a tall, stylish woman appear at the entrance. Light glinted on her dark hair as she stood, surveying the place and presented her ID to Georgie the Texan. They exchanged a few words, Georgie looked over, spotted Digger and Maria, and pointed to their table.

Maria saw Carmen and rushed to greet her. They hugged. Carmen then pulled something from her shoulder bag and presented it to Maria.

Digger had seen Carmen many times on the TV news, or in photos in the papers but she was struck by how uncannily alike they looked; faces the same shape, arching eyebrows, and full lips. Carmen could have been an older sister, she thought.

As they approached, Digger heard Maria say, "Oh, you shouldn't have."

"I thought you could use it to get something for your studio." Carmen smiled and turned to face Digger. "And this must be?"

Digger stood and Maria put an arm around her. "This is my wife, Elizabeth Doyle. Everyone calls her Digger because she's a great investigative reporter."

Carmen clasped Digger's outstretched hand in both of hers.

"I've been looking forward to this for a long time. Maria's said so many great things about you." Her voice was low and resonant, the smile wide and sincere.

Digger hadn't wanted this woman to intrude on her evening with Maria, and she did not even want to like her but as their eyes met, she felt Carmen's genuine warmth and was in awe. She knew instantly why Maria admired her, why many people admired her.

The moment passed and the bar sounds crowded in. She needed to say something.

"I'm glad you could join us. Can I get you a beer or something?"

Carmen surveyed the table, noticed the bottles, and asked for the same. Digger went to the bar and ordered. Lexi produced another Corona and pushed it across to Digger. She nodded over at Carmen. "Who's that with Maria?"

"She's a state rep. Helped Maria up in Santa Fe."

Lexi shot Digger a skeptical glance. "They look pretty cozy over there. You okay with that?"

Digger looked back at the table where Carmen and Maria sat heads together in animated conversation. A twinge of doubt stirred in her gut.

"Yeah, Lex. I'm fine with it," she said, failing to keep the edge out of her voice.

Lexi held up hands in surrender. "Okay, okay! I'm just always looking out for you, remember."

When she got to the table Maria and Carmen were deep in conversation. Digger put the bottle down, sat, and put an arm around Maria.

"Thanks." Carmen nodded at her. "Hey, since you're a reporter I wondered if you'd be interested in covering an event I'm planning."

Digger had been expecting the question and was moved by Carmen's enthusiasm, but Lexi's words echoed in her head. Was Lexi right to be suspicious of Carmen? No, that was ridiculous, she told herself. She shrugged. "I guess you better tell me about it first."

Carmen leaned on her elbows, bringing her face closer to Digger and Maria. "Look," she said, fervently, "we are in a serious crisis because of climate change. You remember the fires last year–tens of thousands of acres burned. Hundreds of homes were destroyed! And the drought! We had half the normal amount of rainfall this monsoon season. It's going to get worse, much worse unless we do something and do it fast. That's why I will propose legislation to get the ball rolling and Maria has helped me with the research. She's done an awesome job!"

Digger knew about Carmen's politics and her polarizing reputation in Santa Fe. Environmental groups loved her but New Mexico was a state that depended heavily on revenue from the oil and gas industry. Her call to quit reliance on fossil fuels had pissed off people with a lot of influence and money.

"Did you know," Carmen continued. "In two weeks, it will be the twentieth anniversary of the opening of the first major wind farm in New Mexico?"

Digger shook her head.

Carmen nodded. "Right. I don't think many people remember that. But I'm planning to use the event and the location to announce a proposal that could put this state on a path that will keep us safe from a real climate disaster."

Face animated, eyes fierce, Carmen jabbed a finger on the table each time she made a point. Digger clenched her teeth. She'd wanted a relaxed evening with her wife, not this speech. Then she caught Maria's pleading expression.

"Okay," she agreed. "I'll run it by my editor and see what he says."

"It'll be a terrific story, you wait!"

In the background, the music switched from country to salsa. As the Latin rhythm kicked in, Carmen's face brightened and she clapped her hands, "Oh, I love salsa!" She looked at Maria and raised an eyebrow. "Do you dance?"

Maria shrugged. "Of course. Been dancing since I could walk." She flashed a smile at Digger. "It's my birthday, you don't mind, do you?"

Without waiting for an answer, she took Carmen's hand and they sauntered to join the other couples. Digger's heart ached as she watched their feet move in sync, their arms arcing as they turned effortlessly in time to the music. It was like a language they understood, a culture Digger would never truly be part of.

At the end of the set, they walked back to the table, all smiles. Carmen laughed. "Your wife is a wonderful dancer."

"I know." Digger smiled tightly, gripped Maria's hand, and led her back to the dance floor.

Maria leaned close and murmured in her ear. "It's okay," she said sliding her arms around Digger.

Digger felt the reassurance and relaxed. "I just wish I could dance like that with you."

"You dance with me like nobody else and I love it," Maria said, smiling.

When the song ended, they headed back to rejoin Carmen. They found her staring intently at a young woman sitting at a table on the other side of the bar. Tears glinted on Carmen's cheeks.

"Is something wrong?" Maria asked anxiously.

Carmen's eyes closed for a few seconds, her face contorted, then she shook her head. Voice husky, she replied, "No. It's just that woman over there—" A shuddering sigh. "She reminded me of someone I lost a long time ago."

Chapter 3

Two Weeks Later

In eastern New Mexico, the wind blows nearly all the time. It scours the land, sucking scarce moisture from the earth, whipping up swirls of dust and sand that sting the eyes. People say it drives them crazy. There is no escape from the endless battering, the moaning of the wind.

Out on the eastern plains, there are precious few trees to offer cover and the flat terrain stretches on for miles. Out there, ranching has always been a tough, hardscrabble life. But in the last few years, the dwindling number of ranchers and the hardy inhabitants of little towns like Fort Sumner and Melrose have a reason to be thankful for the wind. It's the God-given force that drives the giant blades that generate the power for folks far away, and that brings them a steady check each month.

State Representative Carmen Lawlor's news release announced a ceremony at the Eastern Plains Wind Center where she would unveil a plan to 'revolutionize' the state's renewable energy sector. The event would mark the twentieth anniversary of the wind center opening. The press trip from Albuquerque to the wind farm site was supposed to take around three hours.

Roscoe took one look at the email and scoffed. "You know the oil and gas folks are going to go ballistic over this. Those folks spent a ton of money trying to defeat her at the last election. I don't know how she got reelected."

Roscoe Bremmer was the editor and publisher at *The Searcher,* the online paper where Digger Doyle was easing her way back into journalism.

He shook his head. "If that woman got her way, she'd shut down the coal and natural gas-fired power plants and have everyone riding electric bicycles."

"Well, if she's that controversial, it could be a good story," Digger responded.

Roscoe scowled.

"Come on, Roscoe. You said yourself we need stories that rile people up." She gave him her best 'pretty please' smile.

"Oh hell, alright," he grunted and turned back to his monitor.

On the morning of the trip, Digger parked on Second Street and she and Maria walked the two blocks to the meeting point at High Desert Power and Light. As they rounded a corner, Digger spotted Manny Begay.

Digger grinned at the sight of him. They'd developed a camaraderie when they were reporters at the *Courier.* Before the paper closed, Manny was the hot-shot crime reporter and she covered city politics. After the paper shut, he landed another reporting job in Santa Fe. She worked for the state Cultural Affairs Department. Manny was the guy she turned to when she discovered her new boss was behind a phony solar project scam.

Manny caught sight of them and called. "Hey, Digg! Maria! How you guys doing?"

Digger pointed a finger at his ponytail. "Love the new hairstyle. It suits you," she teased.

"Proud to be Diné." He chuckled. "You look different too."

"New job, new hair." Digger had worn her short blond hair

gelled into spikes for the past few years, she now had it in an asymmetrical style, short on one side and the other flopping down over an eye.

Manny laughed. "Yeah, I heard about your new gig at *The Searcher.* How's it going?"

Digger shrugged. "It's different. Still getting used to it."

Manny gestured at the tall, bulky guy next to him. "This is Jim. He's shooting photos for me today. Any other news people here?"

They looked around and Maria cocked her head at a woman smoking by the edge of the sidewalk. "Is she with us?"

Up until then, Digger hadn't noticed her. Tall, with neatly layered gray hair that complemented her pastel blue pantsuit, the woman caught their look and nodded at them. She tossed her cigarette on the sidewalk, crushed it with one high-heeled shoe, and approached.

She ignored Digger and addressed herself to Maria. "Are you Representative Maria Ortiz? I heard you were going to be on this trip."

Maria shot Digger a look that said, *who the hell is this woman?* Aloud, she said, "Yes, that's me." She gestured at Digger. "And this is my wife, Elizabeth Doyle."

The woman gave a tight smile. "I'm Nancy Harford, I'm doing a piece for radio."

Before Digger could ask which station, another figure emerged from inside the building. Digger recognized her as Joan Bishop, the spokeswoman for High Desert Power and Light. On the few occasions they'd had contact, Digger had found Bishop irritating. The woman had made it clear she didn't consider online papers like *The Searcher* legitimate news sources.

Bishop stopped at the entrance of the building and looked around at them impatiently. "Oh, is this everyone? I expected at least three other reporters and someone from one of the TV sta-tions," she said, her voice clipped. "I'll be riding with you on the bus this morning. We're just waiting for Representative Lawlor." She glanced at her watch, frowned, pulled out her phone, and punched in a number.

The rest of them waited. The conversation was brief and it was clear that Bishop wasn't happy with what she heard. She clicked off her phone, pursed her lips, and shook her head.

"Well," she said, barely containing her frustration. "That was Ms. Lawlor, saying she'd decided to drive. She's on some kind of deadline and needs to be back in Albuquerque by six this evening. She'll meet us at the wind farm."

"Bummer," Manny grunted. "I wanted to interview her before we got to the site."

Digger saw disappointment on Maria's face too. "That's weird. I just talked to her last night, she never mentioned anything about having to drive today."

Bishop shepherded them to the small bus chartered for the event. Digger and Maria sat near the front gazing at the flat tawny colored land as they headed east on Interstate 40. Two hours later they left the freeway and continued for several miles through flat ranch land, past the small town of Fort Sumner, and on through a tiny, dilapidated village. The bus halted in front of a small one-story building that served as the wind farm operations center.

Even though it was October, the gust of wind that hit them as they descended from the bus was warm, like a blast from a hairdryer on medium-high. A tall lean young man with wavy red hair came to greet them.

"Welcome y'all. I'm Jake Reynolds, I'm the site supervisor. If you come inside a minute, I'll tell you a little about this place, then we can go out and see one of the turbines up close."

Joan Bishop interrupted him. "Have you seen State Representative Carmen Lawlor? I noticed her car parked a little ways back."

Reynolds looked puzzled. "No ma'am. I thought she was coming with you. I haven't seen anyone and I was wondering about that car. I had some stuff to do in Fort Sumner and I just got here shortly before y'all arrived."

Bishop huffed impatiently. She pulled her phone out of the voluminous black bag slung over her shoulder. The rest of the group stood waiting while she dialed a number and listened.

She waited a moment then shook her head and put the phone away. "She's not answering. I don't know what to say. This trip was her idea. She was very excited about coming here. I got the impression the location was very symbolic for her."

Maria walked over and touched Bishop's shoulder. "Is there any way I can help? Carmen and I worked closely at the Legislature in Santa Fe and I've done a lot of research for her on the initiatives she's planning."

Digger had to smile. It was so like Maria to jump in. Life with Maria was like skiing down a mountain, with lots of twists and turns, always at exhilarating speed.

Joan Bishop glanced skeptically at Maria and sighed. "Let's wait for a few more minutes. Maybe she got here early and went out to explore." She looked back at Reynolds. "Is that okay with you, Jake?"

He shrugged. "Fine by me. Ya'll can come in. I've got some coffee going."

Digger followed Maria and Manny into the building. Nancy, the radio reporter, stayed outside to smoke. Reynolds ushered them into an office furnished with plastic chairs, a couple of metal desks, and a large filing cabinet. A drip coffee maker sat on a table in the corner.

Digger poured herself a cup and sat between Maria and Manny. She leaned over to him. "What are you thinking?"

Manny's dark eyes roved back and forth. He pursed his lips, then whispered, "I'm thinking this is a shit show."

Joan Bishop sat in the far corner of the room hunched over her phone. They could hear her voice growing increasingly agitated.

It sounded as if she was trying different people to locate Carmen and not having any luck.

Nancy entered, glanced around, and approached the three of them. She addressed Maria in a bored tone. "Do you know what Carmen Lawlor was going to talk about? I hate to waste all this time waiting around."

Maria frowned, clearly worried. "Carmen is not the kind of person to let people down. I think we owe it to her to wait a little longer. What I can tell you is that she was planning to talk about the bills she was going to introduce at the next session. Stuff that will transform the way the state handles these wind farm projects. If you want background…" She paused, rummaged in her shoulder bag, pulled out a sheet of paper, and began reading aloud. "These are notes Carmen gave me. According to her, this wind farm began operating in 2003. The wind turbines are two hundred and ten feet high. There are 136 of them and each one can generate up to one megawatt of power. A megawatt is—"

"Un-huh," Nancy said, unimpressed. "I was here twenty years ago at the inauguration. I know all that."

Digger sensed the anger that radiated from Maria. She slid an arm around her, gave a comforting squeeze, and smiled up at Nancy. There was enough tension in the room already without a catfight.

Five more minutes went by. Digger was beginning to wonder just how long they would wait when Jake Reynolds reappeared in the doorway.

"I'm thinking if that was her car back there, then she got here early and decided to go on up. I bet she's probably waiting for us there. So, if y'all will follow me, we can head out now."

Reynolds led the group to the back of the building and gestured for them to climb into a faded red Suburban. "Y'all don't look like you've got the right shoes to go hiking so this'll get us up to the site quicker." He laughed.

The Suburban bounced along a washboard gravel road for a couple of minutes then ground up a steep incline to the top of the mesa. Digger couldn't help wondering why Carmen would park so far away. She didn't seem the type to enjoy hill climbing.

Reynolds parked about one hundred and fifty feet from the base of the nearest turbine tower. Once out of the vehicle, Digger stood gaping at the sheer immensity of it, her body vibrating as the giant blades swept rhythmically through the air. Swoosh, swoosh, swoosh. The constant motion was like standing in the middle of a freeway with giant trucks whizzing past.

"Come on y'all," Jake called. "I'll take you to the base and you'll get a feel for how tall it is."

Digger and Maria walked behind Joan Bishop who was still grumbling to herself about Carmen. "I don't understand it. Where can she be?"

They stood for a moment at the base, staring up at the soaring white structure, then at the plains stretching out below them. A dark bank of clouds hung over the plains to the west, boding rain. Moisture was always welcome in this parched landscape, but today, the clouds looked ominous. Reynolds took them around the base to where a metal staircase led to a door about thirty feet above the ground.

That's when they saw the body.

CHAPTER 4

The body lay face down a few feet from the bottom of the staircase. From the clothing, it looked like a woman. Her head was twisted around at an impossible angle and it was obvious she was dead.

They froze as if held by an unseen hand. No one spoke. Finally, Jake stepped forward, moving gingerly, the way someone would approach the edge of a cliff. When he reached the body, he eased down slowly, reached out a hand, and turned the head so they could see the face. Digger already knew it would be Carmen. But when she saw that face again, so similar to Maria's, a jolt shot through her.

"No!" Maria screamed. She lurched forward and dropped to her knees beside the lifeless woman.

Joan Bishop stood a few feet away, motionless, mouth open, one hand clutched at her neck.

Digger's stomach flipped and she thought for a second, she might vomit.

Manny abruptly turned his back to the sight.

A thought flashed through Digger's mind. Manny was Navajo. In their tradition, they must avoid contact with the dead for fear of bad spirits

Jake took off his jacket and laid it over the body. He stood gazing around, as if uncertain what to do next.

"Don't just stand there, man! We don't know what happened here. You gotta call the police or somebody. Call 911!" It was Jim, the photographer.

Jake looked at him, dazed, then pulled out his phone and made a call. They heard him describe the situation, he said, "uh-huh" a few times then hung up. He looked around at the group. "I'm real sorry folks, they're gonna send somebody out from Tucumcari. It could take a while."

"You mean we have to wait here!" Joan's voice was high and shrill.

Jake shifted his feet uncomfortably as if he wished someone else would take charge. "Look ma'am," he said. "I'm sorry, but they'll probably want to take statements from all of us here."

"I don't believe this!" Joan shrieked. She covered her face with her hands and her shoulders began to shake.

Jake and the others huddled around Joan to comfort her. Meanwhile, Digger took a breath to quell her nausea, stepped forward, and stared at the form on the ground. She remembered how she'd first seen Carmen that night at Frankie's, how confident and elegant she had looked.

Maria was now crouched over her, hands tracing the outline of Carmen's form as if she could bring her to life. After a long moment, she lifted her head and blinked. Digger saw Maria's eyes settle on something. She turned her head and saw a small turquoise backpack that lay a short distance away from the body as if Carmen had let it go as she fell. Maria staggered to her feet and retrieved the backpack from the ground.

"You shouldn't do that!" Digger warned. "The sheriff will want to secure the scene."

Maria ignored her. "I want to find her phone. I need to know why she was up there."

Digger watched anxiously as Maria unzipped the backpack and shoved a hand inside.

"It's not there!" she said, voice cracking.

She dug frantically into the bag and pulled out a small purse. Digger stood over Maria as she opened it. Hands fumbling, she picked through the contents: a driver's license, credit cards, twenty-three dollars, and some change. She dug down again and pulled out an envelope that had been opened. She eased out the letter and took a picture with her phone.

"You should not be doing that!" Digger whispered again, urgently. "Quick, put it down! Jake's coming!"

They jumped to their feet. Digger hoped Jake hadn't seen Maria handling the backpack. To distract him, she pointed to the top of the staircase, which looked more like a ladder affixed to the side of the turbine. At the top was a tiny platform and a door.

"What's that staircase for, anyway?"

Jake looked up confused, as if he was having trouble focusing on the situation. "Uh, the staircase? The maintenance workers use it to get inside the tower. I've told the others we should go back and wait in the office." He sighed heavily and walked off.

Maria and Digger stared up at the platform.

"Why didn't she wait for us at the site office?" Maria said softly. "I can't understand why she would come here alone?"

Digger put an arm around Maria and kissed her cheek. "I don't know. She must have had a reason." She tried to sound calm but her mind was racing. She'd come here to write a routine story that readers would probably breeze through and forget. Now, suddenly, the stakes were so much higher. She knew Maria wouldn't like what she had to do next, so she moved round to face her, kissed her again, and said, "I need to contact Roscoe."

Maria gave her a disbelieving look. "This is just news to you, isn't it? Someone I care about is dead. How can you be like this?"

"Maria I..."

Maria turned away. "Oh, alright. Go talk to your editor if that's what you need to do."

Digger saw the anguish on Maria's face. They'd gone through this tug-of-war before. She was torn but she knew she had a job to do. She took out her phone and tapped a brief message to Roscoe:

Rep. Carmen Lawlor found deceased at base of wind turbine, appears to be an accident, waiting for law enforcement to arrive.

When she finished, she looked around and saw Manny was on his phone too. The photographer was snapping shots of the scene.

Jake walked over to Jim waving a hand. "I don't think you should be taking pictures. We should wait for the police."

The photographer shrugged. "We're in the news business. That's why we came here today. This is news."

Jake shook his head and huffed but said nothing.

Digger's phone rang—Roscoe calling back. "I got your message. How soon can you get me something?"

"I don't know. We're up here on the side of a mountain and my laptop is back at the site building."

"You're breaking up. Shit. Tell me everything you can now and I'll jot it down. Then get back down there and start writing. I want something online before every other outfit in the state has it."

Digger closed her eyes, trying to shut out the constant noise of the wind turbine blades so she could focus her thoughts. She remembered a black-and-white movie she'd seen as a kid where a reporter called in a story from a pay phone. She'd never imagined she'd have to do it. She took a breath and held it for a second until the words flowed.

When she finished the call, she looked up and saw Maria huddled beside Joan. Manny, the photographer, and Jake were about fifty feet away, at the point where the road reached the top of the escarpment. Digger assumed they were watching out for the sheriff.

All this time she had forgotten about Nancy. Now she noticed the radio reporter calmly walking around in front of the tower. She held a notebook in one hand and her gaze was on the ladder. Then she swiveled around, scanning the ground as if mentally measuring the trajectory of Carmen's fall. She jotted something in the notebook, took some pictures with her phone, then spoke into it. Digger guessed she was recording.

She ambled over and stopped beside Digger. Opening her purse, she stuffed the notebook and phone into it and pulled out a pack of cigarettes.

They heard the sound of a vehicle grinding up the incline.

Nancy lit a cigarette, took a long drag, and eyed Digger. "Well, I guess we'll find out whether she fell, jumped, or was pushed."

CHAPTER 5

Roscoe Bremmer worried about finances. It was a chronic condition. He had started *The Searcher,* as an online paper when the business publication where he was working shut down. At first, he'd been lucky, landed some grants, attracted some investors, and launched operations in a small 1950s-era house on Harvard a few blocks from the University of New Mexico campus. But figuring out how to pay the bills month-to-month gave him heartburn.

When Digger arrived at work the morning after the ill-fated trip to the wind farm, she found Roscoe leaning against his desk, sleeves rolled up, hairy forearms folded across his chest, frowning. His face was paler than usual this morning, a sign he'd had a bad night.

"So, what do we know now?" he asked, eyeing her from under eyebrows that bristled like twin caterpillars on his forehead.

Digger's nerves were jangling. Thoughts of Carmen lying dead on the ground, and the relentless whoosh of the wind turbine, had interrupted her sleep leaving her exhausted and irritable. She dreaded having to face Roscoe, knowing he wanted answers and she didn't have many.

In the six months she'd worked for him they'd developed a solid working relationship. He reminded her of Halloran, her mentor at the *Courier*; cranky and demanding, but he knew his craft.

She took a breath. "Not a lot more than we did yesterday, except that police are treating it as an 'unattended death', which means the Office of the Medical Investigator gets involved. At this point, there doesn't seem to be any way of knowing whether she fell accidentally or…"

"Or whether it was deliberate," Roscoe broke in, finishing the sentence.

She shot him a look but he ignored it, so she took a calming breath and continued, "Carmen's car was there when our group arrived. Joan Bishop, the utility company flack, told us she'd had a call from Carmen saying she'd changed her plans and was going to drive instead of taking the bus because she had to get back to an appointment in Albuquerque. So, we were expecting to meet her at the site."

Roscoe interrupted again. "How did this Bishop woman react?"

"She seemed pissed off even before we left because so few reporters showed up. Carmen was the one who pitched the trip idea in the first place. She made a big deal about it, telling Bishop she wanted to use the twentieth anniversary of the launch of the wind farm as an opportunity to unveil some new plan for her renewable energy policy."

"Do we have any details of the plan, or why she had to get back to Albuquerque?"

Digger shook her head.

"Well, find out." Roscoe fired back. He frowned and rubbed his hands through his graying wiry hair. Finally, he exhaled loudly. "So, what do you plan to do for a second-day story? Have you found out anything more about this Carmen woman?"

Digger consulted her notebook. "She's a three-term state legislator from a district just outside Santa Fe. She's big on renewable energy and recycling, hates pollution. That's made her unpopular with the oilfield types around Farmington and Hobbs but the Sierra Club loves her."

Roscoe waved a hand, dismissively. "We pretty much covered that yesterday. What about her personal life?"

"She's been a realtor for about six years. Lives in Eldorado, outside Santa Fe, grew up in New Mexico, divorced, no kids…"

Roscoe interrupted again, "Okay. Get in touch with the ex-husband and…" He paused as though he had a sudden inspiration. "Hey, didn't you say she and Maria worked together on some bills in the last session? They must've talked, see if you can get more from Maria."

Digger didn't like where this was going. "Maria is my wife," she said, tightly. "I'm not going to drag her into the middle of any investigation."

Right now, Maria was grieving. From the way she talked when they finally got home, Digger understood the bond that had grown between Carmen and Maria was deeper than she at first realized. The niggling suspicion she'd felt watching them dance at Frankie's, still lurked. She didn't want to probe while Maria was in such a fragile emotional state.

Roscoe's frown deepened. "Do you want me to get Ginny to do the story?" he snapped. Ginny was the only other full-time staffer at *The Searcher.*

"Ginny?" Digger stared at him; mouth open. "I was the one who was there on the ground. I was the one who got you the story before any of the other papers or TV got it. Remember?"

Roscoe squeezed his eyes shut for a moment, then exhaled slowly. Finally, he opened his eyes and nodded at her. "Look, I hired you because of your reputation at the *Courier* and you know your way around city hall and that 'rat's nest' in Santa Fe."

The 'rat's nest' was how Roscoe scornfully referred to the state legislature.

Digger took a long, calming breath, met his gaze, and nodded. "Okay. Thanks for the vote of confidence. I'll get you something by deadline." She made for the door.

"By the way," Roscoe called. "Good job yesterday. That was a tough call."

Digger blushed. Roscoe wasn't free with compliments and this was a big one. "Thanks. I appreciate it. I really didn't think I'd be able to do it."

When Digger emerged from the house, she crossed the front yard and stood for a moment on the sidewalk. Working for an online paper was a whole new experience. Since they didn't need staff to design the pages or print the paper, it was usually just her, Roscoe, and Ginny, who came into the office. Many articles came from freelancers based around the city or state who worked from home. She missed the hubbub and bustle of the busy *Courier* newsroom. But the *Courier,* like a lot of other newspapers, was gone, and she was lucky to find another reporting job.

She checked her phone—nearly ten o'clock—maybe five hours to deadline. Roscoe would want to beat the TV evening news. Craving coffee, she instinctively headed toward the Frontier Restaurant on Central, a place she knew from her student days. If she was lucky there wouldn't be many people in the back room and she could work there, away from Roscoe's interference.

The warm October sunshine gave the buildings that lined the street a soft glow. In front of the restaurant, there was the usual tangle of bicycles. Mid-morning the Frontier was moderately busy and the mingled smell of coffee, baking, and humanity brought back memories of late nights and laughter with friends from the dorm. At the smell of food, her stomach growled, reminding her how hungry she was. She'd risen early with Maria who had to teach a class at eight-thirty, but she couldn't face breakfast and had left the house without eating.

She ordered a latte and a breakfast burrito smothered with

green chile sauce. Wanting to avoid the noise near the front entrance, she took her tray through the Frontier's connecting rooms and picked a table in the farthest corner. After finishing the coffee and managing half the giant burrito, Digger pushed her plate aside and pulled her laptop out of her backpack.

Okay, Carmen, let's see who you really are.

She spent the next half hour scouring Google, social media sites, and news reports. Images of her popped up everywhere. Carmen as a high school cheerleader in a short skirt, holding pom poms; Carmen at a UNM debate; Carmen the winning candidate—always beaming that big smile. When she found a picture of Carmen with her husband she stopped.

The link she clicked took her to a story in the *Albuquerque Journal*. The piece was about an official dinner they'd attended together. Karl Lawlor, it seemed had a law practice downtown. With another quick search, she found his website and the address. Glancing at her notes, she decided to check out the husband first and circle back to the other names.

Grabbing her laptop, she stuffed everything into her backpack and headed out of the restaurant and back to her car. She had no idea if he had yet learned of his ex-wife's death, but if he was in his office and he would talk, a face-to-face interview would give her the best chance of getting details about Carmen.

Cruising down a side street in an older residential neighborhood on the edge of Downtown Albuquerque, Digger kept her eyes peeled for the address. The bossy woman's voice on her phone's map app told her the destination was just ahead on the right.

She spotted it, the faded sign hanging in front of a small, one-story wooden house that said, 'Karl Lawlor, Attorney-at-Law.' A woman in a faded red sweatshirt was standing on the sidewalk, dog leash in hand. Her canine companion relieved himself on the post supporting the sign. Leg down, the dog paused to sniff a patch of scrubby grass poking through the fence before his owner tugged the leash and they moved on.

Digger parked a short way down the street and walked back. She passed a driveway where a husky bandana-wearing guy was bent over the engine of a 1960s Mustang. The blinds were drawn in the front windows of the house behind him and the wooden deck needed a coat of paint. She glanced around, uncomfortable. The house across the street looked vacant. Odd place to have a law office, she thought.

Whatever grass had been in Karl Lawlor's front yard, had long ago died, replaced by sandy earth and gravel. She climbed the two front steps and pressed the doorbell. Seconds ticked by. In the distance was the rumbling sound of traffic on the two freeways that intersected, cutting the city into quarters. From inside she heard footsteps, then the door opened. The thin, pale man who stood just inside, had a pencil mustache and reddish hair receding from a high, freckled forehead. His eyes, behind large, black-framed glasses, looked surprised and slightly confused.

She had a hard time imagining Carmen being married to this man.

"Karl Lawlor?"

He blinked. "Yes?"

"I'm Elizabeth Doyle, I'm with *The Searcher*, do you have a few minutes?"

His face became even paler. "I suppose you want to ask about Carmen. The other reporters just called me. Why did you come in person?"

Digger swallowed. She had been dreading this conversation and all the words she'd rehearsed deserted her now. "I was at the wind farm. We found her on the ground." She blurted it out and the statement hung between them like a cloud of cold air. She heard him gulp.

His eyes shot around, then back at her. "You'd better come in."

She followed him through what had been the living room of the house but was now crammed with file cabinets and a large, cluttered desk. They continued into one of the former bedrooms which was now his office.

He lifted a stack of papers off a chair and gestured for her to sit. "My assistant quit recently and I haven't been able to replace her," he commented apologetically.

He slumped into the chair behind the desk and wiped his forehead. Digger waited. She knew he would talk, pressuring him right now was not a good idea. In the stillness of his office, she was aware of a fly buzzing, cars passing in the street outside, and the distant wail of a police siren.

Finally, Lawlor spoke, and the words came out in a long, low sigh. "What do you want to know?"

Digger stared at him. What had Carmen ever seen in this man? She was so vibrant, so full of passionate conviction, and he was so very pallid. She made a show of consulting her notebook. "I've got the basic background details, but I'm trying to find out more about her as a person. Can you tell me what she was like?" She gave him what she hoped was an encouraging smile.

He didn't smile back. His eyes remained fixed on his hands splayed on the desktop. After a couple of seconds, he said, "We weren't married very long and I haven't seen her in a few years. That's what I told the other reporters. But you probably know all that. So, I'll go back a bit." He paused, shot her a glance, then continued, "I met her at a seminar on real estate law. Those things can be pretty dull and she was one of the realtors there that stood out. At that time, I was almost finished law school. We sort of clicked. Everything moved very fast and we were married within a few months. I was supposed to go into my dad's law practice in Las Cruces and she kept saying how glad she was to get away from Albuquerque. We spent a year in Las Cruces but I didn't want to be under my dad's thumb so I got a job here in Albuquerque. I knew coming back here upset her but I didn't expect how much it would affect our relationship."

"How so?" Digger asked.

"She started acting weird. Fearful. Like she was hiding something. I thought she might be having an affair. Finally, I confronted her and accused her of cheating on me. She just blew up. Said she was leaving me. Next thing, she filed for divorce and moved to Santa Fe."

"Did you ever find out if she was seeing someone else?"

Lawlor shook his head. "No. If she was, I never heard about it from any of our friends, and believe me, I asked around. As far as I know, she's hardly even dated since we split. I think it must have been something else. Her parents would never talk to me and they're both gone now. You might try her sister."

"How can I reach her?"

"I'm not sure. We didn't stay in touch. Her name is Elena Perez. At least that was the family name. I don't know if she's gotten married. Last I heard she was working for a software company." He sighed, shoulders slumping. "I'm sorry, I can't help you anymore."

She knew she couldn't use anything he told her unless she could track down the sister and get confirmation. She checked the time. She had three hours to get enough to keep Roscoe happy. She had a lot of phone calls to make. No more time for in-person interviews.

She stood. "Thanks for your help. I am sorry for your loss," she added the last part knowing it sounded trite, but he looked so deflated.

"Thanks," he said, with a weak smile. "Even though it's been a long time, it still hurts."

She drove back toward the office, wondering if she could sneak past Roscoe and finish the phone calls before he slammed her with a barrage of questions. Luckily, he was on the phone when she crept in and Ginny was hovering over him impatiently waiting for his attention. She escaped to her desk.

She found the software company Lawlor mentioned, got a number for Elena Perez, and left a message. The next name on her list was one of Carmen's fellow legislators. Thankfully, the woman took the call.

"Oh yeah, Carmen and I served on a couple of committees together. She was incredibly hard-working and dedicated, but frankly, I found her hard to get to know."

Digger then tried the real estate agency where Carmen worked. She was put through to Paula Riley, a breezy-sounding woman with a Chicago accent. According to Paula, the appointment Carmen didn't keep was to show a house in an upscale foothills neighborhood of Albuquerque. Paula had to step in at the last minute because the would-be buyers threw a fit when Carmen didn't show.

"I mean, nobody knew what had happened to her! And these people were from New York and you know what they can be like!" She gave an exasperated sigh. "Then we found out what happened. It was so awful!"

A scroll through Carmen's Facebook contacts led her to a college friend. She sent a message figuring her chances of a reply were slim to none. But not half an hour later she got a call.

"Terrible news about Carmen," the friend said. "We saw a lot of each other after her divorce. She'd never say it, but I think she felt lonely. You know what it can be like when you're over forty and you're suddenly single."

Digger had no idea what it would be like to be single at forty or even what it would be like to be forty, but she was glad the woman was chatty.

The friend continued in the same vein. "I was really surprised when I saw that news report about her being up on that ladder."

"How so?"

"Well, we got together for a meal a couple of weeks ago and she mentioned she'd been having dizzy spells."

"Had she been to see a doctor about it?"

"Carmen? A doctor? If she did, she wouldn't have told me. Like I said, she could be very private."

Deadline time arrived and she filed a story.

Roscoe read it quickly and shrugged. "Okay. This is good as far as it goes. But you should have talked to someone from one of the groups that campaigned against Carmen at the last election."

Digger closed her eyes. Damn, she was tired. Tired and jittery, she'd never found a dead body before. "Yeah, you're right Roscoe. I'll keep on it."

Back at her desk, she pored over the notes she had taken. The image of Carmen that emerged was a kaleidoscope; the popular high school teen, the gutsy politician, the successful realtor. Then, there was the ex-husband's suspicions about an affair. She wondered if it was worth trying to call him again. She looked back at the notes. The comment from the Facebook friend about dizzy spells jumped out at her. Was Carmen hiding some health condition, if so, how serious was it?

CHAPTER 6

The first stars were peeking through the gathering darkness as Digger drove up the canyon road to the village of Los Jardines. Digger and Maria had moved into her grandmother's tiny adobe house the previous year, shortly before they were married. They had made the move so Maria would be living in the state house district she wanted to represent.

Maria's grandmother, *Abuela*, as they called her using the Spanish word, had just turned eighty. Living with her was supposed to be a temporary arrangement until they could buy or rent a place of their own. But the two of them found they loved her company. Abuela had even won the heart of Digger's cantankerous cat, Lady Antonia.

Digger parked her Subaru in the narrow street next to the adobe-brick wall that partially hid the house from view. Maria's car was in the carport and lights glowed from the living room window. She walked through the sheltered garden and entered, feeling a sense of relief. She was exhausted.

Maria was lying on the sofa with Lady Antonia on her lap. When Digger walked in, she pushed the cat aside, rose, and came to hug her. "Rough day?" she asked.

"Rough two days," Digger said, burying her face against

Maria's neck and kissing her just below the ear. Right now, she wanted to push away all thoughts of Carmen Lawlor and wrap herself in Maria's presence.

Abuela came out of the kitchen dressed in her winter uniform of corduroy pants, a check flannel shirt, and a fleece vest. She beamed at them, hands on hips, and greeted Digger. "Hola Cowgirl." Cowgirl was the nickname Abuela had given Digger because of the boots she wore. "I knew you'd be hungry so I've made enchiladas for dinner."

Digger rushed over and hugged her. "Abuela you are the best!"

After dinner, Maria went straight to their bedroom while Digger helped Abuela clean up the kitchen.

When the last plate was put away, Abuela laid a hand on Digger's shoulder. "What happened yesterday, that was some bad business."

Abuela's voice, low and steady, made Digger think of cello music. She looked up and met the old woman's eyes. "Yeah," she sighed. "It hit Maria hardest. I know she admired Carmen. Kind of like the way she admires you because you always stood up for what you believed in back in the sixties."

Abuela smiled, and the way the wrinkles stretched around her face reminded Digger of the bark of an ancient olive tree. The old woman patted her arm. "Go to her now, Cowgirl, I think Maria needs you."

Digger hugged Abuela and went to the bedroom. She found Maria sitting in front of the old-fashioned vanity. She had released her long hair from the twist she habitually wore and was slowly brushing it. Digger bent and softly kissed the back of her neck. All she wanted to do at this moment was to take Maria in her arms and feel the warmth of her body. But despite what she'd told Roscoe, she knew she needed to ask her more about Carmen.

She plunked down heavily on the bed and let out a long weary sigh.

"That's exactly how I feel." Maria nudged in beside her on the bed. "I keep thinking about yesterday."

Digger reached over, cupped Maria's face in one hand, and looked into her dark eyes. "What do you think happened out there?"

Maria looked down, rubbed her hands on her thighs, and exhaled. "I want to think she fell by accident, but…"

"But what?"

"It's just… we spent a lot of time together during the session, she was always confident, upbeat. But remember when I had to go to Santa Fe recently? I had lunch with her that day and something about her seemed different. She was nervous and tense. She'd get off-topic when we were talking. I asked her if anything was wrong but she just laughed it off. Said she was super busy—you know the housing market is crazy right now."

"You think she was depressed?"

Maria frowned and pushed her hair back from her face. "More distracted. She'd been working on a proposal for a bill that could streamline the permitting process for wind farms. That's what she was going to talk about yesterday."

Digger got up and began pacing while she thought about Maria's words. From outside, came the sound of a dog barking not far away. Señor Jose, the neighbor, had a nervous old terrier that woke her some nights. He must have heard something, a coyote perhaps? There were always animals lurking around.

She kept asking herself why Carmen would park at such a distance from the wind turbines, walk all the way there, climb those stairs—and do all this alone? It made no sense. Suddenly a thought struck her.

"Wait a minute, did you ever look at the letter you found in her backpack?"

Maria's hands flew to her face. "No. I guess I got distracted. Here, the picture is on my phone."

She grabbed it from the top of the vanity and opened the photos app. The picture of the letter was the last shot she had taken. They sat together on the bed and stared at the screen. The insignia at the top showed it was from a doctor's office. It was the result of a blood test Carmen had recently undergone. One column of figures showed the typical range for each item tested, the other showed Carmen's results. Comparing them, Digger could see several tests showed Carmen was well outside the normal parameters. They looked at each other.

"What do you think this is?" Maria said.

Digger took her laptop from the bedside table and typed in a Google search. Her eyes scanned the results. Maria's hand gripped Digger's thigh as she read over the text. "I'm not sure, but it looks like it's serious. Something to do with her liver."

They were still staring at the laptop screen when Digger's phone rang. She had left it on the dresser when she came into the bedroom.

"You going to answer it?" Maria looked at her, eyebrows raised.

Digger rose, retrieved the phone, and peered at the number. She didn't recognize it. Later, she was unsure what prompted her to answer the call but she was glad she did.

"Hi, am I talking to Elizabeth Doyle, or should I call you Digger?"

She recognized the edgy smoker's voice. "Hi, Nancy."

"I saw your stories about Carmen and the little incident at the wind farm. We need to talk."

The aspen trees on the flanks of the mountains above Los Jardines shone golden in the morning light. Digger drove down the winding road to the interstate headed toward Albuquerque. Nancy wanted to meet at the Nutty Squirrel, a cafe in the Nob Hill area, not far from *The Searcher* offices. As she headed toward the city Digger realized she knew little about Nancy except that she said she worked for one of the radio stations. But even that was suspect. She hadn't shown up in any of Digger's searches.

Traffic on the freeway slowed to a crawl as she approached the first exits to the city. It happened every October as tens of thousands of tourists flocked to the annual hot air balloon fiesta. The ten-day event drew enthusiasts from all over the world. The pilots launched shortly after dawn and by the time Digger was driving to work, the sky west of the freeway was polka-dotted with balloons that spanned the horizon. As a kid, she loved the special shape balloons, especially the one that looked like a giant panda bear.

The congestion had thinned by the time she reached the university area and she parked in her regular spot near the office. As she approached the gate she spotted a familiar figure.

"Rex! What are you doing around here? I thought you were taking pictures of those fancy houses in the foothills."

"Hey, Digg!" He waved. "Your boss Roscoe called me. Asked if I'd do some shooting for you guys." Rex, her favorite photographer at the *Courier*, undid his worn yellow barn coat and then adjusted the camera bag slung over his shoulder before lighting a cigarette. "Heard about that crazy stuff at the wind farm."

"You saw the stories? I'm doing some follow-up, meeting Nancy Harford, she was on the trip with us."

"Nancy! She's still around?"

"You know her?"

Rex chuckled. "Oh yeah! She was with the *Courier* about twenty years ago, got crossways with the then editor and he fired her. She kicked a trashcan across the room on her way out. Made quite a stir!"

"Really?" Digger tried to imagine the staid woman she'd seen on the wind farm trip having a public meltdown. "Well, thanks for the heads up. Good luck with Roscoe. He can be… well, you'll see."

She wondered why Roscoe would call in an outside photographer, but she was glad he had. The last time she had seen Rex he was working for a real estate agency taking pictures of expensive custom homes and hating it. She waved goodbye and hurried to the meeting spot, arriving at the cafe a few minutes late.

Every table in the small space was occupied. Several young singles with headphones were bent over laptops, beyond them was a group of twenty-something women, and at the next table was a gray-haired couple in hiking clothes—but no Nancy. She wasn't in line at the counter either. Digger thought for a moment then remembered the courtyard. Of course, Nancy would probably be out there smoking. Sure enough, she spotted her at a table, a coffee mug in one hand, cigarette in the other. Digger ordered a cappuccino and briefly considered a blueberry muffin. No, she needed to focus on Nancy. Coffee in hand she went out to join her.

"Ah, Miss Doyle, you're late." Nancy peered at Digger over large, blue-framed glasses.

Digger picked up her mug, licked at the foam on top of her coffee, and sipped. "What is it you want to talk about?"

Nancy's eyes narrowed. "There are things you should know about Carmen Lawlor," she said.

Digger's chest tightened. She thought of Nancy's comment at the wind farm as she looked at Carmen's body. "Okay," she said. "I'm listening."

Nancy shoved a hand into the oversized purse on the bench beside her. She pulled out a manilla envelope, extracted a folded newspaper clipping, and spread it on the table for Digger to read.

It was a *Courier* article from 1998. Under the headline, *'Las Vistas Girl Missing in El Malpais lava beds'* was a picture of a teenager in shorts and an AC/DC tee shirt. The caption said, *'Julie Mondragon, 18, was last seen near a picnic ground in El Malpais, a rugged area of lava beds near Grants.'* The story said the girl had gone on a day outing with friends and had wandered off when they stopped for lunch. Search efforts had so far been unsuccessful.

Digger recalled references to the story. It was one of those weird cold cases people mentioned occasionally. She looked at Nancy and frowned. "What's this got to do with Carmen?"

Nancy retrieved the article and placed it back inside the envelope. "Carmen," she said. "Was one of those friends."

Digger wondered if Nancy was some kind of conspiracy nut. "Okay. I'm still missing something here."

Nancy crushed out her cigarette and leaned over the table. Her voice was low and earnest. "Those *friends*," she raised her fingers in air quotes, "knew what happened to Julie."

Digger's heartbeat quickened. Did Nancy mean the friends, including Carmen, were responsible for Julie's disappearance? "Didn't the police question them if they were the last to see her?"

Nancy gave a short harsh laugh. "Of course, but they all said she just wandered off. The four of them even joined the searches. They never found her."

"And just how do *you* know all this?" Digger asked, suspiciously.

"I was in the same class with them at Las Vistas High." Her voice had an edge that could have been anger but her expression was impossible to read.

Digger studied her face: the fine lines around the eyes, the deep crease between the eyebrows, and stray gray hairs. She'd probably be in her mid-forties. Based on the newspaper article, she could have been in high school in 1998. "You think they were covering up? What makes you think that?"

A smile spread slowly across Nancy's face, but it wasn't a happy look. Her lips thinned in a grimace and her voice sounded bitter. "Oh, they were this little pack; Carmen, Sylvia, Donna, and Billy Switzer." A pause. A hard laugh. "Somebody once called him Swiss Cheese. Billy punched the kid."

Nancy pursed her lips. Her eyes, behind the blue-framed glasses, had a far-away look. Digger cleared her throat. "What about Julie?" she prompted.

Nancy's penciled-in eyebrows lowered in a frown and she shrugged. "After Julie disappeared, they just clammed up any-time anybody mentioned it. I think they call it *omertà*, it's an Italian word. Look it up if you don't know what it means."

Digger knew what it meant alright—four friends keeping a secret. Her heart pounded. Why was Nancy telling her this? Aloud, she said, "If you knew–or suspected this all along–why didn't you go to the police?"

"Hah! I tried. No one listened to me. They thought I was just a mean girl who wanted attention because she hadn't been part of that little clique. I haven't got the best reputation. I burned my bridges at a couple of the places I worked."

Digger recalled Rex's story about the trash can episode. "What do you want me to do with this?"

Nancy gave Digger a pitying look as if she were explaining a simple math problem to an obstinately slow student. With that, she stood and grabbed her purse and said, "Go find them. Ask them what happened to Julie. Ask them why Carmen is dead."

Chapter 8

Digger sat and stared at the shafts of sunlight that dappled the high wall of the cafe courtyard. The clattering of plates and hiss of the espresso machine jolted her nerves as she mentally wrestled with how to handle Nancy's story. She had a thousand questions but sat rooted in her chair unable to go after her. Was the woman delusional, Digger wondered, or was there more than a kernel of truth in what she said? If so, where did that lead?

She took a few calming breaths and decided to call her buddy Manny. He'd covered the police beat at the *Courier* and knew more about police procedure than she did. Last year, they collaborated when he helped her investigate the politics behind a phony solar project. Pulling out her phone, she tapped on Manny's number. It rang so long that she was about to give up when he answered.

"Hi, it's me. You got a minute?"

"Just a couple. I'm on deadline."

Digger quickly recounted her conversation with Nancy and when she stopped, she heard him make a long whistling sound with his breath.

"Whew! That's a whole new can of worms. Do you know if she's talked to anyone else about this?"

"I don't think so. She called me last night out of the blue. I'm not even sure I trust her."

"Well, police are still going with it being an accident. Even if they suspect it was suicide, unless there's some indication of foul play, they can't get a warrant to search her home, and the OMI report won't be available for weeks."

Manny was right. Any time there was a sudden, violent, or unexplained death anywhere in New Mexico, the Office of the Medical Investigator was always involved. Digger realized she was so preoccupied with Nancy's story that she hadn't told Manny about the letter with the blood test results. "There's something else, and it's big. Could you meet me tomorrow?"

"Let me check something."

He seemed to be hesitating and she wondered if he was weighing the implications of joining forces on the story. She trusted him because of the work they'd done together in the past. She was sure that trust was mutual. But this time they worked for different newspapers and that could cause problems.

At last, he said, "Okay babe, meet at the usual place for a burrito?"

"Definitely. Eleven o'clock and the burritos are on me."

She left the cafe and, on a hunch, headed for Las Vistas. She hoped the high school had an archive where they kept old yearbooks. If she could get her hands on the book from the year Carmen graduated it might show pictures of her and the friends Nancy mentioned.

The school was in a jumble of tan stucco buildings on a bluff overlooking the Rio Grande River. A parking lot the size of a football field was filled with an assortment of old cars, motorcycles, and bicycles. She followed signs to the office, identified herself to the security guard, and stepped through the entrance. The smell of cleaning fluid and floor polish hit her as soon as she walked through the door. A voice stopped her before she took another step.

"May I help you?" The chubby woman seated behind the front desk frowned over her glasses at Digger as she patted down the mass of auburn curls that sprouted from each side of her head like the ears of a large spaniel.

Digger introduced herself and explained the reason for her visit as briefly as possible. Giving too much detail invited complications.

The woman huffed and her frown deepened. "I'll have to ask the principal." She picked up the phone and dialed. "Miss Cantrell, I've got a reporter here who says she's doing some research into that girl that went missing back in the late nineties. She wants to look at some of the old yearbooks."

Miss Cantrell had no problem with Digger's request. The chubby woman led Digger out of the office and down several hallways to the school library. She pointed at a bookcase near the back of the room. "You can look through those over there. If you need any help, just ask the librarian. She's on a break at the moment but she'll be back in five minutes." Then she left.

Digger scanned the spines of the books and, spotting the year 1998, she pulled it down and took it to the nearest table. She recognized Carmen in a photo of the school cheerleaders. She appeared again on the class picture page next to photos of the students Nancy had mentioned; Sylvia, Donna, and Billy. Near the bottom right-hand corner of the group was a pretty dark-haired girl with a big smile. The caption identified her. It was Julie Mondragon, the girl who had gone missing and was never found.

If Nancy was right, Carmen and the other three knew what had happened to Julie. And now Carmen was dead. She studied the faces, pulled out her phone, and took a picture.

Back at the office, she found Roscoe fuming over a city council story Ginny had written. The story claimed a counselor had
stormed out of a meeting. Ginny named the wrong counselor and
the guy had gone ballistic. Hearing their raised voices through the
closed door of Roscoe's office, Digger decided it was not a good
time to tell her editor about Nancy. She retreated to her corner.

She spent the next two hours poring over old news reports
about the search for Julie Mondragon. The little group of friends
Nancy had mentioned featured in many of the stories. Police had
interviewed each of them multiple times over the years. Each
time they described the outing to the Malpais area of lava beds,
the picnic, the moment when Julie wandered off, and their frantic
search efforts. Sylvia's account was always the most emotional.
Through her words, Digger could envision how easy it would be
for a person to disappear into the fantastical landscape of twisted
black lava rock that covered more than a hundred square miles.

As the years progressed, there were fewer and fewer articles
and some of the details changed. She noticed that the girls married and took on different last names, Billy became William Switzer. Julie's parents, who sounded the most desperate of all, died
without ever learning what happened to their daughter.

Then, in a story from 2018, she noted that Sylvia had also died.
The woman was only thirty-eight and that made Digger curious.
She searched Facebook and found a Neal Logan, maybe Sylvia's
husband, had memorialized her account. There were dozens of
comments from family, friends, and co-workers. With a little more
checking, Digger found a work contact number for the husband.

She dialed.

Digger had made a lot of tough phone calls in her years as a
reporter and had developed a tone that blended courtesy with just
the right level of firmness. She'd also honed the skill of repeating
the question multiple ways. "Always ask the second question,"
Halloran, her mentor at the *Courier*, had said.

When Neal Logan answered, she thought she was prepared.

"Hi, I'm Elizabeth Doyle, from *The Searcher,* I'm working on a story about the recent passing of Carmen Lawlor and I'm trying to get comments from people who knew her when she was younger. I know she and your late wife were close friends for many years. I—"

Neal's voice was clipped and angry. "Oh, not again. I thought I was done with this. Yeah. They were friends in high school but that whole thing with the Julie Mondragon case made their lives hell. Every time Sylvia thought she could get on with her own life, some cop or reporter would be calling wanting to interrogate her about it all over again."

Digger decided to risk a tougher question. "I'm sorry about your loss. I saw that your wife was very young, had she been ill?"

He exhaled loudly before answering. "No, it happened out of the blue. One day she seemed fine, I mean she was always kind of depressed, but then suddenly she was gone."

"Was there an autopsy?"

"What? No. They said it was a massive heart attack. They said it can happen to women without warning, without any symptoms. Me, I think it was all the stress, I mean she felt like the police were harassing her. And Billy, you should talk to that asshole."

"I thought he and Sylvia were friends?"

"Huh!" The laugh was short and sharp. "He used to call her now and then. Every time he did, she'd have one of her migraines. It was right after he came to visit that she had her heart attack."

"You think there was any connection?"

He cut her off. "No. But he sure upset her. Just go talk to him."

Chapter 9

Digger escaped from *The Searcher's* office shortly after five-thirty. Traffic was already inching down Central Avenue toward the freeway interchange. That was the drawback of working in an old part of Albuquerque.

During the previous year when she worked in Santa Fe, she enjoyed the long drive south to Los Jardines. Sometimes she took the RailRunner train and daydreamed as she watched the mountains slide past; their flanks rocky blue-gray in summer, gold-flecked as the aspens turned in the fall, and snow-capped in winter. Now her commute took just as long but all she had to look at were sprawling suburbs, industrial buildings, and highway billboards.

Dusk was gathering as she turned off the main road into Los Jardines and the sunset pink of the Sandia mountains had yielded to the encroaching blue shadows by the time she reached the house.

The sound of Cumbia music and the scent of chile that reached her as she walked through the gate signaled that Maria was cooking.

Abuela emerged from the side of the house where she had

been checking on her chickens. The six Barred Rock hens were the old lady's latest project. "Only two eggs today," she said, holding up a small basket. "It's getting dark too early. I need to put a lamp in there to give them more light."

"Well, you know it doesn't matter to me because I don't like eggs." Digger kissed her lightly on each cheek and they walked into the house together.

She was savoring the first few bites of green chile stew when Maria set down her fork and spread her hands on each side of her plate. "I have something I want to announce."

Maria's face had taken on the determined look that Digger knew well. Whatever it was she was about to announce, it was big.

"What is it? Mi'ja." Abuela shot Digger a look of alarm.

Maria regarded both of them, then folded her arms across her chest. "I've decided I will sponsor the bill that Carmen was working on. She helped me from the first day I entered the legislature and I believe in her vision. I owe it to her."

Maria's decision might have seemed sudden if it had been anyone else, but Digger knew she was never one to sit on the sidelines. Maria needed a cause to champion the way most people needed air to breathe.

"How are you going to do that?" Digger asked, keeping her tone neutral.

"You know Carmen asked me to help her with the early research and we had been working together on some proposals," Maria said, surprised by Digger's question. "I want to continue that work and I'm going to focus on getting a bill drafted before the next session starts in January."

Abuela frowned. "But Mija! What about your paintings for the Christmas show?"

Maria waved a hand impatiently. "Abuela! I thought you'd be pleased. You supported me in running for office. I did it because I want to make a difference! The stuff Carmen was working on could make a huge difference for small communities and pueblos all over the state."

"I get that," Digger interrupted. She wanted Maria to know the risk she was taking. "You know there are people out there who weren't happy about what Carmen was doing. If you take on her work, they could go after you. I don't want to see that. Abuela and I went through a lot to help you get elected."

"You don't get it!" Maria snapped, her dark eyes flashing. "There are lots of groups out there that support what she stood for. Just because Carmen is gone it doesn't mean her work stops. She meant a lot to me!" Maria's voice cracked as she said the last words.

A stunned silence settled over the table. A chill spread through Digger's gut. Her mind flashed back to Maria's birthday, the night Carmen joined them at the bar, the way Carmen had asked to dance with Maria, the sight of them on the dance floor. A flame of jealousy flickered in the cold pit of her stomach. "Just how much did Carmen mean to you?"

Maria glared at her. "You sound just like Izzy." She stood, grabbed her plate, walked to the trash can, dumped her barely-touched dinner, and walked out, slamming the door behind her.

Digger looked over at Abuela.

"That wasn't fair," said the old woman. "You're nothing like Izzy. That woman was bad news for Maria."

Digger's heart pounded. The accusation that she was like Maria's old girlfriend Izzy stung. She didn't want to sound jealous but couldn't quell the fear that Maria might have had an affair with Carmen. With Maria's new announcement came the dread that her decision to take on Carmen's work could put them all at risk. This life together, with Abuela, the three of them safe in the adobe house. Life could change in an instant. It had happened. The accident had taken her parents.

She went out to look for Maria and followed the narrow street to where a gate led to a foothills trail. Cold ate at her. In her hurry to leave she hadn't grabbed a jacket. Get a grip, she told herself. Shivering, she walked slowly back toward the lamps that illuminated Abuela's blue gate. Once inside, she saw Maria standing by the front door. How did she not see her in the lane? Maria must have turned toward the main street when she went out the gate.

"I'm sorry," Digger mumbled. She hung her head, uncertain of Maria's reaction. Life with someone as impulsive and passionate as Maria could be draining, but she couldn't imagine being away from her.

Footsteps approached and Maria's warm arms encircled her. "Preciosa," she murmured. "You have nothing to worry about. I admired Carmen, but that's all."

Digger realized she'd been holding her breath. Now, she exhaled slowly. "I just want you to be careful. We still don't know how Carmen died, and maybe even why she died."

"I know. And I know how hard you're working to find answers. That's who you are. Taking on Carmen's fight is who I am. Now, come in, you're freezing. And there's still some stew left."

Chapter 10

State Representative Paul Marquez stared at the post that just showed up on his phone.

'Happy to announce I will be carrying on the great work of Rep. Carmen Lawlor. She is a tremendous loss to us all. With your support I will continue to press for changes that will bring more renewable energy to this wonderful state.'

He knew the woman who had posted it only slightly. Maria Ortiz. She'd been a freshman representative at the last session in January. He recalled their first encounter in the lobby of the Roundhouse, it was just a mundane question, she needed directions to the ladies' room, but she projected an air of confidence. Marquez had been around the legislature for nearly a decade, long enough to recognize the signs. No wonder she and Carmen Lawlor became fast friends. They were two of a kind. He had admired Carmen's spirit and still couldn't grasp how she died. The circumstances were so weird.

Now this Maria was going to take on Carmen's quest. Marquez knew she would face tough opposition. The governor made no secret of his support for the drilling companies that brought so many jobs to the southeastern part of the state, towns like Artesia and Hobbs. Those companies were like a flock of geese laying a whole clutch of golden eggs.

Well, he thought, he'd find out just what the opposition was thinking tonight. He put his phone away, scooped up his laptop case, and left his law office. He had a dinner to attend.

Half an hour later, Marquez was driving the winding narrow road to the exclusive Hyatt Regency Tamaya Resort which was nestled in a remote corner of Santa Ana pueblo land. He wasn't looking forward to the dinner. He knew he'd been invited because he was a longtime member of the House Commerce and Economic Development Committee. They probably wanted assurances that he would support them in the next session. He hated the quid-pro-quo approach but it was all part of politics. But since his divorce he had a lot of free evenings and he enjoyed a good meal especially when someone else was paying.

The resort parking lot was located a discreet distance from the front of the hotel. Marquez parked his Lexus and began walking toward the lights that glowed softly around the entrance. As he approached, he heard the recorded sound of Native American flute music. Entering, he crossed the lobby and made his way to the restaurant. He stopped in the doorway to scan the room. Overhead chandeliers cast a bright glow over the dark leather-backed chairs, picking out brighter colors in the geometric pattern of the rug.

The group expecting him was already seated in a far corner. There was the heavyset guy from the oil and gas association, he'd met the man at least a dozen times but was blanking on his name. Across from the O & G guy was the loud-mouthed rancher type from Roswell who liked to remind you just how many leases he owned, and there was Martin Granger, the lobbyist. Granger's presence bothered him. He'd noticed him for the first time during the session this year. Dressed in an expensive-looking suit, blond beard neatly trimmed, and hair so perfect it looked like a toupée, he reminded Marquez of the salesman at his Lexus dealership. He'd seen him frequently, haunting the hallways of the Roundhouse touting for a range of different causes. Marquez got the feeling Granger would shill for anyone who would pay him.

Granger caught sight of him first and waved him to the table. "Hey Paul, great you could make it. We were just saying it wasn't like you to be late." He jumped up and thrust a hand out.

Marquez found this gesture uncomfortably familiar. They weren't friends. The man's pale blue eyes weren't friendly either. Marquez debated with himself whether to take the proffered hand, but he had to keep up appearances. He didn't want the men at this table as enemies. So, he shook Granger's hand and nodded at the other two. "Sorry, I didn't see the turn in the dark, had to double back."

After they'd all ordered and the appetizers arrived, the oil and gas guy leaned over to him. "I suppose you heard about Carmen Lawlor?"

Marquez slid a look around the table, trying to gauge what the others were expecting from him. He knew their stance on what Lawlor had been promoting and suspected her untimely demise was a boon to them.

The rancher from Roswell, broke in before Marquez could answer. "I know it was a terrible shame, a real tragedy."

Marquez knew exactly how much Lawlor had been a thorn in the side of the organization, but the rancher, with his deep, resonant voice, managed to make his sentiment sound sincere. The man's next comment confirmed Marquez's cynicism. "But I have to say—and Fred here agrees with me," the rancher gestured at the guy from the O & G association. "We're relieved because the direction she wanted to go would have been bad for this state."

I bet you are, Marquez thought. He recalled now that the O & G man's name was Fred Carter.

During this exchange, Marquez noticed that Granger's eyes remained focused on the shrimp cocktail in front of him.

"What do you think, Martin," Marquez asked.

Granger cleared his throat and ran a hand through his well-groomed gray-blond hair. "I didn't know her personally, so I can't comment."

The remark struck Marquez as odd. He hadn't asked Granger whether he knew Lawlor, he just wanted to get his reaction to her death. Marquez set his elbows on the table and leaned forward to press Granger for an answer. "Martin, you must have some opinion, surely?"

Carter interrupted. "Let's face it, Paul, our goals were diametrically opposed. So, I have to say, without her grandstanding in Santa Fe, we can move forward. The County Commission will have to pick someone to fill her place, but that could take a while, and…" He paused, looking around the table, "I think we can have some sway with the commissioners, give them some names, you know."

Marquez stared at Carter, a flicker of anger burning in his chest. He had expected some bland, pseudo-sympathetic statement, but nothing so blatant. The sour taste of disgust filled his throat. He wanted to hit Carter but the message that he'd seen just before he left his office would work just as well, he thought.

"Well, I'm guessing you guys didn't see the same Tweet I saw a little while ago."

Blank looks all around.

"Some state rep. just put out a message that she's going to take up Carmen Lawlor's cause and carry on her work."

The Rancher slammed his glass on the table sloshing beer onto the pristine white tablecloth. "What! Who the hell is it?"

"Name's Maria Ortiz. She's pretty new, so you maybe haven't come across her."

The rancher scowled. "Well now," he drawled. "That's not good news."

Carter stared at Marquez, his jowls reddening. His shoulders rose as if he were taking in a big breath but before he could say anything the server arrived with their meals.

Granger smiled over at Marquez. "Thanks for letting us know, Paul."

Carter shot Granger a look, frowning. "Let's you and I meet next week and talk about this situation."

Chapter 11

As Digger drove north toward her meeting with Manny in Santa Fe, she passed her favorite cottonwood tree. Half the branches looked dead, the other half glowed vivid gold. Behind the tree the rumpled brown blanket of low hills west of the freeway was tinged with green from recent rains. The colors and the intense blue of the fall sky lifted her mood.

She had spent a restless night with the image of Carmen lying dead at the base of the tower preying on her mind. A thousand questions had raced through her brain. Beside her, Maria slept peacefully, her breathing regular. Maria's assurances about her relationship to Carmen had eased her mind. But in the middle of the night, as she thought about Maria's commitment to Carmen's work, she worried again that it would bring trouble. According to all the news reports she'd read, Carmen had stepped on a lot of toes and those people could turn on Maria.

Just outside Santa Fe, she left the freeway and took the next turn to pull into the gas station. Manny's ancient orange VW Beetle was in the parking lot. She had suggested meeting here because the gas station store had a cafeteria counter where travelers could get a freshly made breakfast burrito any time of day. As soon as she walked through the door, she spotted Manny's battered brown leather jacket. He had his back to her as he leaned over the counter making his order. When she joined him, her mouth watered at the sight of trays filled with crisp crumbled bacon, scrambled egg, hash brown potatoes, and green chile sauce.

The server piled spoonfuls of each onto a warmed flour tortilla wrapped it deftly, slipped it into a paper bag, and handed the bundle to Manny.

"Watch out, chile's super hot here." She grinned slyly.

"Just the way I like it," Manny said.

He turned, spotted Digger, and chin-pointed toward a table. "I'm over there."

Moments later, laden with a burrito and coffee, she joined him. Apart from the trip to the wind farm, she hadn't seen Manny in several months. From Instagram posts, she knew he'd taken up running with his dog. He looked fit and the long hair and ponytail suited him.

"What?" he said, looking up from his food.

"Your hair, it looks good like that, better than the hat." The last time they worked together he wore a tweed flat cap that was a gift from his girlfriend.

"Yeah. Lina took the hat when she broke up with me."

Digger recalled the afternoon last year when he met Lina. They were at a cafe in Santa Fe discussing how to investigate the suspicious behavior of Digger's boss. The pretty young woman who served them commented on Manny's hair. Back then, he wore it in a crew cut. She was from Crownpoint, the Navajo community near where Manny lived as a boy. From the way Manny smiled at her, Digger knew he was interested. She was happy to see them together a few weeks later. Too bad things didn't work out, she thought.

"I'm so sorry."

"Don't be," he said, shaking his head. He took the last bite, wiped his mouth, and pulled out a notebook. "Anyway, you didn't come here to talk about Lina or my hat."

Digger rummaged in her bag and handed him the printout of the letter Maria had found in Carmen's backpack, showing blood test results.

Manny was silent for a moment as he read it, then he looked up, eyes wide. "Where the hell did you get this?"

Digger explained how Maria had found the letter. He blew out a long breath, shaking his head slowly. "Did it occur to you, or her, that you could be in trouble for tampering with evidence?"

Digger nodded. "Yup. That was my thought too. But Maria took the picture and left the original in Carmen's backpack so the police would find it as well. It just gives us a jump on requesting information."

"Maybe," he said. "Do you think it has any bearing on what happened out there?"

Digger had been wrestling with that question. If, as she suspected, the numbers in the test results indicated a serious medical condition, would Carmen have decided to take her own life? But why do it in such bizarre circumstances?

It didn't make sense.

Manny studied the printout more closely. "Can I take a picture of this? A friend of mine is a doctor. I'll ask him to look. It might give us a better idea of what it means."

"As long as he's somebody you can trust. And make sure you blur out all the personal information."

Manny's face remained impassive but she knew his mind was crunching through the details and he would speak when he was good and ready. As a cop reporter at the *Courier*, Manny had been relentless, focused like a hound on a scent.

She waited, aware of the sound of steel utensils banging on cooking pots from the kitchen behind the cafeteria counter. Music played faintly in the background. She recognized the song but couldn't remember the name. The inability to remember irritated her, the same way the details piling up around Carmen were beginning to irritate her. Right now, she wished she had Manny's ability to focus. She felt like a hiker stuck at the intersection of a dozen different trails, uncertain which one to take.

"Okay," Manny said, at last. "Here's what we have." He reached out a hand and began plucking packets of sweetener from the container in the middle of the table. One by one, he laid them down. "This is Carmen as a state representative who is crusading for renewable energy. This one is Carmen who has pissed off a lot of the fossil fuel boys. This is Carmen who may know something about the missing Julie Mondragon. And—based on that letter you just showed me—this is Carmen who may have serious health problems."

Digger stared at the row of pale blue sweetener packets on the table between them. She wondered if they were making too much of this. Perhaps there was a simple explanation. Carmen decided to make a big splash, get to the wind farm early, climb up and practice her speech and she got dizzy and fell.

Digger's inner voice screamed NO!

"What's the latest you've heard from the cops?" she asked.

He shrugged. "I keep calling the sheriff's office and my source says they're still looking into it. When I pressed him about an autopsy report, all he would say was that her injuries were consistent with a fall from thirty feet—or whatever it was."

"Do you think she just fell by accident?" Digger demanded.

"At this point we don't have any way to prove she didn't."

"Okay, then. Maybe if she just found out she has some terrible diagnosis, she might be depressed and…"

He shook his head. "I don't buy that. She could just take pills and end it all at home Why go to the other side of the state and throw yourself off a wind turbine."

He was right of course. She pushed away her coffee cup and propped her chin on her hands while she thought. Something was tugging at the back of her mind, just out of reach, like the name of that song. Then it came to her. *Nancy.*

"What if she was pushed?" she said, slowly.

"Pushed?"

"That's what Nancy said. She was standing beside Maria and me and she said something like, 'guess we'll find out if she fell or was pushed.'"

"Hmm." He stared upward as though he could read something in the stains on the ceiling tiles. Finally, he looked back, leveled his dark eyes on Digger and asked, "Why do you suppose Nancy wanted you to know about Carmen and the Julie Mondragon case?"

"I don't know." Digger wasn't sure what Nancy's motives were, or even if she trusted her. "She told me to track down the friends that were with Carmen the day Julie disappeared. She said they knew what happened to her."

"And you did?"

"I thought I had. Someone named Sylvia. I found her on Facebook and I talked to her husband. He told me she died a few years ago. It was a heart attack. He blamed it on stress; said police and the press kept harassing her about the case." She paused, remembering the man's angry tone. "He told me I should talk to Billy Switzer. Sounded like he hated the guy."

"You think his wife had something going with this Billy guy?"

"No, I didn't get that feeling," she said. "But the way Nancy talked and the stuff he said is making my gut tell me there's a connection between what happened to Carmen and what happened to Julie."

CHAPTER 12

Wind moaned through the window frames at the field office. Today it was just a low hum, but when spring gales blew full force, Jake worried a gust would lift the flimsy building off the ground, whirling it through the air like Dorothy's home in *The Wizard of Oz*. The steady whoosh of the giant turbine blades beat in his ears like a pulse.

Jake missed his home and family in Houston. He felt it most acutely on mornings like this when he looked out over the dry New Mexico landscape. Houston was where Cassie was—Cassie and the thousand petty arguments over details that never deserved the energy she devoted to them. He wanted the relationship to work, God knows he wanted her so badly he was able to absorb the attrition.

Until that last argument.

The stupid, senseless argument over the way he'd done the laundry was the last straw. That was when he'd walked out and enrolled in a training course for wind technicians at the community college in Tucumcari.

So, here he was. It was a great job, but lonely, and until last week, boring.

The woman falling from the ladder shook everyone in the

area. Some of the local ranchers had taken to dropping by, eager for gossip. His office window had a view of the gravel road and he could spot them coming by the cloud of dust.

He'd just poured a cup of coffee when he glanced out and saw a vehicle approaching fast. It halted abruptly in front of the building. When the dust cleared, Jake could see it was an old tan-and-white Ford F150. A slim figure in faded blue jeans and a checkered shirt emerged. He couldn't tell if it was a man or a woman because a black cowboy hat covered their face.

Thirty seconds later he heard the sharp rap-rap-rap. Opening the door, he found a woman, maybe late thirties, hat in hand, with short-cropped brown hair and weathered skin. She pushed her wrap-around sunglasses back on her forehead.

"Hi," she said. "You the guy in charge here?" She had a dry, raspy voice.

"Yeah. Can I help you?"

She pointed past him. "Okay if I come inside?"

"Oh, sure." He led the woman into the office space, indicated a chair, and offered her coffee.

Mug in hand, she settled on a metal-framed chair and crossed a booted foot over her knee. "My name's Eileen, husband owns the ranch up there a piece."

Jake had met a few of the ranchers since he'd worked here. They liked to talk about the old times. How tough life was before the towers went up on their land and they started getting the steady checks. He sipped his coffee, eager for her to get to the point of her visit. Eileen took her time, stirred in two packets of sugar, glancing around the temporary building as if she were appraising the furniture.

Finally, she picked up the coffee mug and leaned toward him. "You're new here and you don't know the sheriff. He can be… well, this is kinda awkward. Let's just say him and me, we don't see eye to eye. That's why I thought I'd pass this on to you and you can talk to him yourself."

Jake wasn't sure he liked where this was going. Being an outsider in a place like this put you at a disadvantage. "Well, I'm not sure if—" he began, but she cut him off.

"You know, the morning of that accident, I was out checkin' fences. I was passin' by the end of your road here and I seen a coupla' cars headin' up toward this building."

Jake bolted upright. "You said a *couple* of cars? What time was that?"

"Yeah. That's right. Maybe about nine." She nodded slowly. "That's why I thought I'd better come in here and talk to you. All the news reports said that woman came up here on her own. But I seen two cars. There was a silvery gray sedan and a big dark-colored SUV, could've been black or real dark blue." She paused and pulled a pack of Marlboro Lights out of her breast pocket. "Mind if I smoke?"

Jake didn't like smoking in his office, but he wanted her to keep talking. "No problem. You said around nine?"

"Yeah, around then," she said, shaking out a cigarette. She lit it, took a puff, and gazed around, thoughtfully. "You know, I see work trucks coming up here all the time, but not a lot of cars, especially clean ones that look like they've come from the city." She took another drag off her cigarette and blew smoke from one side of her mouth. "I was real curious so I hung around. I saw the cars stop and two people get out. There was a woman in the sedan and a man in the SUV. They headed up toward the towers. My husband called me just then saying he couldn't start his car, so I had to run home."

The knot that had formed in Jake's chest tightened. For the umpteenth time since the day of the accident, he cursed himself for being late to work that morning. If he hadn't stopped in Fort

Sumner on his way in, he would have been at work by eight. Maybe none of this would have happened.

"You're sure about all this? There was only one car when I got here. The sedan," Jake said, hoping he didn't sound as nervous as he felt. "Can you tell me anything more about the other car you saw?"

"Like I said, it was dark blue or black. I don't know much about the different makes and I wasn't close enough to get a license number."

"And the people?"

She shrugged. "They was pretty far away. About all I can say is the woman had dark hair and the man's looked blond but it might just have been really short, or he may have been bald."

"Well, thanks for coming by, Eileen. I'll let the sheriff's people know." He gave her his most confident smile. Gossip traveled faster than the wind out here.

She smiled back, swung her booted foot to the floor, and retrieved her cowboy hat from the back of the chair. On her way out she patted his shoulder. "You do that, hon. By the way, nice place you got here."

Jake closed the door behind her and stood for a moment, eyes closed, breathing slowly to calm the erratic beating of his heart. He thought about that morning again. Normally he was at work by eight but the day the press group was coming from Albuquerque he'd had a message saying he had to pick up paint supplies in Fort Sumner.

It was a wasted trip.

The man in the hardware store said he'd never received an order. At the time, Jake had dismissed it as a mix-up. Maybe it wasn't. Did someone deliberately send him on a phony errand? He pulled his phone from his back pocket and searched through old messages. Damn, he'd deleted it.

He thought about the sheriff, the man's hard face, his questions. The way he made him feel guilty just for being at the wind farm when the body was discovered. He gritted his teeth and made the call. The deputy he spoke to was terse and non-committal. Irritated, Jake searched his call log again and found another number. Maybe this would stir things up, he thought.

"Hi, it's Jake. You told me to call if I had any new information. I do. Somebody just told me they saw a second car here early that morning, but it was gone when I arrived."

Chapter 13

Digger was halfway back to Albuquerque when her phone pinged an incoming message, she glanced at it, Roscoe wanted to ask some questions. Right now, she didn't want to talk to him, her mind was still churning from the conversation with Manny. A few minutes later, she was passing an exit when a call came through.

It was Manny. "Hey, I just heard from Jake; you remember the site supervisor at the wind farm. He said one of the local ranchers told him she'd seen a second car there that morning before he got to work."

"Are you serious!" Digger swerved into the slow lane as a van sped past her. "Can you check it out?"

"Yeah, he gave me her number and I've left a message. I'm going to call the sheriff."

As soon as Manny disconnected, she peered over her shoulder to check traffic, swung back into the fast lane, and floored the Subaru.

Back at the office, she found Roscoe in a rage.

"Those assholes!" he said, banging down his phone.

He winced and reached over to a family-sized jar of Tums on

his desk, opened it, and popped one in his mouth. He sucked on it for a minute, eyes closed, then he groaned. Digger knew better than to interrupt Roscoe when he was having a heartburn episode. Lately, he'd been having a lot of those. He was always worried about the paper's finances. She worried too; job hunting was hell.

Finally, he opened his eyes. "What gives?"

Digger filled him in on what she'd heard from Nancy, and the bombshell from Manny.

He frowned and looked thoughtful. "I remember the Julie Mondragon case." He paused, shaking his head. "But don't put any of that in a story until you find out if that Harford woman is bull-shitting us." He took a breath and winced again. "Oh, and call the wind farm guy, and that rancher about the second car. Get something online as soon as you can, I don't want TV beating us on this one."

She went back to her corner, found the number from Nancy's late-night call, and tried it. The call went straight to voicemail. It was then that she realized Nancy had never said which radio station she worked for. Digger did a Google search. She drew a blank at the first three stations that popped up. On the fourth try, she found Nancy's name among the reporters. She called. The young woman who answered apologized and said Nancy was away from the office and no, she didn't know when she'd be back.

Digger left a message and switched focus to check out Manny's tip.

Jake answered on the third ring, sounding breathless. "Oh hi, my phone's been blowing up for the last hour. I guess you talked to Manny Begay?"

"Yeah, I'm following up on that, and I'd like to talk to the rancher too."

"Sure." He gave a long sigh. "There's been some other stuff."

"Okay. I'm listening."

Jake told her that after the visit from the rancher, he had gone to check the surveillance camera outside the office. "I looked at it before but didn't notice anything unusual. The internet out here is sometimes a little unstable so it can be iffy. But this time, I slowed the playback way down and I think I saw two people go by."

Digger's heart leaped. "For real?"

He hesitated "Well, the camera angle was off, so it just caught the lower legs. At first, I thought it was just the wind blowing some debris, we get that all the time here. But I played it back a few times and what I saw was definitely two sets of legs."

"You tell the sheriff?"

"Yeah. He sent someone out to pick it up and they're going to analyze it."

"Wonder why they didn't do that in the first place?"

"Dunno. Could be they're busy. Maybe they're just not on the ball. And maybe there's people who want it kept kinda quiet."

Digger chuckled. Manny always had good instincts.

Her next call was to the number Jake gave her for Eileen the rancher. Eileen sounded as though she was sitting on a tractor, or maybe it was just the wind in the background, making it difficult to hear.

"Oh hey, you're the second reporter that's called me today, and I've got some TV people on their way here."

Shit! thought Digger. She had hoped she and Manny were the only ones chasing this so far. Jake must have called the TV people. That made it all the more urgent to get a story out.

Thankfully, Eileen confirmed everything Manny and Jake had said. Next, she called the Quay County Sheriff's Office. She had to repeat herself twice to the receptionist.

"No, I'm with *The Searcher*. It's a paper based in Albuquerque. Yes, we're new and we're mostly online." Finally, she was put through to a deputy.

"Yes, ma'am. I can confirm we're looking at some video footage from the wind farm, but that's all I can say at this time." Click.

Digger wanted to pound on the desk but was aware that Ginny had come into the office and was hovering nearby.

"Is something wrong?" Ginny asked in her faux-sweet voice.

Digger shook her head. She wondered why Ginny annoyed her so much. Was it the 'I'm-a-New-Yorker attitude'? Or the clothes she wore, the dresses that looked as if they cost a whole paycheck.

She managed a smile. "I'm fine. Just chasing down information. You know how it goes."

She put on her headphones to block out distractions and began typing:

New information has emerged that may be related to the mysterious death of State Representative Carmen Lawlor...

Half an hour later she ran the story by Roscoe, he made a couple of suggestions and posted it. Whew! They beat TV and the Albuquerque and Santa Fe papers.

She looked at her phone.

A missed call and a message from Maria: *Did you forget we're meeting Rex tonight for a beer?*

She texted back. *Sorry. Deadline. Leaving now. See you soon. XX.*

Maria greeted her at the door wearing a dark, shimmery calf-length skirt and loose white linen blouse. Digger wanted to kiss her and carry her off to the bedroom immediately.

"Do we really have to go meet Rex?" she murmured, nibbling at Maria's earlobe.

"You're the one who made the arrangement," she teased.

Rex had asked them to meet him at the Pioneer Saloon. The downtown bar was a popular journalist hangout back when reporters could still smoke at their desks and people read newspapers instead of iPhones. She knew he was nostalgic about the bar, he and her mentor Halloran used to drink there before the cranky old guy got sober. When Halloran died a group of *Courier* reporters had gone there after his memorial service to reminisce and commiserate. Two months later the paper closed and they were all out of a job.

Rex was seated at one of the rustic tables along the back wall beneath a faded print of cowboys roping cattle. A half-empty bottle of Dos Equis sat in front of him and by the look of his face, Digger could tell it wasn't his first.

"Hey ladies."

They each hugged him. Moments later, Bo Sampson the bar owner appeared at the table.

"Hi there, I hear congratulations are in order," he said in his hearty voice. When Digger and Maria looked blank, he grinned. "I heard you two got married."

Digger laughed. "That was more than a year ago, but thanks Bo. Maria here was elected too. She's a state rep now."

He looked incredulous, rubbing at the gray beard that splayed over his ample chest like Spanish moss. "Whoa! You guys need to come here more often. What'll it be?"

"Corona for me and Maria and some beef tacos. You want one Rex?"

Rex nodded. "Thanks and I'll take another one of these," he said, waving the empty bottle at Bo.

While they waited for the tacos, Digger asked Rex what Roscoe wanted him to do for the paper.

"I was waiting for you to ask that." Rex grinned. "He wants me to go down to the border and do a photoshoot at the Bridge of the Americas in El Paso."

"What? He never told me anything about that!" Digger was incensed. She'd been begging Roscoe to let her write a piece about border issues.

"He told me that other reporter would be going with me, Ginny something."

Now Digger was upset. "Ginny! As in 'I'm-from-New-York-and-I-always-wear-designer-dresses, that Ginny?"

Rex took a slug of beer. "Guess so. Said she speaks fluent Spanish. Claims her mom is Puerto Rican."

Maria laughed, nearly choking on her beer. "Oh yeah, Puerto Rican Spanish will get her a long way. She should go to Miami, not El Paso."

Rex shrugged, looking at Digger. "Plus, you're busy with this Carmen Lawlor thing."

Digger couldn't argue with that. It occurred to her that Rex had worked with Nancy in the past. Now would be a good time to ask him about her.

"Okay, maybe you can help me with something," she related the strange conversation she had had with the radio reporter. "What do you think?"

Rex had just taken a bite of taco. He pointed at his mouth as he chewed. Digger glanced at Maria, who rolled her eyes. In the background, Toby Keith was singing 'I love this bar'. She smiled thinking of her old friend Halloran. This place was his favorite before he got sober. Finally, Rex stopped chewing and wiped his mouth with one of the thin paper napkins.

"Hmm. The Las Vistas girl that went missing. They searched and searched and never found her, nobody even knew if she was kidnapped or killed. Yeah, I remember that. So, you're saying Nancy told you that Carmen and the girl were friends and she believes Carmen knew what happened to her and that she somehow thinks it's tied to what happened at the wind farm."

Digger nodded. Rex picked up his nearly empty beer bottle and stared at it thoughtfully. He drained it, set it on the table, and eyed Digger.

"I don't know what's been happening with her in the last few years, but the Nancy I remember was a good reporter, the kind that didn't let corporate flacks get away with bullshit. As I recall, she was chasing a story about a company in town. A source told her the company wanted the governor to give them an exemption for the air pollution from their plant. Nancy was all over it but the editor told her to back off. She couldn't accept that so she quit." He paused. "If it were me, I'd trust her."

Chapter 14

Paul Marquez leaned into the mirror, smoothed the thinning swath of hair over his scalp, and adjusted his glasses. He wasn't sure what he was going to say to the young woman he had asked to meet him this afternoon. He had debated with himself whether his law office was an appropriate place to meet but decided it was better than a cafe. It would avoid the risk of someone snapping a photo of them and trying to use it against him. It was only six months since his divorce.

He had asked her here because the dinner at the Hyatt Tamaya had unsettled him, something about the glances between the other men. He sensed menace in the unspoken communication that night and his conscience told him he should warn her.

He left the men's room and returned to his office on the top floor of the downtown building. Moments later his assistant buzzed letting him know his visitor had arrived. He remembered seeing Maria Ortiz a few times during the last legislative session. She stood out among the group of newly elected representatives for the confident way she handled herself, with that clear voice, and the way she showed she had studied the details. He recalled that he'd often seen her huddled with Carmen Lawlor, deep in conversation. As he thought of Carmen his chest tightened. The woman had shown such courage in the few years she had served in the legislature. But there was no time for those thoughts now. There was a knock and his assistant opened the office door.

"Paul, it's Miss Ortiz."

He rose, straightened his tie, and went to the door to greet her. "Thank you for coming to meet me. I hope I didn't inconvenience you."

He had forgotten how impressive she was with those large dark eyes and the sweep of mahogany brown hair. She was striking, even in the plain blue blouse and white slacks she wore. She reminded him a little of his wife when they had first started dating. The thought was as sad as it was sweet. He held out a hand and she smiled at him.

"Hello, Mr. Marquez…"

"It's Paul."

"Paul, I'm sorry I'm a little late, I teach in the school at San Fermin and I hit a lot of traffic on my way into Albuquerque."

He waved a hand, dismissing her apology, and gestured to a chair opposite his desk. "Not a problem. I don't keep banker's hours. Can I offer you water, coffee?"

"No, thanks, I'm fine." She took her seat, giving him a smile that was both expectant and curious.

He sat and glanced around for a second, wondering where to begin. Then it came to him. Her family, that was always a good way to connect. "Your grandmother is Conchita Chavez Ortiz, no?"

"Yes," Maria answered, puzzled.

"My mother had great admiration for her. They volunteered together, with Dolores Huerta in California one summer."

That put her at ease. Her smile widened and her body relaxed. "My Abuela is a strong woman. Still is," she said proudly.

Marquez nodded. He remembered the way his mother had

spoken of Conchita Ortiz. He barely knew the young woman sitting in front of him, but he'd seen her speak at the Roundhouse and he sensed she had the same kind of strength as her grandmother, calm on the outside and steel on the inside.

"You're probably wondering why I asked you to come here today," he began. "I suppose I could have phoned but it seemed better to talk in person." He leaned back in his swivel chair wondering again if he was being an alarmist. "As you know, I am on the House Commerce and Economic Development Committee. As such, I get a lot of requests from people who want my support. Now, I know you recently announced that you plan to continue the work Carmen was doing…"

"What happened to her was a tragedy!" she broke in, her face animated. "Carmen invested so much in her work. It has to continue. We have some of the best renewable energy resources in the country right here. We need to take advantage of that. It makes sense for everyone, and I'm including the business community in this."

Marquez was taken aback. He hadn't expected her to be this forceful. He wondered how she would react to what he had to say next. "I happen to agree," he said carefully. "But there are people who do not." He paused, letting that sink in. "The other night I was invited to dinner with a group of men whose interests are, shall we say, not aligned with Ms. Lawlor's."

Maria's eyes met his, and he could see her nostrils flare as she took in a breath, but she said nothing.

"I think you should be aware that you will get strong pushback as you continue her work. These people have deep pockets and they have experience in exerting influence in Santa Fe, if you get my drift." Marquez hoped he sounded gently avuncular, he wanted to warn her to be careful. He had seen too many high-minded young people ground down under the subtle but relentless pressure of politics. He often thought it was no coincidence that the Roundhouse, the building where the legislature met in Santa Fe, looked like a Spanish bullring.

Maria leaned forward, eyes flashing. "Mr. Marquez, Paul, I don't know if you're familiar with my district, but it is deeply divided between the rural areas and the city of Las Vistas. Families like mine have gradually been pushed out by the developers who cater to retirees who move to Las Vistas from California or Michigan or Long Island because they can get a bigger house for their money. Your family is from Los Lunas, no? I'm sure you've seen something similar there."

He nodded and she continued. "The reason I'm saying this is because I want you to know that my first experience in local politics was a fight over a road that would have ruined a historic site. I won that fight and the Spanish chapel is still standing. I don't give up easily!"

Marquez nodded again. This young woman impressed him. "From what my mother said about your grandmother, you have inherited her spirit. That's good. Because I know you will need it."

He hoped she understood the seriousness of his words. His eyes met hers briefly, then she looked down at her hands as if thinking. Outside the light was starting to fade, the Sandia range was beginning to glow and the lowering sun glinted on the windows of homes in the foothills.

Finally, she took a deep breath. "Can you at least tell me who these men you met with are?"

Marquez considered. If he were talking as a lawyer, he would probably decline. But this was a matter of public interest he told himself. He was unnerved by what had happened to Carmen and he wanted to help this young woman. He pulled a notebook out of his desk drawer, wrote down the three names, and handed it to her. "If you need any help in the future. Call me."

They shook hands and she turned to leave. As she slipped out the door he called after her, "Give my best wishes to your grandmother."

CHAPTER 15

Digger arrived home from work to find Lady Antonia curled up on the edge of the couch and a note on the kitchen table from Abuela. It said, *Felt tired so am taking a nap. Maria called saying she'll be late. She has a meeting in Albuquerque after work. She didn't say what kind. I made some posole. We can heat it up for dinner. Abrazos.*

Digger thought it odd Maria hadn't messaged her. With the prospect of Abuela's posse for dinner, she decided to go for a run. Ever since the trip to the wind farm she'd been too busy to get in her usual exercise. She hoped the run would help calm the tangle of questions roiling in her head. Changing quickly, she headed to her regular route on the foothills trailhead at the end of their street.

Daylight was ebbing making the aspen trees higher up the mountainside glow like beaten gold. Gradually the shadows crept upwards and Digger had to switch on the headlamp she wore to make out the trail. The air cooled swiftly, biting at her cheeks and ears.

By the time she returned, it was fully dark and Maria's car was in its place, snug beside the house. Once inside, she saw Abuela standing at the sink, her back to the door.

At the sound of Digger's footsteps, she called out, "Maria went straight to her studio when she came home."

Abuela didn't need to say more, Digger knew that meant bad news.

"Thanks, I'll go see her."

She slipped out the back door, crossed the walled yard, and stood outside the partially glassed-in shed tacked onto the back of the house that served as Maria's art studio. This place was Maria's refuge in times of stress. A few canvases hung around the room; more paintings leaned against shelves. Every surface in the small space was covered: cloths, photos, stacks of paper, drawing pads, and toolboxes. Maria was sitting in front of her easel, staring at a half-finished landscape of Navajo Lake.

Digger went to her and laid her hands on Maria's shoulders. "What happened?" she asked softly.

Maria gave a long, deep sigh. "It's started," she said.

Alarmed, Digger moved around the side of Maria's stool and knelt in front, looking up at her. "What? What's started?"

Maria sighed again and folded her arms across her chest. "One of the state reps asked me to meet him today. Paul Marquez, he's on one of the legislative committees. He wanted to warn me about taking on Carmen's work. He was nice about it, but I got the feeling he knew a lot more than he was saying."

"Did he threaten you?"

"No. He just said there were people who could exert pressure. He told me to watch out."

An icy wave gripped Digger's stomach. Carmen had been outspoken and upset people; now Maria wanted to take on her mission. Could that put her in danger?

People with vested interests could take revenge in different ways. Her old boss Julia Montoya had tried to ruin someone's career to even a score.

Maria's ex-girlfriend had tried to get Maria fired from her

teaching job by planting a rumor that she was bringing drugs to the school.

She wished Maria would change her mind, but she knew it would be pointless trying to persuade her.

As if she had been reading Digger's thoughts, Maria shrugged and stood up. "Come on. Don't look so worried. You know I can handle pressure." She took Digger's face in her hands and kissed her. "I will be all right. Carmen had a lot of people on her side and they will work with me."

Abuela was stirring a big pot on the stove when they returned to the house and the kitchen was suffused with the rich scent of slow-cooked pork. "I've heated up the posole. it'll be ready in a minute. Cowgirl, can you feed Lady Antonia, I forgot, and don't forget the teaspoon of tuna."

Digger chuckled. Abuela had not been enthusiastic about Digger bringing her cat when she and Maria moved in, but Digger insisted. Lady Antonia had won the old woman's heart with her deep blue eyes, soft gray fur, and diva-like personality.

Over supper, Digger noticed the deep crease between Abuela's brows as she eyed Maria and knew she was worried.

Maria looked up from her bowl and seeing her grandmother's expression, she set down her spoon. "Okay, I get it, you want to know where I was."

"M'ija, you looked upset when you came home. What's going on?" Her voice was strained with concern.

As Maria related her meeting with Paul Marquez, Digger noted how she soft-pedaled the implications, trying to reassure her grandmother. "And he said his mother volunteered with you and Dolores Huerta back in the day in California."

Abuela knit her brows. "Marquez? From Los Lunas?" She sat for a moment, deep in thought. Then her face softened. "Ah yes, I remember. She helped me when I came back here, too. After your grandfather left me with four children. Yes, she was a good woman. Her son, he's a lawyer now?"

"Si, Abuelita, and he told me to call him if I ever need any help," Maria said. She laid a hand on her grandmother's arm. The old woman smiled but Digger could see tears glistening behind her glasses.

After they'd finished the meal and cleared up, Digger suggested a short walk. "There's going to be a full moon tonight. We can see it rise over the mountain crest."

Abuela made a face. "It's too cold for me. You two go."

Maria and Digger put on their jackets, wool caps, and gloves and headed outside. The night air was so sharp it took their breath away. They strode swiftly up the deserted street toward the trail Digger had run a couple of hours earlier. A few feet beyond the trailhead, they stopped and squeezed together to perch on top of a rock.

Already the flanks of the mountain were bathed in silvery light. A glow at the highest point of the crest grew brighter as they watched. A sliver of brilliance grew imperceptibly as if the rock itself were giving birth to a ball of pure light. The full moon crowned the ridge line of the crest, hanging above them huge and yellow.

"My father used to call the October moon the Hunter's moon," Digger said.

"Do you think of them? Your parents? How many years is it now since the accident?"

"Nineteen. Yes, I dream about them sometimes. I wonder what they would look like now, Digger murmured, "But Abuela has made such a difference in my life. She brought me into your family and I am so grateful."

"She has such a great heart. That's why I don't want to hurt her. I know she will worry about me because of what I heard today."

Digger wrapped an arm around Maria and whispered in her ear. "I want you to know I believe in what you are doing," she said, "but I'm glad he warned you. There will be people who will want to stop you."

CHAPTER 16

Digger had just pushed her way into crowded traffic on Interstate 25 when Roscoe called, his voice blared from the car speakers.

"Christ, have you seen your friend's story in the *Daily Post*? He included the rumor about Carmen and the Mondragon case. What the hell was he thinking?"

Digger shrugged eyes focused on the swarm of freeway traffic. "Well, it's not our problem, is it?" she said. "I left it out of my story. I'll check with him to see if he's getting pushback." She ended the call.

Twenty minutes later, she was hunting for a parking place near *The Searcher*, silently cursing Roscoe for putting the office in an old residential area with impossibly narrow streets. Manny called.

"Hey Digg, you see the story?"

"Not yet. Gimme five, okay."

She gritted her teeth and squeezed into a tight spot. Sighing with relief, she picked up her phone and returned Manny's call. "No, I haven't read it, but Roscoe told me you used some of Nancy's story."

Manny gave a scornful laugh. "Yeah, well. I talked to her, and did some research, I thought it was fair game. Then she called me this morning, she was totally unglued, saying she wants to meet me later. She wants you there too."

"No shit. Where?"

"Get this. She said she'll be in front of Saint John's Cathedral on Silver at eleven-thirty."

"You're kidding, right?"

"Yeah. Kind of a weird place. You'd think she'd suggest a cafe or thing. Oh well, I guess she's had a come-to-Jesus moment. Anyway, see you there?"

"Okay."

As soon as she entered *The Searcher's* cluttered newsroom—formerly the livingroom of the tiny house—she noticed the tobacco smell, indicating Roscoe had started smoking again. He routinely quit each month, and just as routinely lapsed. Digger wished her editor would take up vaping. When she relayed Manny's news to Roscoe he clamped his lips. His expression meant. 'Don't bother wasting your time with this shit!'

She chose to ignore the warning. "Look," she said, "gimme an hour. We'll meet with her and put it to rest. Okay?"

"Okay," he grumbled and turned to answer the phone ringing on his desk.

Checking the time, Digger calculated she had about an hour before she had to head downtown to the meeting spot. Enough time to look into Paul Marquez and the industry group he met with at the Hyatt Tamaya. She figured if he was worried enough to contact Maria, he must think they presented a real threat.

A search of the New Mexico Legislature website showed Marquez had represented a district in the Albuquerque area for ten years and sat on several committees, including one for commerce and economic development. He was also an attorney at a big-name law firm. So far, everything Maria had said about him checked out.

Next, she looked at the industry group.

Maria had only been able to give her first names, so she browsed the website. There she found details showing how much the industry contributed to state coffers, education, and so on. Maria had also said there was a lobbyist, but she couldn't remember his name. Digger tried the Secretary of State's website but there were so many options she realized she needed more information to narrow her search.

Right now, she didn't have time.

Outside, a light rain was falling. The shower had turned to a downpour by the time she reached downtown. Lacking a rain jacket, she searched in vain for a parking space close to the cathedral, finally ending up in a vacant lot off First Street between a shuttered movie theater and a second-hand store.

She texted Manny. *Be there in ten.*

Shortly before eleven-thirty, she rounded the corner from Lead Avenue onto Fourth and spotted him on the steps of the tan stone-faced entrance to the cathedral. Rain penetrated her fleece and created damp patches on her jeans. Manny stood with his jacket pulled over his head, irritated.

Digger joined him and cast a glance around. "Guess she's late?"

He nodded, eyed the clouds, and said, "Haven't heard from her. Let's give it a couple of minutes."

While they waited, Digger glanced in each direction hoping to see Nancy. Looking left she noticed a shopping cart piled high with what looked like clothing and boxes. Behind the cart stood a figure swathed in layers of dark clothing so voluminous it was hard to tell if it was a man or a woman, or even a human being. The cart approached slowly, creaking along the sidewalk. When it drew level with Digger and Manny, it stopped. A hand emerged from the cloth, palm dark and creased with grime.

"You live around here?" Digger asked, pulling her wallet out of her backpack.

A voice rasped from behind a brown cloth head covering.

"Found a space down the street last night, been checking it out this morning."

It was still hard to tell whether the person was male or female. Digger placed a dollar in the outstretched palm. "We're supposed to meet somebody here. Did you see anybody while you were checking out the street?"

The hand swiftly disappeared into the folds of the cloth and the head covering moved in what could have been a nod. Then the voice said, "Yeah. Little bit ago, a couple went inside. I didn't see 'em come out but I wasn't watching the whole time."

The outstretched palm reappeared. Digger gave Manny a nudge in the ribs. He dug a few coins from his pocket and handed them over.

"Thanks." The cart creaked again and the figure moved off.

Digger pointed at the door. "Let's go in. Nancy probably didn't want to wait out here and get wet."

She took a few steps inside the cathedral and stopped. It reminded her of a church in Ireland her grandmother had taken her to see. The still air, the filtered light, and the solemnity of the surroundings weighed like an unseen force. She wondered if Manny felt it too.

Twin ranks of pews stretched out before them leading to the altar rail. On the left, a bank of organ pipes gleamed a dull silver. Above the altar, daylight shone dully through three long narrow, stained-glass windows, the colors glowed like jewels.

They saw no one.

Manny whispered, "Let's go this way." He led and they walked slowly along the pillared arches gazing along the rows of pews.

"There." Manny cocked his head, indicating someone in the second row back from the altar rail on the far side.

It looked like the person was kneeling, with head in hands deep in prayer. As they approached, they saw it was a woman, wearing a red coat. Digger recognized Nancy's layered hairstyle.

Sliding into the pew beside her, she murmured. "Nancy."

No reaction.

Manny approached from the other side, sat, and stretched a hand over to touch her on the shoulder. "Hey, Nancy, you wanted to meet us here."

Still no reaction. Manny gently pushed her head to one side. The eyes were open, but the pupils in the dim light of the church were mere pinpoints, her lips ashen. As the head turned, one arm flopped toward the floor.

Manny recoiled.

Digger stared, horrified, unable to move. Around them the church was silent, her pulse deafening. As if from far away, she heard Manny say,

"Call 911. She's overdosed on something."

Of course, she thought, Manny did the cop beat. He knows these things. In a fog, she pulled her phone out of her backpack, and made the call, stammering out the words. Then they sat transfixed. It seemed an eternity before they heard the front doors flung open and footsteps pound toward them. Digger started to explain how they found Nancy.

The tall, beefy young EMT who led the crew held up a hand. "We got it, ma'am," he said.

Manny pulled her aside. "Give them some room. They'll give her naloxone, it should revive her."

The next moment another EMT, who was bent over Nancy, said, "No pulse."

Minutes went by as they watched the medical team examine Nancy and answered questions about how they found her. Then a police officer arrived, a burly young man with heavy dark eyebrows and a prominent jaw.

He surveyed the scene, then turned to address Digger. "I understand you were the one who made the 911 call. What were you doing here?"

They went through the story again, describing how they'd arranged to meet Nancy to interview her for a story they were working on. Digger was relieved when Manny told the officer the story was about renewable energy. The last thing she wanted was for Carmen Lawlor's name to be mentioned. The officer didn't ask for any further details, just questioned them why they were inside the cathedral.

Digger answered. "It was raining while we waited for her outside. We thought she might have gone inside to get out of the weather."

The officer's eyes slid back and forth between the two of them, then he nodded, apparently satisfied. "I may have to call you later, okay." He turned his attention to the older man in a tweed sports jacket and gray slacks who had just bustled in looking worried.

"Oh, my goodness, what's going on here?"

"Are you a church official?" the police officer asked.

"Not really, I'm the organist. This is my regular practice time."

The medics had just lifted Nancy's body onto a gurney. The officer lifted the sheet covering her face. "Do you recognize this woman?"

The organist gaped and answered, nervously, "No, but then I don't see the congregation. My back is to them while I'm playing during the services."

Later, after they had watched the EMTs load the gurney into the ambulance, Digger nudged Manny. "Let's see if we can find that homeless person and talk to him again."

They searched for half an hour, walking in a pattern all around the cathedral, venturing into the gaps between buildings, peering behind parked vehicles, clumps of trees. Finally, Digger noticed a battered blue tent in an alley on the edge of a parking lot. As they drew near it, they saw the familiar shopping cart. Digger called out several times before they saw movement. The dark shape emerged from within the tent.

"What d'you want?" The gruff voice sounded suspicious.

"Hi," said Digger. "We talked to you outside the church a little while ago."

"Yeah. What about it?" The tone had changed to anger.

"You said you'd seen two people walk into the church a little while before we got there. Can you tell us anything about them?"

A vigorous movement disturbed the layers of dark clothing, Digger interpreted it as a head shake.

"Don't know nothing more. Just two people. Could have been man, woman. Dunno. Go away! I don't want no cops finding me." The form disappeared into the tent.

As they trudged across the parking lot, Digger said aloud the question that had been churning through her mind. "You think Nancy was addicted, or?"

"Or somebody slipped her something on purpose?" said Manny, finishing the sentence. He shrugged. "OMI will investigate, but it'll take a while before we'd be able to get our hands on the autopsy report."

Digger immediately thought of Carmen but before she could say anything the rain started again. She hunched her shoulders. "I gotta go talk to Roscoe. Later," she called, waving back at Manny.

CHAPTER 17

Paul Marquez sat staring at the rain pelting his windshield. He knew it was welcome, the monsoon rains had been light and every part of the state was in moderate to severe drought. Still, he didn't have a raincoat with him and he knew he'd get wet before he reached the entrance to the Country Club. At least he had his car. He usually walked to the office since he worked downtown and lived a few streets away, but he'd taken the car today because of the rain.

A few rays of sun poked through the clouds and raindrops glistened on the sweeping lawn in front of the low building. Exiting the vehicle he dashed toward the clubhouse. At the entrance, he had to pull his jacket over his head to ward off water dripping from the edge of the red tile roof.

Inside the restaurant, the bright young woman at the reception desk greeted him by name and offered to get him a towel to dry off. Marquez declined her offer and went straight to his usual table. Once seated, he checked his watch. He'd made the reservation for twelve-fifteen, to give himself a few minutes to gather his thoughts before his guest would arrive.

He took a tiny notepad from his inside pocket and skimmed through what he'd written. He had plenty of practice eliciting client information without alarming them and didn't anticipate Fred Carter would pose a problem. It was his own emotions he had to keep in check. The more he thought about the meeting at the Hyatt Tamaya, the more the uncomfortable feeling grew. Something about the death of Carmen Lawlor struck him as sinister. That's why he had felt bound to contact the young woman, Maria Ortiz. He'd seen just how powerful and persuasive the oil and gas lobby could be. The industry provided almost half the state's revenue. If she wanted to curb their power, he knew it would be a tough, and maybe ugly battle.

He gazed out the window at the green fairways of the golf course, ran his hand through the hair on his scalp, and took a couple of the deep breaths as his yoga teacher had taught him. He used to think yoga was a 'woman's thing' but agreed to try it at his wife's request.

When he looked around, he spotted Carter's tall bulky form approaching.

"Hey there Paul! Great to see you, man." Carter's voice grated on him like the sound of a goose honking.

Carter's rust-colored hair and the tan fabric of his jacket were dark from their recent shower. He grinned at Marquez and as he leaned forward to shake hands the curve of his belly brushed the table. As soon as they were settled, Marquez signaled the server and she bustled over.

"How y'all doing today, can I tell you about our specials?" She was short and curvy, with shoulder-length blond hair that bounced as she walked.

"Why sure." Carter beamed at the young woman letting his eyes linger on the spot where the neckline of her blouse was just low enough to afford a glimpse of cleavage. Marquez noticed the look and frowned. He'd hate to think of a guy like Carter ogling his daughter.

Carter ordered a beef tenderloin, and Marquez settled for a

lasagna. While they waited for their meals, chatting about the unusual weather, Marquez took the opportunity to study Carter. From what he'd read about him since the dinner meeting, he learned that the man had moved into his job with the industry group after a career in the field. Marquez guessed he was likely to be defensive and unreceptive to new ideas.

Marquez decided to test the waters. "Fred, I was thinking about the dinner at the Tamaya resort."

Carter flicked a glance at Marquez then helped himself to one of the rolls from the basket on the table, spread it generously with butter, and took a bite. He took his time chewing then finally set down the remains of the roll and said, "Glad you brought that up, Paul. I hope we made ourselves clear that night. As you know, some of our members donated to your last election campaign." He let the sentence hang.

A twinge of disgust stirred in Marquez's stomach. Money was always the sordid underside of politics and he hated it. But the next election was still a long way off and he could afford to stick to his principles. He smiled and responded to Carter's unsaid implication. "And you expect me to support your agenda."

Carter nodded and took another bite.

Just then the server brought their meals, interrupting Marquez. He waited for a few minutes while Carter tucked his napkin into his collar and took a knife to his steak. "Well, the next legislative session is a few months away. I'm sure you're going to be very active in planning for it. I know you were very focused on Carmen Lawlor in the last session, but now?"

Carter set down his knife and fork. "Well, we had a strategy all planned out. Now, I'm not sure."

Marquez sat up, alert. "How so?"

"It was Marty Granger. Even though he's kind of new to our field, he's a smart guy and he can sure charm people. I've seen him catch legislators in the hallways right before committee meetings at the Roundhouse. Folks who were dead against bills we favored, and he'd have 'em eating out of the palm of his hand." Carter grinned, took another bite, chewed it, then continued. "Anyways, Marty followed the fights we had with Carmen during the session and he came to me right after it ended. Said he knew her from way back and had an idea how we could cooperate together."

Marquez frowned, he remembered Granger had said little during the evening at the Hyatt Tamaya, leaving the conversation to Carter and the Rancher. He clearly recalled Granger saying he didn't know Carmen personally. That was just before Carter said Carmen's goals were diametrically opposed to his group's. So, what kind of game was Carter playing now?

He watched as Carter made steady progress through the pile of French fries on his plate. He wanted to catch him unawares, so he ate a few mouthfuls of his lasagna. A few moments later, when the other man had loaded a forkful into his mouth. Marquez commented. "That sounds creative, given the very different goals you have. What was Granger's idea?"

Carter shot him a look but had to continue chewing for a few more seconds before he could respond. "Well." More chewing. "It was like this." Another pause. At last, he swallowed and took a breath. "We discussed pooling our lobbying resources so we could minimize delays on some projects, that kind of thing."

Carter's group represented companies that drilled for oil and gas, operations that routinely polluted groundwater and the atmosphere. Marquez failed to see how they could possibly find any way to merge interests with Lawlor's green energy platform. But he was curious, so he remained silent.

Carter continued, "Marty told us he pitched the idea of making a big splash at some event where he and Ms. Lawlor could lay out their goals to a shared audience."

"And you thought you could make it look like you were all in the same boat together and get the environmental types to accept you?"

"That was his idea, more or less, except…" Carter waved his fork around as if he expected Marquez to guess his next words.

"Except what?"

Carter shrugged as if the answer was obvious. "Well, Marty couldn't follow through because she went to that wind farm and had that accident."

Marquez nodded and returned his attention to the half-finished lasagna on his plate. Thoughts ricocheted around in his mind. What Carter said made no sense, there had to be more he wasn't saying. If Martin Granger was lying that night at the restaurant, then whatever plan he pitched to Carter and the others probably had more to do with some relationship he had with Carmen Lawlor than any real possibility of getting members of Carter's organization and the environmentalists to sing from the same hymnbook.

"What about this Ortiz woman that says she's going to carry on Lawlor's work?"

Carter frowned. "Well, I think we're done trying to accommodate. It's just not in our interests. We need to keep the governor focused on our agenda and we've got the right connections. If this gal thinks she can sweet talk the legislature, she's got another think coming."

Marquez leveled his gaze at the other man and they stared at each other over the empty plates for a few seconds. "Just what are you planning to do?"

"You know I'm not going to answer that, Paul," Carter said, a smile creeping slowly across his face. He reached over and plucked a toothpick from the holder in the center of the table and poked at his teeth. With his free hand, he signaled the server who bustled over to their table.

"Any desserts here? I can recommend the key lime pie."

"No darlin', just the check," Carter said.

"Separate checks, please," Marquez said. He was not going to have Carter pick up the bill.

Chapter 18

By the time Digger got back to her car after leaving Manny, her hands were shaking so much she didn't trust herself to call the editor. When she walked into the office Roscoe was in the middle of yet another phone call meltdown. While she waited, she filled her water bottle and sat down to let her heartbeat return to normal. At last, Roscoe finished the call. She let another sixty seconds go by before she approached. Sometimes he needed a minute or so to calm down. The minute went by and hearing no further explosions she went over and filled him in on what had gone down at the cathedral.

He screwed his eyes shut, grimaced and forced words out through clenched teeth. "That woman was always a disaster! Now she OD's! I don't have time for this!"

"But Roscoe! Don't you see, this is…"

He cut her off. "Digger, look, I get it that you're upset," he said tightly. "But right now Ginny is out at a SWAT scene going down and there's a major storm forecast. So put Nancy on the back burner and get on the phone with that weather service guy!" He turned and picked up the phone on his desk that had been ringing throughout their brief exchange.

Digger retreated to her corner and set to work. A weather story! She'd give Roscoe the rest of the day but she knew Nancy's story was way more important.

When she got home that evening she went straight to the refrigerator and pulled out a cold beer.

Abuela was on the old corduroy couch with Lady Antonia on her lap watching Jeopardy. She eyed Digger as she flopped next to her, beer in hand. "Another bad day, Cowgirl?" Abuela punched a button on the remote to turn off the TV and reached out to take her free hand.

"You could say that," Digger replied.

A chill swept over her as she recalled Nancy's sightless eyes in the filtered light of the cathedral interior. What was Nancy doing there? Had she gone from prescription pills to scoring drugs on the street, and this time been unlucky? Digger read the stories daily, the problem was everywhere, and now it was here, beside her, slumped in a pew a few feet from the altar. She blew air through her lips, took a sip of beer, and told Abuela about the scene in the cathedral.

"It's not your fault. You're safe here, Cowgirl," Abuela said quietly.

She didn't need to say more. Digger closed her eyes and let out a long slow breath. She was grateful for Abuela's calming presence. She hadn't wanted to move in with Maria's grandmother, she had agreed to it because Maria had to be living in the district she represented. They were in a bind and Abuela offered them her home. That was more than a year ago. They could have found their own place after the election but it was in moments like these that she knew how much she had grown to love the old woman.

At the sound of Maria's car parking outside, Digger roused herself, squeezed Abuela's hand, and headed for the door. Before she could open it, Maria came rushing in.

"I'm sorry I'm late, you must be starving." She set two large bags on the table. "I know it's my turn to make dinner so I brought a casserole from Rosario's."

They were halfway through their meal when Maria made the announcement. "Guess what!"

Digger looked up from the rice, beans, and corn casserole. She was used to Maria's sudden revelations, but they still made her wary.

Maria caught the look on her face and laughed. "No, it's good news, *preciosa*. You know I contacted three of the solar companies that your grandfather recommended. He said he'd looked into them and was fairly certain they were interested in New Mexico. I told them all about the work done last year to prepare the site near San Fermin Pueblo. Anyway, I heard back from one of the companies today and we're setting up a meeting."

Digger still felt shaky about the scene in the cathedral, but Maria's words intrigued her. Last year she had been investigating a suspicious-sounding company that was supposed to build a solar array on state land near the San Fermin Pueblo. She knew her grandfather had experience in the solar industry so she contacted him to check on the company's background. Besides helping her with the research, Grandpa Jack had given her names of other companies interested in New Mexico.

"Are you working with anyone else at the state on this?" she asked.

Maria grinned. "Funny you should say that. Remember Chris Lovington, the State Land Commissioner pushing that solar project as part of his campaign for governor last year."

"How could I forget? Last I heard he found religion and was starting some church."

"Well, he's got another job now. Come on, let's let Abuela watch her TV shows. We can go out to the studio. I'll show you what I've found out so far."

Maria stood and gathered the plates. Once they had finished cleaning the kitchen she led Digger out to her studio. She opened the voluminous canvas bag she called her 'life support system' and pulled out her laptop and a bundle of folders. She pushed aside some tubes of paint and rags and spread a map on the worktable.

"You're right," she said. "Chris Lovington is involved with some kind of church, but he's also working for the Energy Minerals and Natural Resources Department and part of his gig is to scout sites for solar projects. See here is where they were proposing the project last year." Maria tapped her keyboard and called up a map. She pointed at an area northwest of Las Vistas.

"The project that never happened." Digger laughed. She didn't need to study the map. "Guess he'd have plenty of experience since he proposed that fiasco. Is he going to be at this meeting you're setting up?"

Maria nodded. "Yeah, it's next week. I've invited someone from the state economic development department and I'll invite that guy Paul Marquez too. I think he could be useful."

In one way, Digger was glad Maria was moving ahead with her plans undeterred by the concerns Marquez had raised. Still, the questions about Carmen Lawlor's death and now Nancy Harford's made her uneasy. If Paul Marquez was concerned enough to warn Maria, he probably had a good reason.

CHAPTER 19

The threatened storm eased off to the west during the night and by the next morning the only signs of the nighttime downpour were clumps of gravel and leaves accumulated like sandbars at the edges of the streets.

Digger headed to the radio station where Nancy worked. It seemed the best place to start fishing. She hoped to find someone who could shed light on Nancy's personal life. Maybe she could get an insight into whether her colleagues were aware of a drug problem or some other addiction. She put her chances at fifty-fifty. What little she'd seen of Nancy; she got the impression the woman could be blunt and hard to like.

The radio station offices were located in a one-story 1960s-era stucco building near the old industrial part of the city. There were spaces for about half a dozen cars in the parking lot. Runoff from the heavy rainstorm had left a pile of soggy clothing, broken liquor bottles, and crumpled fast-food containers along the sidewalk in one corner. A sprinkle of glass from a broken window glittered in the sunlight near where she turned in. Digger locked her car and hoped it would be intact when she returned.

A pale, twenty-something woman was sitting at the front desk immediately to the right of the front door. Her thin blond hair was parted in the middle and she sported a nose ring, and false eyelashes. The nameplate on the desk said 'Chelsey Fornier.' She had the desk phone clamped to one ear and was in the middle of a discussion that was not going well. As she spoke, she tugged nervously at the sleeve of her Halloween-themed black-and-orange T-shirt. Digger was glad to have a few moments to gather her thoughts. She wondered if Nancy's co-workers had even heard about what happened to her. Overdose deaths were a dime a dozen in this city.

The young woman finally ended her conversation and plunked the phone handset down. She eyed Digger. "Are you here for the interview?"

Digger shook her head. "My name's Elizabeth Doyle and I'm here because of Nancy Harford."

Chelsey's eyebrows furrowed. "Where is she? She was supposed to host a show this morning and she never showed. We had to scramble to keep on schedule."

Digger cleared her throat. "Could I talk to the station manager. I've got some news he or she should probably hear."

"Oh, I'm sorry, she's so busy. Unless you have an appointment, she probably can't fit you in till this afternoon."

Digger leaned over the desk and said quietly, "I'm sorry to break the news, but Nancy passed away yesterday."

The young woman's eyelashes sprang open impossibly wide. "What? That can't be!" Chelsey's eyes searched Digger's face as if pleading for her to take her words back. "Oh my God! When she didn't come home last night. I just thought she maybe hooked up with someone."

"How do you know she wasn't home last night?"

"Um… she… she…" Chelsey stuttered. "She's been letting me stay at her place till I could find a new apartment. Oh God, this is terrible!"

"Don't you think I should talk to your boss about this?"

Chelsey looked around nervously. "Not yet, please. It's too awful! Let's go somewhere else to talk. Give me a minute, I'll get someone to sit here for me."

She sprang out of her seat and disappeared down a hallway. Moments later she returned with a tall young man whose dreadlocks hung halfway down his back. "Thanks, Robert, I'll just be a little while. I have to go check something at the post office."

Robert shrugged and took Chelsey's seat without a word. Chelsey grabbed her handbag and jacket from behind the desk and signaled Digger to follow her.

They left the building, walked across the parking lot, and turned left. They continued walking for a few minutes and came to a wooden shack that served as a burrito stand.

"You want something?" Chelsey asked.

"Coffee, an Americano if they've got it. Just black."

"Okay, it's on me. There's a bench round the back. I'll be there in a minute."

Digger walked in the direction Chelsey had pointed and found a table and bench beneath a cottonwood tree. In the summer the tree would provide shade, now its fallen leaves formed a yellow carpet around the table.

Chelsey appeared a few moments later with two coffees and handed one to Digger. They sat side by side, facing the open bay of a garage. A pair of legs in grease-stained blue overalls protruded from the underside of an old pickup. Cars passed. Voices from the men in the garage floated over to them.

Digger sipped her coffee while she waited for Chelsey to speak.

After a long moment, she swallowed a couple of times, took a breath, and said, "Nancy was so good to me." She paused, struggled to control herself, then continued. "When I told her I couldn't pay my rent, she offered to let me stay at her place." She turned to face Digger. Tears rolled down her cheeks. "Can you tell me what happened to Nancy?"

Digger bit her lip. She didn't want to scare Chelsey, but she needed information. "I'm a reporter with *The Searcher.*" She studied Chelsey's face but there was no reaction, so she continued. "Another reporter and I were supposed to interview her yesterday for a story we were working on. She asked us to meet her in front of St. John's Cathedral." Digger paused.

"And what happened?"

"She wasn't there and it started raining so we went into the cathedral. We found her in one of the pews, bent over like she was praying. But when we tried to talk to her, she was unresponsive. My friend was a cop reporter. He said it looked like she had overdosed."

"What?" Chelsey was incredulous. "Nancy didn't do drugs. Alcohol yes. Everyone knew Nancy liked a drink. Drugs? Not a chance!"

Digger sighed. If Chelsey was right about Nancy, somebody must have slipped her something. "What made you ask if something bad might have happened to her?"

Chelsey gulped and fidgeted one of her dangly earrings. "She'd been acting a little weird the last few days. A couple of nights ago, she asked me to go for a drink with her after work. We went to Marble Brewery, it's just down the road. She had a couple of beers then she knocked back a couple of shots and started talking about an old case, saying she knew a lot of background about it that none of the investigators had uncovered."

"What was it?" Digger had a pretty good hunch Nancy had been referring to the Mondragon case, but she asked the question anyway.

Chelsey shook her head. "You know, Nancy had a kind heart but she wasn't the easiest person to get along with sometimes.

When she started drinking heavy, I got to feeling pretty uncomfortable so I left. I heard her stumbling around when she got home and she came in to work looking awful rough the next day."

"So that was the day we were supposed to meet her?"

"Uh-huh." Chelsey sat for a few seconds staring at the ground. Then she frowned as if a thought had just occurred to her. "Yeah, she came in late, stayed for about an hour. I could hear her talking to someone on the phone, it sounded like she was mad. Then she rushed out of her office and said she had to meet an old friend. I'm guessing that wasn't you guys?"

Digger tried to remember the timeframe. The morning they found Nancy, Manny told her that Nancy had called him, furious about his story. That's why she wanted to meet. Was the phone call Chelsey mentioned the one she made to Manny? It seemed odd that she would refer to Manny as an 'old friend'. If she wasn't talking to Manny, who was she planning to meet?

Chapter 20

Digger left Chelsey sitting on the bench behind the burrito shack and headed to her car. As she walked, she debated what to do next. Since Chelsey had briefly shared a living space with Nancy, she figured the young woman's information was more valuable than anything she might get out of the radio station manager. Chelsey said Nancy left the office intending to meet someone else before she went to the cathedral to talk to Manny, it had to be somewhere nearby. On a hunch, she drove back to the cathedral area, parked, and set off along Silver Street. She remembered it was raining that morning, so Nancy probably would have agreed to meet indoors. She walked another block and spotted a small cafe on a corner.

Maybe there.

The sign said "Mother Road Cafe" in looping turquoise letters. Beneath it was a stylized picture of a 1950s Chevrolet on a highway with a rocky landscape and a Route 66 sign in the background. Inside, the air was warm and smelled of coffee and baking. There were half a dozen tables covered with red-and-white checked tablecloths. The walls were lined with black-and-white photos of Central Avenue in downtown Albuquerque in an era when the sidewalks were full of men and women wearing hats.

Two of the tables were occupied by what looked like office workers on an early lunch break. The table nearest the door was empty. She slid into a seat and picked up a menu. Moments later a plump woman in a red apron bearing the cafe logo, ambled over to take her order. Her gray hair was scraped back in a bun with what looked like an old-fashioned nurse's hat perched on top. The name tag on her generous bosom said 'Sally.' Digger ordered coffee.

"That all? We've got some great maple walnut pancakes. Sure, I can't tempt you, hon?" Sally smiled.

"Maybe a muffin with the coffee," Digger conceded. She didn't want a muffin or coffee, but she needed to get the woman talking.

Sally returned a few minutes later with the coffee and a plate with a muffin the size of a grapefruit. "You're gonna love this," she promised.

Digger smiled. "Say, were you working a couple of days ago? The day it rained so hard?"

"Hon, I'm always here, rain or shine."

"I was supposed to meet someone nearby that morning and she never showed up. I wondered if I got mixed up and she wanted to meet here. The woman I was supposed to meet is in her mid-forties, has short hair, wears glasses with blue frames, and usually a red coat. She's got kind of a loud voice. Does that ring a bell?"

"We get a lot of people in here. Let me think," Sally said. She paused, scanned the room, then nodded. "Yeah, come to think of it, it does. I remember she came in and looked around, then sat at that table over there. She seemed real nervous."

Sally pointed to a table against the opposite wall. The photo above the table showed a high-rise downtown building Digger recognized as the Sunshine Theater. She'd been to concerts there as a student.

"Was the woman here on her own?" she asked.

"No. I was just coming over to the table when this guy came

in. He nearly bumped into me but he never even said excuse me. I notice that kind of thing." Sally wiped her hands on the front of her apron.

"What was the guy like? I'm wondering if he was someone she told me about."

"Oh, about the same age, I guess. Good looking fella, if you ask me. I brought them coffee and they just hunched together talking. They didn't look too happy. At one point she got up from the table like she was going to leave, but she caught sight of me, then just asked where the bathroom was."

"Really?" Digger wondered if Nancy had used her trip to the bathroom to make the call to Manny. But why then?

"Any idea what they were talking about?"

Sally shrugged. "I dunno. I try to mind my own business. I've seen customers get into pretty big arguments. The boss doesn't like it. I've had to ask people to leave, but I always make sure they pay."

"Did they cause trouble?"

"No, she came back, they were there a while longer, drank their coffee. I remember they left me a pretty generous tip." Sally shrugged. "You say you were supposed to meet with her? Maybe you're right and she got mixed up, agreed to meet this guy here and forgot about you. It happens you know."

Digger nodded. "Yeah. I guess so."

She took a sip of coffee and a couple of bites of muffin. She decided to leave Sally a good tip as well. The coffee and the muffin weren't worth it but the information was.

Heading back to where she'd parked, she passed St. John's. She stopped a moment and stared at the entrance, then pulled out her phone, and called Manny. He picked up on the third ring.

"Yo, Digg, what's up?"

"I went by the radio station this morning to check up on Nancy and I talked to the receptionist. She hadn't heard about what happened and she freaked out when I said it looked like an overdose. Said Nancy used to drink pretty hard sometimes but drugs, no way! She told me Nancy came in late that morning, got a call and rushed out to meet someone. I've just been talking to a waitress at the cafe down the street from the cathedral and she remembered a woman wearing a red coat came in and met with a guy. She said they were kind of arguing, had coffee, and left. They could have gone to the cathedral."

The homeless person of indeterminate gender they'd seen on the street by the cathedral entrance that morning mentioned seeing two people go inside. "Do you suppose…" she started to say.

Manny broke in. "You're thinking the guy she met at the cafe might have slipped her something in the coffee, right?"

"Well, think about it," Digger said. "You had experience on the cop beat. If he did give her something, how quickly do you think it would take effect?"

"Some of those street drugs work pretty quick."

Digger piled on. "Like the time it would take to walk a couple of blocks and dump someone inside the cathedral?"

He grunted. "I dunno, Digg. Maybe we should go to the police with this."

Digger snorted. "You know I don't trust the police."

There was a long pause, then he said quietly, "You want to talk about it?"

His words touched a nerve. She hung her head and let out a long, slow sigh. "Not right now."

She had issues with the police. The driver who caused the accident that killed her parents got off with a slap on the wrist. She spent years trying to find out why. When she finally tracked him down and confronted the guy, he admitted his father—a longtime sheriff—had pulled strings to delay vital evidence so that it wasn't admissible in court. She'd finally been able to let go of her anger with the driver, but trusting the police was a whole different story.

It pained her not to be able to explain it to Manny, she appreciated his steadiness, his loyalty. But right now, she had more pressing matters.

She took a breath and said, "I think there's some kind of connection between what happened to Nancy and Carmen and we're just not seeing it."

"Like this guy might be involved with both of them?" He paused as if thinking. Finally, he continued. "We need to find out who he is."

CHAPTER 21

Maria called late in the afternoon with news about her meeting with the solar company representatives. Even before she gave any details, Digger could tell it had gone well by the excited tone of her voice.

"They are so interested they want to look at the site tomorrow. Do you think you could persuade Roscoe to let you cover it?"

The site was about an hour northwest of Albuquerque. Digger estimated that reporting on the event would take up several hours of an already busy day. Hours she wanted to spend tracking down the man Nancy had met at the cafe. Time Roscoe would want her to follow his own agenda.

"I'll pitch it," she said, cautiously, "but I can't make any promises. I'm just about to leave the office. See you soon, okay?"

The sun was setting as she drove home and traffic was heavy. The southbound side of the freeway was a solid stream of headlights from commuters heading home from Santa Fe. Digger was stuck in a slow-moving line of red taillights bound for Rio Rancho, Bernalillo, and points north. She loved living in Los Jardines, but the drive could be a bitch.

When she arrived home, Abuela was in the kitchen. A scraping sound indicated she was whisking something in a bowl. Lady Antonia, the cat, watched from her favorite perch on top of the refrigerator.

"Hola Abuela! Something smells good. You roasting chiles?" At the sound of Digger's voice, the cat leaped down, raced across the room, and wound herself around her owner's legs.

"So fickle! She only loves me when I give her tuna," Abuela commented dryly,

Digger laughed, hugging the old woman. "We can both love her, just like we both love Maria, no?"

As if on cue, a car pulled up outside. Moments later Maria breezed through the door. She looked tired but elated and rushed to kiss Digger and then her grandmother. "I have so much great news!" she said, breathlessly. She flung off her scarf and undid the buttons of her coat. Digger and Abuela exchanged glances. They were used to Maria's dramatic outbursts.

"Okay, how long are you going to keep us in suspense?" Digger said, head cocked to one side.

"Patience, *preciosa*!" Maria said. She plumped down on the couch and pulled off her shoes.

"Ah, that feels better!" She sighed, dropping them on the floor. "Okay, the best part is that the San Fermin governor, José Archuleta, has agreed to meet with us before we go to the site."

Digger knew Archuleta's support would be critical. The site's location meant access to the nearest electrical transmission line would require an easement through a portion of San Fermin land. Maria explained that Chris Lovington would pick up the NovoSolar representatives at their hotel and bring them to San Fermin. Meanwhile, Paul Marquez had agreed to attend. He would pick her up and drive to San Fermin in his car.

"Did you persuade Roscoe to let you go?"

"Let's say I'm working on it." Her mind was focused on

investigating Nancy's death but she was curious to hear about this new solar project. Were the people behind this one legit or would they be as shady as the last bunch?

By ten o'clock the next morning, Digger had wrangled a grudging "Okay" and an eye roll from her editor and was driving northwest on US550.

The meeting was set for eleven-thirty and she had agreed to meet Maria and the others at San Fermin Pueblo. The last time she had driven along the route was about a month before the elections, more than a year ago. Back then, Digger was trying to discover who was behind the shell company that had announced plans to build a solar array close to the Pueblo. In the end, the project turned out to be an elaborate cover scheme to swindle a hefty chuck of taxpayer money and wreck the former State Land Commissioner Chris Lovington's political career.

She was thinking about Lovington during the drive. Then, about four miles before the turn-off to San Fermin, she noticed a side road on the left. Something about it rang a bell. She slowed, signaled, and pulled over. After staring at it for a few seconds she remembered it was supposed to be the access road to the phony solar site. Now, however, a sign beside the road said, 'Coming Soon, Mesa Vista Luxury Gated Community and Retreat Center.'

Of course, she thought. Las Vistas developer, Danny Murphy, had pledged to invest in the phantom project. He wanted the solar site road to access his planned subdivision. At the time, Murphy and Maria were campaigning for the same legislative seat. It was a bitter fight and a close call on election night. Murphy had contested the results but a recount confirmed Maria as the winner. Digger stared at the sign. She wondered where Murphy was getting the money to go ahead with the fancy new development.

San Fermin lay at the edge of the district Maria now represented. She and Maria had made several visits to the pueblo during her campaign. Turning off the highway, Digger followed the winding paved road for about a half mile before hitting washboard gravel for the last quarter mile into San Fermin. The dirt street through the village was almost deserted. The pale brown, flat-roofed adobe homes looked sad and neglected. Some had chain-link fences that kept a clutter of dusty machinery, old bicycles, and vehicle carcasses from invading the street. A couple of dogs barked hysterically as she passed, straining at the chains that held them staked to the ground.

She stopped at a large white building which served as the governor's office. It looked like an old rural post office. Two vehicles were parked out front. She guessed the large black SUV belonged to Lovington and the black Lexus was probably Marquez's.

A tall middle-aged man with gray hair scraped into a ponytail greeted her in the lobby and led her into a conference room. José Archuleta stood at the far end of a long table. Maria was on his right. It looked like she was introducing him to the two men in dark suits who stood beside her. One of the men had longish wavy hair and he towered over Archuleta's bulky form like a eucalyptus sapling, his companion was broad and squat with close-cropped red hair. Lovington and another man, whom she took to be Marquez, stood a few feet away, like courtiers waiting to be presented to royalty.

Eventually, Archuleta turned to Digger. Recognition flickered in his dark eyes. "You came here once before," he said quietly.

Digger nodded. Her boss at the Cultural Affairs department had asked her to accompany Lovington when he was touting the solar project as part of his election campaign.

Archuleta's lips moved in the faintest hint of a smile at Digger, then he turned and gestured for everyone to sit. He took the seat at the head of the table, folded his hands in front of him, and nodded at Maria expectantly.

She began with a short speech about renewable energy and the environment and the benefits the solar array could bring to the tribe. Digger knew Archuleta had heard it all before the last time a solar company had come seeking his blessing for an easement to the transmission line, but his face remained impassive.

When Maria had finished speaking, the tall man took a stack of brochures from his briefcase and passed them around the table. "Governor, it's an honor to be with you here today. I'm Jim Spencer, I'm a project manager at NovoSolar. This brochure gives you an overview. We're a ten-year-old company based in Houston, Texas. We specialize in commercial and residential solar power solutions and we had revenue of more than $200 million last year. We are very interested in expanding into New Mexico and we think this location offers the perfect opportunity for a twenty-megawatt facility."

He paused and nodded at his red-headed colleague who continued smoothly. "Yes, thank you, Governor Archuleta. I'm Gary O'Neill and I'm a chief engineer at NovoSolar. Ms. Ortiz, or I should say, State Representative Ortiz, has told us about the solar array plan that fell through last year. We want to assure you that we are a solid company with a good track record."

Digger noticed Chris Lovington's eyes were closed and his mouth crimped tight. O'Neill's words must bring back bitter memories, she thought. Lovington was ahead in the governor's race when he promoted the solar project. Then the whole thing turned out to be a scam and he lost in a landslide.

Archuleta listened to the presentations, his eyes traveling over the two company men. When they finished, he nodded slowly. "I am glad to hear this. It is important to me that this will benefit my tribe. I hope you understand. We will have to negotiate. But first, we will go look at the site."

The governor rose and ushered them out to where two jeeps were waiting. Digger climbed into the nearest, beside Maria, Marquez, and Lovington. The pony-tailed man who had greeted her drove. Archuleta drove the other jeep carrying the NovoSolar men. They left the village and bumped along for about twenty minutes through a landscape of tan-colored earth dotted with Chamisa and Cholla bushes. Archuleta stopped at the edge of a ridge and they piled out of the jeeps and stood looking out over a flat plain. Digger imagined rows of iridescent blue solar panels stretching into the distance.

She approached the NovoSolar men and asked the tall one, Spencer, "How soon could you start a project like this?"

Spencer rubbed a hand along his jaw thoughtfully. "If negotiations go well with the governor and we can lock in a power purchase agreement with a utility, we're probably looking at ground-breaking within three months."

Digger mentally calculated that would put the start date in January, just in time for the next legislative session. She asked them a few more questions about investment and jobs, then went to find Lovington.

She wondered if he felt shame or vindication today.

CHAPTER 22

Paul Marquez stared out his office window which faced east to a view of the Sandia Mountains. It was just past five o'clock and he heard the sounds of the office staff leaving. He saw the mountains beginning to glow their iconic watermelon pink as the sun sank over the mesa on the west side of the city. Caught in the rays of the dying sunlight, the windows of homes that clung to the foothills sparkled like Christmas lights.

He watched deep blue shadows creep up the flanks of the mountain. He thought of Maria Ortiz and the sheen on her hair, smooth and dark as the surface of a grand piano. The passion in her eyes and in her voice as she addressed the San Fermin governor reminded him again of his wife when they met as students at the University of New Mexico.

As the memories surged back, so did the pain. Every time he relived that conversation, the one when his wife said she was leaving to go be with a woman, his gut twisted. His daughter blamed him for driving her mother away because he spent so much time at his office or at the legislature in Santa Fe. He tried to explain, saying it was for the family, for the people who depended on him, he wanted them to know he cared. Just as he cared about Maria Ortiz.

Abruptly he pushed away thoughts of Maria's hair. After they had visited the solar site, she introduced the slender blond woman as a reporter with *The Searcher*, then added that she was her wife. *Her wife!*

He went back to his desk. On it lay a copy of the *Santa Fe New Mexican* that someone had left on a counter beside the door to his office. Clients were often forgetful. Judging by the date, the newspaper must have been sitting there for a couple of weeks. Marquez had been about to throw it in the trash but a headline caught his eye.

Questions swirl over state representative's death at eastern NM wind farm.

Beneath it was a photo of Carmen Lawlor standing outside the Roundhouse. The caption said it had been taken on the opening day of the session.

Lawlor's unexpected and unexplained death had been extensively covered by TV, radio, and the local press, but he hadn't seen this story before. He picked up the paper and read the opening section, then flipped to the inside page where the story continued. When he came to the paragraph that mentioned the Julie Mondragon case, he stopped. The article quoted someone called Nancy Harford saying Carmen had been one of the friends with Julie on the day she disappeared. The back of his neck tingled.

As a young man, Marquez had been obsessed by the story of the missing girl and the fruitless investigation. It was one of the factors that led him to pursue a law degree. His pulse raced as he turned back to the front page and saw the byline, *Manny Begay*. Who was this reporter and why did he mention the connection between Carmen and Julie Mondragon? Marquez looked back at the window and saw the sprawling blanket of city lights sprinkled like diamonds in the darkness.

It was after six o'clock when Maria arrived at the little house in Los Jardines. She rushed in, hugged her grandmother and flung her arms around Digger. "Thank you for being there today, sweetheart. We need to go out and celebrate!"

Digger, mindful of the gnawing in her stomach, had been thinking the same thing. "If we're talking Thai food, I'm in."

Maria looked contritely at Abuela. "I know I was meant to cook tonight, but you won't mind will you Abuela?"

Her grandmother laid a gnarled hand on Maria's shoulder, smiling. "You girls deserve a night out. You work too hard. Lady Antonia will keep me company."

A couple of hours later, stomachs satisfied with generous helpings of curry—massaman for Maria and green for Digger, they decided to continue the celebrations at Frankie's.

At the entrance, Georgie greeted them in mock surprise. "You guys back already!"

"Good to see you too, Georgie. Is Lexi here tonight?"

Georgie gave an eye roll. "Come on, Digger, is the Pope Catholic? Lexi's always here."

Halloween was a few days away, and Lexi had the place decked out. Fake cobwebs hung from the pillars that supported the mezzanine floor, a cardboard black cat nuzzled around a portrait of Frida Kahlo and a broomstick-mounted witch sailed across the wall above the bar. The DJ was playing Darius Rucker's 'Wagon Wheel' and couples were two-stepping around the small dance floor.

The TV over one end of the bar showed highlights from a World Series game. Digger and Maria slid onto a couple of stools and waited. Lexi was arguing baseball with a tough-looking Hispanic woman whose arms were covered in tattoos.

"I'm telling you it was the Cardinals," Lexi said, one elbow propped on the counter.

"Yeah, yeah," Tattoos said. "You Google it and you'll see I was right." She waved a hand and walked away.

Lexi shrugged, turned and when she caught sight of Digger and Maria, she put her hands on her broad hips and grinned. "Well shit! Always good to see you two. The usual?"

Digger nodded and moments later Lexi slid two bottles of Corona toward them. They chatted briefly, catching up on what they'd been doing since Maria's birthday. Then Lexi shot a glance toward the other side of the bar and leaned close.

"A woman came in here this evening looking for volunteers to help with a fundraising walk. I thought maybe you," she nodded at Maria, "being in government and all, and you," a nod at Digger, "being in the press, might have some ideas. She's with a group that helps families of women who went missing. Here's the flier she's handing out."

Missing. The word pricked, unwelcome, dragging her thoughts back to Nancy. She knew Maria was worn out, they needed time together, not thinking about Carmen, politics, or whatever un-expected threats might be lurking in the future. She stared at the flier, turned the beer bottle around in her hands, and a kernel of an idea formed at the back of her mind.

If this woman's organization helped families of missing women, maybe she would be willing to help find out more about Julie Mondragon. If Nancy was telling the truth, then there must be more people out there who knew details the police had never found. Would someone like that be willing to talk to this organiza-tion if they used the walk to publicize her case? It was a complete long shot, but why not try?

She slid a glance at Maria who raised an eyebrow and gave the slightest of nods

Digger turned back to Lexi. "Sure, where is she?"

Lexi pointed to a group of women standing around the pool

table. "That's her there, the tall Native American woman with the braids."

Away from the bar, Maria took Digger's arm and led her to a quiet corner. "Okay. I know that look. Let's have it."

Digger cocked her head towards the woman with the fliers and outlined her plan.

Maria pursed her lips, frowning. "It's a stretch. But if you think it might work. Okay. Let's go talk to her."

Holding hands, they threaded their way around the dance floor waving at familiar faces. The woman Lexi had pointed out was leaning on one end of the pool table talking to the players. She had a messenger bag slung over her shoulder and a leaflet in one hand.

Digger hailed her. "Hi there, Lexi told us about your group, can we talk?"

The woman's head swung around, flinging braids over one shoulder. She looked surprised. Digger pointed to a table in the far corner, away from the dance floor.

Once seated, the woman looked from Digger to Maria, eyes wide. "I'm not in trouble, am I?"

"No, not at all. Lexi thought we might be able to help you. My name is Maria Ortiz and I was elected last year to represent the district around Las Vistas. This is my wife, Digger Doyle, she's a reporter."

"Well, as long as we're doing intros, I'm Lynda Bernal and I run a small nonprofit."

"Oh yes," Digger interjected enthusiastically. "Lexi told us about what you do and showed us your flier. You want help with a fundraising walk you're organizing, right?" She leaned her elbows on the table, chin in her hands.

"That's right. It's in a couple of weeks. The walk is on a track around that private school on the north edge of town."

"We'll be happy to help, but we think there's a way you can help us too," Digger said.

"Okay." Bernal's eyes darted suspiciously from Digger to Maria. "What do you need?"

"Could you name the event in honor of someone who went missing a long time ago? Her name was Julie Mondragon."

Bernal looked puzzled. "I've heard of that case. Nobody ever found her. Has something new turned up?"

Digger decided to keep details to a minimum. "I'm following a story that might link to her disappearance. I thought that if you put her name on the event, it might attract somebody who could give me more information."

Bernal's eyebrows knitted in a skeptical frown. "I'll say yes because her case fits our mission but only if you guys will help us on the day. We need people to register participants and hand out water."

"We'll be there," Maria said, giving Bernal the 500-watt smile she used at campaign events.

——➤

It was past midnight by the time Digger and Maria drove up the winding road to Los Jardines. A half-moon cast a pale light over the rumpled foothills terrain and here and there a lamp still glowed from a window of one of the fancy homes along the ridge line. But Abuela's street was dark.

Maria parked her old RAV4 and they stepped quietly through the walled garden. Even though it was almost November, the day had been warm and the scent of roses still hung in the air. As she stepped inside, Digger felt Lady Antonia brush past her legs to escape out into the night. The cat would return before dawn, leaving some treasured offering on the doorstep.

Maria closed the door behind them and reached for Digger's

hand. They fell into each other, their mouths hungry, hands grabbing at clothing.

"It's been too long," Digger moaned as Maria kissed her breasts.

"Shh, we don't want to wake Abuela," Maria whispered, pulling her toward the bedroom.

———

Later, when she woke to the faint sound of the radio coming from the kitchen, Digger realized she had slept through her alarm. Reaching out a hand she felt for Maria, but her side of the bed was empty. She was still groggy and disoriented by a dream she'd had. It was one of those dreams where she was lost in a city. The city itself was familiar, but somehow, she couldn't find her way to the place she needed to be. There was someone she was supposed to meet and she was going to be late. She tried to call them but her phone wouldn't work.

"Ah, you're awake." Maria stood in the doorway, wearing a robe and had a towel wrapped around her head. She sat down next to Digger and stroked her forehead. "Are you okay? You were very restless."

Digger sat up and rubbed her head. "Yeah, it's just… this stuff with Carmen and then Nancy. I feel like I'm following something, but it's like smoke."

Maria put an arm around her and laid her head on Digger's shoulder. "It's okay. You'll figure it out. I wanted to tell you some good news. Chris Lovington messaged me this morning that the solar array is going ahead."

CHAPTER 23

Manny called as she cruised slowly down the street by the office eyes alert for a parking spot. She let it go to voicemail.

Damn, she thought for the umpteenth time, why did Roscoe pick this place for the office? She knew exactly why. The cramped little house belonged to his cousin and he could rent it dirt cheap. Sometimes she wondered why she'd jumped at Roscoe's job offer.

She also knew exactly why she'd accepted. Newspaper jobs weren't growing on trees in New Mexico and when the Cabinet Secretary she worked for was fired *The Searcher* gave her a chance to get back to what she loved doing best.

When she finally squeezed the Subaru into a free and legal parking spot, she called Manny back. "What's up, friend? Haven't heard from you in a couple days or so."

"Been busy."

"So, who hasn't?" she retorted, hastening her pace toward the office.

She had a feeling Roscoe would be in one of his moods this morning so only half-listened when Manny said he'd read several archived stories about the Mondragon case. Manny's next words stopped her in her tracks.

"I just got hold of one of the guys involved in the early investigation. His name is Chuck Mathers. He's a retired sheriff's deputy and he agreed to talk to me this afternoon. I just thought I'd let you know."

"Hey, I know we're kind of writing parallel stories here, but can I tag along?"

A few seconds of silence.

Sure, they'd collaborated before, but now they worked for different newspapers. She counted on the fact that Manny's paper had a much larger reach than *The Searcher's* online readership.

"Mmm. Yeah, I think that's okay."

"You are awesome! What time? Where can I meet you?" Her heart raced. Manny always came through.

"I told him three o'clock," Manny said. "He's living out near Edgewood. I'll be driving from Santa Fe on North 14 so maybe we could meet in Tijeras just off I-40 and take one car from there, okay?"

➤

By noon she had cranked out a piece about the solar array and how it would contribute to the state's clean energy goals, plus a fluffy article about a new 1960s-themed diner that Ginny had promised to write. Ginny had called in saying she had a migraine. Digger had yielded to Roscoe's pleading but warned him that the next time he asked her to cover for Ginny she'd have a migraine of her own.

Digger slipped out of the office and headed east, leaving Albuquerque behind as she climbed through the canyon. Manny said he would be waiting for her in the parking lot of a feed store in the tiny village of Tijeras. She took the exit and descended into the village. Sure enough, he was lounging against his aging orange VW Beetle in front of the Western Mercantile store.

She parked and got out. "Want to take my car? If this guy Chuck lives on a dirt road I've got all-wheel drive."

He shrugged. "It's your gas."

Shortly after they left Tijeras an accident in the slow lane forced traffic to a standstill. Crawling past a long line of trucks, Digger worried they'd be late. Finally, they reached an exit.

She turned south and followed an undulating two-lane road until Manny, watching the route on his phone, suddenly said, "That's it, on the left."

Digger slowly turned and they bumped along a washboard gravel road, raising clouds of dust. The road dipped and rounded a corner. Up ahead on the right, they saw a high metal gate wedged between two concrete block pillars. Digger stopped and they got out, but as they approached, they could see the gate was chained shut with a sign hanging over one of the center posts that read, 'We Don't Call 911!'

Digger stopped abruptly. People who put out signs like that had guns and they wanted you to know they were ready to use them, no questions asked. On top of that, they were usually deeply conservative and racist. Manny was Navajo and she wondered if that put him at greater risk.

She turned to him. "How much did you tell this guy? I mean, does he really know why we want to talk to him."

Manny frowned and his jaw muscles clenched briefly. "You're not having cold feet, are you? I thought we agreed that whatever happened to Carmen Lawlor at the wind farm was probably not an accident. There must be a reason why Nancy wanted us to know about Carmen's connection to the Mondragon girl. I think we both believe Nancy's overdose wasn't an accident either."

"Okay, okay. I'm with you on all that." She pointed at the gate. "But that sign gives me the creeps. You sure this is the right place and this guy is okay talking to us as reporters?"

"Yeah. This is the address. I'll call and let him know we're here."
The conversation was brief.

A few minutes later a man Digger figured was Chuck Mathers appeared on the other side of the gate. "Hey! You the reporter guy?" he shouted; voice gruff.

Manny shouted back. "Yeah, I'm Manny Begay. We spoke and this is my colleague, Elizabeth Doyle."

"Okay! Leave your car out there!" he commanded, then released the chain, pulled the gate open about a foot wide.

His broad shoulders pulled back as he moved the gate making the snap buttons on his checked shirt strain across the paunch that hung over his jeans.

He scratched the grizzled gray beard as he waved them in. His dark deep-set eyes peered suspiciously at them from under the brim of a black cowboy hat. He stood aside as they walked through but didn't offer to shake hands. As soon as they were inside, he closed the gate behind them. Digger's chest tightened. What if the guy was crazy and wouldn't let them out? Her throat went dry and she fought the urge to run.

Instead, she and Manny followed Mathers past a barn and a huge red Ford pickup truck. Up ahead they saw a pale blue doublewide trailer home. Mathers led them up the three steps to the entrance. From inside came the deep barking of what sounded like a large dog.

"That's Raider. Don't try to pet him. He ain't no lap dog," Mathers warned. He opened the door and a large muscular dog with a wiry brindled coat stood barking at them.

Digger was used to cats but was wary of dogs ever since a neighbor's terrier bit her on the calf moments after the owner swore the dog had never bitten anyone.

They stood aside as Raider charged out through the open door. Mathers took them through a small, cluttered kitchen into his living room and nodded at a sofa covered in faded orange-and-brown tweed. Mathers took the only armchair and the three of them sat looking at each other for what seemed like an eternity before he took off his hat, revealing a pale bald scalp. He reached into his breast pocket and retrieved a pair of reading glasses.

To Digger, that simple gesture made him seem less threatening.

"So, what is it you want to know?" His tone was sharp.

Manny took out his voice recorder but Mathers waved it away. "No recording. I'll only talk on background. That clear?"

Digger and Manny exchanged glances. "Okay," Manny said. "What can you tell us about the friends who were with Julie Mondragon the day she disappeared."

Mathers chuckled. It sounded sour like the laughter in response to an old joke. "Huh! Those kids. We talked to 'em a dozen times and they always told the same story. They went to the Malpais to go hiking. They stopped for a picnic, they had an argument and the Mondragon girl ran off and they could never find her."

Digger wondered if they were wasting their time. Mather's account was exactly what she had found in her research. "Yeah, we read the stories," she said. "But we want to know what you think really happened?"

The retired sheriff glared back, defiant. "What's it to you? That was all a long time ago. Why bother to track me down to ask all this?"

Digger looked at Manny again. He nodded, so she went over what they knew. "We went to a press event a few weeks ago where State Representative Carmen Lawlor was scheduled to make an important speech, but instead we found her dead body at the base of a wind turbine. Then this woman, Nancy Harford, who says she was a high school classmate of Carmen's, contacted me to let me know that Carmen was one of the friends that was with Julie the day she disappeared. When Manny wrote a story about Carmen's death and mentioned the Mondragon case, Nancy asked to meet with us. She sounded urgent, but when we went to the meeting place, we found her dead. That's why we're curious," Digger finished.

Mathers rubbed his hands on his thighs, looking down at the floor as if the answer to Digger's question was written on the worn carpet.

His voice came out low and rusty-sounding. "I've been living out here alone ever since my wife died couple years ago and I've had a lot of time to think about that whole thing." He sighed, wearily. "I don't have no proof, but I think one of them four teenagers killed that girl and they hid her body. I mean we searched, used dogs and all, but there's all kinds of deep holes in the lava. Plenty of places for someone to disappear and never be found."

Silence filled the room when he finished speaking. It lay heavy on them as if his words were an invisible lead blanket. Digger could barely feel herself breathing. The sound of Raider barking somewhere outside the house broke the spell.

Manny spoke then, his tone quiet and firm. "Do you think that the deaths of Carmen Lawlor and Nancy Harford could somehow be linked to what happened out there in the Malpais?"

Mathers began to rock, his hands moving restlessly on the fabric of his jeans. Digger noticed how the backs of his hands were coated with dark hairs, even the first joints of his fingers had tufts of hair.

They waited.

Finally, he exhaled, shot them both a look and said, "I think you guys might be onto something. That's all I'm going to say. Now, get out of here before Raider comes to check on me. He can be protective and it ain't pretty."

CHAPTER 24

Danny Murphy pulled the Range Rover into the slot marked for the club manager and parked. On days when he'd been away from the golf club, he liked to take a minute to look around and admire his work. In the three years he'd run the place he had snagged investment to upgrade the eighteen-hole course and transformed a tired seventies-era clubhouse with faux-leather booths that reeked of french fries and stale coffee, into a farm-to-table restaurant that boasted specialties from local growers. He wasn't sure if anything they served actually grew within the state of New Mexico, but a high-priced PR firm had come up with that pitch and he thought it sounded good. He'd gone upscale with the bar too. It now boasted a variety of local craft beers and trendy cocktails. He looked at the glass and concrete facade of the building and enjoyed that familiar little thrill of satisfaction.

Murphy nodded at the golf pro as he headed for the bar. The place was quiet at this hour, just a few retired-looking guys sitting at the bar counter joking about their game. The barman hustled over as Murphy approached.

"Hi Ricky, can you make me a Negroni?"

"Sure thing, Mr. Murphy." Ricky's man-bun bobbed.

Murphy took his drink to a table in the corner. The low glass and aluminum table stood beside a huge window with a panoramic view of the extinct volcanoes that lay west of the city. He took a few sips while he waited for his guest to arrive. His old business partner Johnny Raposa had contacted him a week ago when he'd been released on parole and suggested they meet.

Murphy spotted Raposa at the entrance. He stood a moment, buttoned the navy blazer he wore over a white turtleneck then bent and picked up a briefcase. Murphy watched him, drink in hand until he approached the bar.

He waved.

Raposa caught sight of him and made his way across the room. He looked thinner, Murphy thought, he had deep lines around his eyes and he'd lost a lot of hair in the nearly two years since they'd seen each other.

Raposa had asked for the meeting and he agreed, but he was wary. They hadn't parted on good terms. Maybe time had helped the memories fade. He hoped so. Raposa seemed in a good mood as he held up the Manhattan he had ordered. Sunlight filtered through the window behind him making the red liquid glow like a jewel.

He gave a lop-sided smile. "You know I can't have too many of these. They let me out early for 'good behavior' but I have to be a really good boy. Huh!" He knocked back half the drink in one mouthful, set down the glass, and leaned closer. "So, Danny Boy. I've been reading about that development of yours, the one out west of Las Vistas. I guess you took my plan to the guys in Arizona and they bought in. Smooth move." Raposa paused, eyeing him.

Murphy couldn't tell whether he was jealous or angry, but he knew something was coming. He didn't have long to wait.

"I want in." Raposa gave a confident smile as he said it.

Murphy had envisioned a lot of possibilities, but not this one. "Excuse me?" he said.

"You owe me, Danny. We were business partners, remember?

But somehow, I was the one who ended up in jail over the Rancho Milagro deal." Raposa's voice was soft, but it had an edge to it.

Murphy gritted his teeth. A twinge of fear gnawed in his gut, but he met Raposa's gaze. "That whole deal was shaky," he said, "and you knew it from the start."

"*We* knew it from the start," Raposa shot back. He gestured at the briefcase he'd set at his feet.

"When I got out I looked through all the old files. It's interesting what you can find."

This time, there was no mistaking the menace in Raposa's voice. Murphy stared out the window. A couple of golfers were standing around the edge of the green on the ninth hole watching a third line up his putt. For three years he had managed this club, Raposa was the one who brought him here from Arizona and got him the job.

They were on a roll back in the day. Then it all started to unravel. It was the fight over the road to the new subdivision and that woman who wanted to protect the Spanish chapel. All the publicity. That's when the newspaper started looking into Raposa's past and found out about Rancho Milagro and the millions they owed the county. Money they'd never paid back. Raposa took the fall, so maybe he was right to be mad.

Murphy watched the golfers for a few more seconds. When he saw the man sink his putt an idea began to form at the back of his mind.

Murphy set down his glass and leaned back into the deep recess of the armchair. "You've got a good point, Johnny." He knew Raposa liked his ego to be stroked. "So, you mentioned that piece of land out west of Las Vistas. You're right I did put together a deal and we've got a development underway. It's very high-end, more like a resort. Now it turns out some Texas-based company is planning to put in a big-ass solar array right next door. I mean it would totally ruin the views."

Raposa sat up, alert now.

Murphy took another sip of his Negroni. He had Raposa hooked so he was going to play it out a little. "Guess who is pushing that solar project?"

Raposa shrugged.

"House Representative Maria Ortiz. Name ring a bell?"

"You're shitting me. She's a state representative?" Raposa was shaking his head.

"I guess you didn't read the newspapers while you were inside. I ran against her in the last elections, but she beat me. And now she's representing the district that includes Las Vistas. I'm guessing she's not your favorite person."

Raposa took another slug of his drink, his face dark. "That woman and her Spanish chapel! And that reporter gal! If she hadn't gone poking around, nobody at the county would have ever started asking about Rancho Milagro. I had it buried."

Murphy laughed. "Well, I've got more news for you. Our state representative and that 'reporter gal' are now married. Anyway, I thought it might be timely to start raising objections to the solar array because it could hurt sales and home values, plus traffic to the site would have to use the access road out to the development. Is that something you'd be interested in?"

Raposa nodded, smiling. "I knew you'd understand, Danny. Let's drink to that."

CHAPTER 25

Digger heard their voices from halfway across the front yard. Roscoe, Rex, and Ginny were yelling at each other. Before she could open the door, it burst open and Rex stormed out, his face furious.

"That damn woman!" he spat, shaking his head, fists balled.

Digger jumped aside. "What the hell, Rex?"

He stopped and registered her presence. He narrowed his eyes, his lips twisted in a grimace. He had his camera bag slung over one shoulder and looked as if he had slept in his old yellow barn coat.

Digger grabbed one of his arms. "Rex! Talk to me!"

He clenched a fist and pounded the air. "Twenty-five years I've been making trips to the border to shoot pictures. Believe me! I know my way around. That woman," he pointed back through the doorway, "barges in talking shit and nearly gets us arrested." He strode off without a backward glance.

Stunned, Digger watched him open-mouthed as he slammed the gate behind him. "Rex, call me later?" He didn't answer.

She guessed Roscoe would be in a major bad mood and her instincts told her to head down the street for a coffee break, but she needed to tell him about Mathers. Heart thumping, she slipped through the door and eased it gently shut.

Roscoe stood at his desk, arms crossed, face a mask of fury. Ginny stood nonchalantly by the window, her head turned away from him. She looked like a bored model, dressed in a long gray jacket over a black shirt, plunging neckline, and billowing pants. Digger wondered why Roscoe hadn't fired Ginny long ago after all the stupid mistakes and stunts she'd pulled, but no. He just grunted and sat down.

"Okay, Ginny, just give me what you've got. At least Rex said we could use his picture, but you're skating on thin ice, understand?"

Ginny rolled her eyes and strode off toward her desk, shooting a sly grin at Digger as she passed.

When she was gone Roscoe popped a Tums and sat down. He snorted, looked up at Digger, and said, "Okay, what have you got for me?"

Sliding into the chair in front of his desk, Digger leaned forward and recounted the interview with Chuck Mathers. Roscoe listened, scribbling notes as she spoke. Then he shook his head.

"Sounds good Digger, but you don't have him on the record. So, story-wise, we're nowhere. If you think there's something to this Carmen-Mondragon angle, you've got to get someone we can put in as a credible source. Meanwhile, I need you to follow up on that city bus contract screw-up."

He was right of course. Digger knew that before she briefed him. That was the problem, every part of this weird story felt like chasing someone through a thick fog. Frustrated, she grabbed her backpack and went to her desk.

Before calling the spokesman for the city's transportation department, she flipped through her notes. She mentally checked off the names of all the contacts she'd reached.

Both Carmen's parents were dead and she'd struck out at

reaching her sister, Elena. She'd sent emails, texts, and messages. She'd even left voicemails but received no response. She looked at Elena's phone number again. Maybe worth another try.

She tapped it and waited, one eye skimming through her emails. Suddenly there was a woman's voice.

"Hello?"

"Oh, uh, hello," she stuttered. "Elena? Elena Perez?"

"Yes? That's me."

"Oh. Good. My name is Elizabeth Doyle, I'm with *The Searcher,* I left you a message."

"Oh. Yes. I got the messages." The tone was clipped. "I've been traveling on business. I just got home yesterday. You want to talk about my sister?"

Digger's pulse raced. "Yes, I explained everything in my email. I was hoping we could meet."

"Um. You know, I'm really tired. I just got home from Australia late yesterday."

Digger groaned inwardly, expecting Elena to refuse. She was surprised then when she continued and agreed to an interview.

They arranged to meet at a local restaurant. After ending the call Digger briefly considered texting Manny but decided against it. She didn't know what Elena's relationship with her sister was like or how she might feel about Carmen's death. Some people found Manny intimidating.

The restaurant where Elena wanted to meet was in a run-down area full of car mechanic workshops and second-hand furniture stores. Digger spotted the name painted in red on the side of an old adobe building. The place didn't seem in character for someone who made business trips to Australia. It was the sort of diner she could imagine Abuela meeting her old friends to gossip and indulge in a *dulce de leche* on a Saturday afternoon. On the opposite side of the street was an old motel that advertised kitchenettes, and next to it a store that sold *'muebles y colchones'*—furniture and mattresses.

She parked and entered through the narrow green wooden door. She stopped at a counter painted Pepto Bismol pink decorated with dancing Day-of-the-Dead skeletons. Peering into the dimly lit dining room she wondered how she would recognize Elena. But as soon as she stepped inside a woman sitting in one of the green-leather-backed booths hailed her.

There was no mistaking the resemblance to her sister. Elena's hair was a little darker and her face was a tad slimmer, but she had similar high cheekbones and dark, arching eyebrows.

"Hi, you must be Elizabeth," Elena said, stepping out of the booth. Digger nodded. They shook hands and settled into the cracked leather seating. As she sat, taking in the rich aroma of corn, beans, and simmered pork, Digger was reminded of her first lunch with Maria at Rosario's, the little restaurant in Los Jardines.

"I hope you don't mind meeting in a place like this. My mom used to bring us here when we were growing up," Elena said. She looked around as if reliving old memories.

"I'm very sorry for your loss." Digger said. She knew it sounded trite but she wanted to come across as sympathetic.

Elena hung her head. "Yeah. I got the news by email when I was in Melbourne. The company I work for has a lot of clients in Australia and it was an important trip. I couldn't even get back for the funeral. Corporate priorities suck!" She grimaced.

A plump middle-aged woman in a red-and-white checked apron spread a paper tablecloth, brought them bowls of salsa and chips, and took their orders. They sat in silence while Elena stared toward the window.

Voices of the other diners mingled with the faint sound of ranchera music in the background. Digger rolled the thin gold neck chain Maria had given her as a wedding present between her fingers and waited for Elena to speak.

After a long moment, Elena turned around and her dark eyes met Diggers. "You were there, weren't you?"

"The wind farm? Yes."

Elena's directness took her by surprise but she had mentally gone over the events of that day so many times that she could tell it now as if it happened to someone else. "It was a press trip. Your sister was supposed to be making a speech but she didn't show up for the bus ride. She told the utility spokeswoman she'd decided to drive because of some appointment in Albuquerque. When we arrived, her car was there, but she wasn't. We walked up to the first turbine and that's where we found her."

The server returned with their meals.

The chile sauce on Elena's plate was blood red. She stared at it and shook her head. "I keep trying to understand it. I can't believe she's gone. We were just eighteen months apart. Mom used to dress us alike—everybody used to think we were twins."

Digger spread her hands on the table on each side of her plate. Dealing with people's raw grief made her uncomfortable but she needed to have this conversation.

"You okay with me taking notes?"

Elena nodded.

Digger pulled the notebook from her backpack and jotted down the date. "You told me you last saw your sister about a month ago?"

Another nod.

Digger continued. "How did she seem?"

Elena took a sip of water. "I thought she'd been doing well this past year. She'd gotten past the divorce. I mean, when she left Karl she said she felt stifled. She told me she was excited about the new direction she was taking at the legislature—the renewable energy thing, but..." Her voice trailed off.

"But what?" Digger prompted.

Elena frowned as though trying to pinpoint a memory. "I got

the feeling she was worried. She said she'd kept quiet about something, but it was time to go public. I thought it was something political, or maybe a work thing?"

Digger wondered if Carmen was referring to what happened to Julie. Focusing on her meal, she let Elena's last words sit. Maybe she would volunteer more, maybe not. The server came and refilled their water glasses. Elena picked at her food. Digger waited. Finally, she decided to ask the question.

She pushed her plate aside and took up the notebook. "How well did your sister know Julie Mondragon?"

Elena's mouth fell open. "What? What's that got to do with this?"

Digger hunched forward. Speaking fast, she said, "There was a woman on the press trip with us called Nancy Harford. A couple of days after we were at the wind farm Nancy called me and wanted to meet. She said she was in your sister's class in high school. She said your sister and Julie were friends."

"Oh God, not that." Elena covered her face with her hands. "Yes, Julie was Carmen's best friend for forever."

Digger waited and when Elena had composed herself, she continued. "Nancy said Carmen and some others were with Julie the day she disappeared. Who were the others?" Digger knew the names but she hoped for more from Elena.

"Billy, Sylvia, and Donna." Elena rolled her eyes. "Funny how you remember people. Sylvia's father had a big job and she always had super expensive clothes. She loved to make snarky putdowns. Donna was weird and arty. I think she clung to Sylvia because she was lonely. Billy Switzer claimed his family originally came from Switzerland. He was good looking, charming, and played football." She shrugged. "You know the type."

"Did your sister keep in touch with them after high school?"

"I'm not sure about Sylvia and Donna, but Billy used to call her sometimes. He did it once when I was having dinner with her. She was upset but wouldn't talk about it."

Now it was time for the question she wanted to ask all along. "Did Carmen ever tell you about what happened out there in the Malpais?"

Elena leaned back in the booth, pushed her half-eaten meal away, and folded her arms across her chest. She sighed. "I've had a lot of people ask me that question over the years and my answer has always been the same. My sister never told me anything she didn't already tell the police." She eyed Digger with weary defiance. "Why is this important now?"

Digger stared back. "The reason I contacted you is that a few days after Carmen died, I went to meet with Nancy and found her dead too. It looked like she overdosed."

Elena's eyes widened but her expression remained defiant. "What makes you think there's a connection?"

"Because a newspaper colleague and I think your sister's death seemed suspicious. Then Nancy told me your sister and the others knew what happened to Julie. Days after she told me that story, Nancy ODs. I checked up on Nancy. Her colleague said she drank, but she was adamant that she didn't do drugs."

Now there was fear in Elena's eyes. Her lips moved but no sound came out. She swallowed and tried again. "You think what happened to Carmen wasn't an accident?" She buried her head in her hands and her shoulders shook.

Digger spotted the server heading toward their table and waved her away. She didn't want any distractions right now.

When Elena looked up, black lines of mascara trailed down her cheeks. "I don't think Carmen ever got over Julie." She paused. Eyeing Digger, she added, "Look, I don't want you to publish this part, but they were... more than just friends. If you know what I mean."

Digger gave a barely perceptible nod. The image of Carmen dancing with Maria flashed through her mind and she knew exactly what Elena meant.

"Okay, thanks." Elena sighed. "Anyway, rumors started about them at school. Then one night Julie's mother caught them kissing. Julie's parents were very Catholic; really homophobic. Her mom came by our house and yelled at my parents. A little while after that Julie suddenly started dating Billy Switzer. Everyone was shocked."

"How so?"

Elena rolled her eyes. "He was the guy all the girls wanted to date, except my sister. He kept after Carmen but she always turned him down. She was really upset when Julie got together with him."

Digger needed clarification. "So why did she go on the picnic with them at the Malpais?"

The sigh that escaped Elena carried twenty-five years of pain. "I don't know. Carmen would never tell me."

CHAPTER 26

Dusk was falling as Digger drove the road that meandered through the canyon to Los Jardines. Lights from the fancy new houses atop the ridge line shone through the gathering darkness like early evening stars. Shortly before the turn-off to Abuela's, she passed the defunct post office that was now a gallery selling pottery, weavings, and paintings by local artists. The present owner, an aging hippy from upstate New York, had been pressuring Maria to finish a couple of landscapes so she could include them in her Christmas show. Seeing the gallery, Digger felt a twinge of disappointment. Maria had all but abandoned her painting in the weeks since the wind farm trip.

Now, as she drove up the narrow street between the adobe houses, she saw Maria's old RAV4 was already snugged in beside her grandmother's wall. On cold nights like this, Digger was always happy to see lights shining across the sheltered courtyard. Opening the front door, she found Maria pawing through the contents of a huge cardboard box. Piles of clothing and remnants of Halloween decorations lay around her feet like an incoming tide.

"Um, what's going on?"

Maria looked up; eyebrows raised as though she couldn't believe the question. "Did you forget we promised to go trick-or-treating tonight with Cristina and her kids?"

Abuela, who was standing behind Maria, gave Digger a mischievous grin.

"Um," Digger answered contritely. "I guess I did. Do we have to wear costumes?"

Maria put her hands on her hips and rolled her eyes. "Of course we do. That's why I'm going through all this shit. Come and give me a hand."

Half an hour later, Maria had rummaged enough from the box to kit them out in almost matching black outfits with cat-face makeup and fake furry ears.

As she stood looking at herself in the long mirror on the bedroom door, Digger recalled the last time she had done the trick-or-treat ritual was with her mother, as an eight-year-old. Four years before the car crash. The memory jabbed like a knife. Funny how small, insignificant incidents brought back thoughts that could hurt so much all these years later.

As they were about to leave, Digger handed Abuela her phone. "Here, can you take a photo of us?" The old woman puzzled over the phone and Digger had to reset it twice. Finally, she took the shots, handed back the phone, and hugged them. "Mija, Cowgirl, you be careful. There's crazy people out there on Halloween you know."

Maria drove them back down the canyon road toward Las Vistas. Her sister lived in an older neighborhood where every third house on the street had a basketball hoop or a project car on blocks in the driveway. Many homes were decorated for the season with Halloween paraphernalia. Cristina's front yard had a pair of life-size inflated ghouls and a glowing orange pumpkin. Trick-or-treating wasn't Digger's idea of fun, but family rituals were important to Maria and she liked Cristina and the girls.

Cristina greeted them at the door wearing a bumble bee costume that accentuated her generous figure.

"Hola!" she said, giving each of them a kiss on the cheek. "You two look so cute! Wait till you see the kids!"

Seven-year-old Anabela burst from behind her mother and flung her arms around Maria. "Tia, Tia! Look at my wings!" The little girl twirled, showing off blue gauzy fairy wings that sparkled under the porch light.

Moments later her younger sister's face peered from behind Cristina's back.

Maria crouched down. "Come on, sweetie, show us your outfit."

"I'm a princess," the toddler said shyly.

Maria beamed up at Digger. "Aren't they adorable?"

Digger nodded. Not for the first time, she wondered if Maria wanted children. She knew women who had taken the leap but she'd never had the courage to bring up the subject with Maria. Maybe there would be a day when it felt right.

Cristina's husband Fernando came to the door and handed the girls tiny orange plastic buckets to collect their candy.

Cristina kissed him and patted his ample paunch. "Don't go eating any of the candy! It's for the kids, remember."

He grinned and nuzzled his wife's cheek, then pointed at Digger. "You take care of them for me Digger, right?"

"Sure bro."

They set off. Pools of light from the street-lamps illuminated the groups of children and adults that milled along the sidewalk, filling the night with chatter and laughter. Cristina held Anabela's hand while Maria pushed the toddler's stroller. Digger put an arm around Maria and together they wandered from house to house.

They'd been walking for nearly an hour and were turning to head back to Cristina's house when they spotted the flashing red lights of a police cruiser ahead.

Digger's reporter instincts kicked in. "I'm going to go have a look, you guys wait here," she said and took off at a jog.

The police car was parked in front of a shabby-looking duplex apartment building with overflowing trash cans by stairs leading to the upper level. As she approached, Digger saw an officer climb the stairs, the other stood right in front of the cruiser. Digger recognized him as Josh Sanchez, one of the officers she used to encounter when she had to cover SWAT scenes for *The Courier*. She approached him, pulled off her fake cat ears, and called his name.

He looked around, saw her, and frowned. "Digger? Is that you? What the hell are you doing here?"

"Just out trick-or-treating with the family, you know how it is. You've got kids." She cocked her head toward the building. "What's going on?"

He shook his head. "You shouldn't be here. We're executing an arrest warrant."

Unfazed Digger shot back. "Well, I may be dressed as a cat but I'm still a reporter. Is it something I should know about? I've got family living a couple blocks away." The last part was a stretch but she knew the family card always worked well with Sanchez.

He shrugged. "Not exactly headline news. The guy's a low-level dealer. Pretty routine."

"You got a name?"

Sanchez scowled, his jaws working. Digger remembered he had a fondness for Dentyne gum. He shook his head. "You never give up, do you?"

Digger grinned. "How do you think I got my nickname?"

Sanchez gave an exasperated sigh. "Oh, screw it. Name's Tony Switzer, but you didn't get it from me. Go do your homework tomorrow."

The hairs on the back of her neck prickled. She'd heard that last name for the first time recently, from Nancy. Nancy who overdosed. Coincidence? Maybe not. Could this drug dealer guy be related to Billy Switzer?

"Thanks buddy. Appreciate it." She patted Sanchez on the shoulder and slipped away. She had crossed the street and was passing a tall juniper bush that overhung the sidewalk when she noticed a figure lurking in the darkness. Fearful, she stopped and peered at the shape. It was an older man wearing a puffy jacket with a collar that hid the lower part of his face. His eyes had been fixed on the police activity but he startled when he noticed her.

Digger stopped and stood motionless. If the old guy tried something she could shout. Josh Sanchez was less than twenty yards away. But the old man turned away and continued to watch the scene across the street. Two figures descended the stairs, the officer and slim man in a white T-shirt. The officer led the man to the cruiser and stuffed him into the back seat.

The old man's voice caught her by surprise. "Sure, glad they finally got that guy." He jerked his chin toward the house across the street. "I complained about them over there a bunch of times. But nobody did anything."

Digger's alarm level dropped a notch. Maybe the old man could tell her more than Sanchez.

"You know the guy they brought out?" she ventured.

"Yeah. He's the only one living there. Downstairs has been empty for a while. 'Course he's just renting. Said his uncle owns the place, some big shot up in Santa Fe. Wish he'd clean it up."

The old man's head swiveled round and he stared at her, taking in her outfit and the cat whisker makeup. He shook his head. "Honey, this ain't the area to be trick-or-treating in. You go on home now."

CHAPTER 27

As if the passing of Halloween had signaled a change in the weather, the next morning dawned crisp and bitterly cold. A thick frost coated the juniper bush outside Digger and Maria's bedroom window and the higher slopes wore a dusting of snow.

They could hear Abuela talking to the cat in the kitchen. The old woman liked to get up early and since Lady Antonia demanded her breakfast at six o'clock, she had switched alliances and went to Abuela for her Iams and tuna, leaving Digger a welcome extra few minutes in bed.

Maria was still in the shower when Digger went to the kitchen to get coffee. She found Abuela seated at the table, studying a large book. It looked suspiciously like a cookbook. Digger thought it odd because Abuela prided herself on never having to use written recipes. 'Everything I need is in my head' was her standard response whenever anyone asked her about a recipe.

"Morning Abuela. Where did you get that?" Digger pointed at the book.

Abuela pursed her lips as though caught in an embarrassing act. "I'm thinking about Thanksgiving."

Digger smiled, knowing how much Abuela loved hosting family at holiday occasions. "Your Thanksgiving dinners are the best!

My grandma never did Thanksgiving, she grew up in Ireland and it isn't a thing there, so we went out."

"Ah but you have Saint Patrick's Day, no? Corned beef and cabbage?"

Digger laughed. "Grandma Betty always said the only corned beef they have in Ireland comes in a can. They have boiling bacon with cabbage."

Abuela looked at her as if she'd lost her mind. "Dios mio! What kind of people boil bacon?"

Digger laughed. "It's actually a kind of ham. I tried some when my grandparents took me to Ireland when I was about sixteen. It's very good."

Abuela's expression showed she remained unconvinced.

Maria came in then, still fluffing her damp hair. She kissed Digger and headed for the coffee maker. Halfway there she stopped; her eyes fixed on the table. "Is that the cookbook I ordered? Abuela, did you open my package?"

Abuela's head sank into her shoulders and she peered guiltily over her glasses at Maria. "The package came yesterday. I thought it was for me."

"Oh, really?" Maria raised her eyebrows.

Abuela straightened, thrusting out her chin. "You don't like my cooking?"

Digger decided it was best not to intervene. Maria and her grandmother had a warm relationship but now and then, feathers were ruffled.

Abuela shook her head and huffed. "Well, this year, I think I will let you and Maria do the cooking for Thanksgiving."

Digger did not expect this. Abuela not cooking the Thanksgiving meal was unthinkable. She was the lodestar. Everything in the little adobe house revolved around her: the Ortiz family, the garden where she grew the zucchini, squash and chile, heck even the chickens. Digger could operate a George Foreman grill and a microwave but no way could she handle the huge family feast. She shot a helpless glance at Maria who looked as shocked as she felt.

Maria came over and put her arms around her grandmother. "Abuela, I didn't mean to upset you. I will send the cookbook back."

Abuela looked at the big book that lay open on the table, tracing a gnarled hand over the glossy picture of a lasagna. "It's okay. Let's keep it. I might learn something." She gave them a sly smile.

➤

The dusting of snow made driving slower than normal. As Digger drove out of the canyon, she kept thinking about the arrest scene she'd witnessed the night before. Normally a low-level drug dealer wouldn't interest her. Roscoe certainly wouldn't consider it worth a story. There were just too many of them. Still, she decided to follow Sanchez' advice and do her homework. She called Roscoe and told him she was checking some court records and would be in late.

The address where the arrest took place was in the northern part of Las Vistas, just a few miles from the county courthouse. It had been a few years since she worked the police beat at the *Courier* and made regular visits to the courthouse, but the place hadn't changed. She entered the echoing lobby, went through the security check and headed upstairs to see if she could get the arrest record.

The second floor bustled with activity around the doors of the court rooms that led off the main hallway. The records room was equally busy. She filled out a request form and waited nearly twenty minutes for an available window. Court records staff still had the weary, harassed look of flight attendants on a low-budget airline. A clerk who attended to Digger looked to be in her late fifties, with a stiff cloud of unnaturally auburn hair and heavy eye makeup. She perused the form, consulted her computer and moments later handed over a document.

Digger found a bench on the other side of the room and sat to read it. Everything checked out; the address, charge and name were all as she remembered them from last night. The weird old man who'd been lurking across the street said the young drug dealer was renting from an uncle. Again, she wondered if Tony Switzer have any connection to the Billy Switzer Nancy and Sylvia's husband had mentioned.

Time to find out just who owned that duplex.

The assessor's office was about a mile down the road in the county administration building, an impressive two-story edifice of glass and salmon-colored stucco. Digger took the stairs to the second floor and followed a long corridor to the assessor's office. She asked for Nick Lopez, a contact she'd worked with in the past. When she reached the right office, she found it just the way she remembered it. Nick, his bushy black beard splayed over his chest like an invasive plant, sat in the tiny cubicle squeezed between two monitors the size of coffee tables.

"Hi Nick."

He swiveled round, saw her and jumped up from his desk. "Hey Digg! Long time no see!"

She shrugged. "Yeah, I was working for the state in Santa Fe for a year."

He laughed. "I heard about what went down. Your old boss Julia Montoya got nabbed for fraud. I'm thinking you had something to do with her getting caught."

"You'd be right. And that's also why I'm not there anymore. I'm back to being a reporter, working for an online paper."

"Well, congrats. What can I do for you today?"

She pulled the arrest record from her backpack, laid it on the desk. "I'm doing some background research. Can you help me get a name for the owner of this property. The guy who was arrested was dealing, but I was told he was just renting."

Nick looked at the paper, frowning as he twirled a spindle of beard hairs in his fingers. "Give me a minute." He sat in front of the computer, eyes shifting from the screen to the document as his fingers tapped the keyboard. The screen flickered with new data. "Looks like this is it. Want a printout?"

Digger nodded. From somewhere beyond the cubicle wall she heard a mechanical chugging sound. Nick disappeared and returned with a paper. He handed it to Digger. "You could have done this online you know," he said, grinning.

Digger laughed. "I just wanted an excuse to renew our acquaintance." She sure didn't want to admit she'd forgotten how to do the online search.

Nick waggled his eyebrows. "Believe me, it's quicker online. But good to see you anyway."

Digger sat in her car, scanning the form in her lap. The property belonged to Margaret Switzer. Disappointment flooded her. She so wanted there to be a connection to the Billy Switzer who had dated Julie, the guy with her the day she disappeared. Her phone pinged a message from Manny.

Call me.

He answered on the second ring. "Hi Manny, I was going to call you anyway. I was hoping I found out something that might relate to Nancy." She told him about the drug bust, the arrest details and what she'd just learned at the assessor's office.

"Well, you can't win 'em all, but I've got something you might want to hear," he said. His tone, dry and matter-of-fact, hinted he was holding back something big.

Digger's heart thumped. "Don't keep me waiting, what is it?"

"I've got a contact over at OMI—we're connected by family—I told him how we found Nancy and what we suspected. He agreed to talk to me off the record."

He paused for a few seconds and the thumping in her chest increased. "What did he say?"

"The toxicology report showed Nancy had fentanyl in her system."

A chill gripped Digger's insides. Hundreds of people overdosed on fentanyl every day. News reports said it was up to forty times more powerful than heroin. Could the man Nancy met at the cafe have given it to her? Cheryl had said, Nancy told her she was going to meet an *old friend*.

CHAPTER 28

The day of the Julie Mondragon Fundraising Walk dawned bright and cloudless with the mountains looming a gunmetal blue, the crest etched against an immense sky. Leaves of the Cottonwood trees glowed like beaten gold.

The crisp cold air made Digger's ears burn when she stepped outside to feed the hens that Abuela kept in a shed at the end of her garden. Normally Abuela fed the chickens but this morning she had complained of feeling tired so Digger stepped in. She liked the sound of the hens and the excited way their heads jerked as they rushed to the feed bowl.

Chores done, she and Maria set off for the event in the Subaru. Digger's eyes were on the cars flowing southward toward Albuquerque. Last night, before they went to bed, Digger had told Maria what she had learned about the drug bust, and at the assessor's office. They'd been too tired to discuss it, but as she tossed restlessly, she kept wondering if there could be a link. Switzer wasn't a common last name, and it kept coming up in connection with Carmen, Nancy and Sally, who all died sudden unexplained deaths.

She'd woken during the night, and as she lay in the dark

listening to the soft murmur of Maria's breath, she thought of Nancy Harford. She recalled the way Nancy stared at Carmen's inert body and her words, 'I guess we'll find out if she fell, jumped, or was pushed.'

Weeks later, Digger still had no answer. The official line was that Carmen suffered a fatal accident. If Nancy thought differently, why didn't she do something about it? Or was that why she contacted Digger? What had happened to Nancy? Her mind kept sifting through the details, looking for a pattern but the threads always petered out.

She was thinking about Manny's news about the fentanyl as she drove toward Albuquerque. Beside her, Maria was studying the flier they planned to hand to the participants. They had obtained permission to use one of the newspaper pictures used at the time Julie had disappeared and then used an AI aging app to create an impression of what she might look like in the present day. The text beneath the pictures read:

'Julie Mondragon went on a picnic in the Malpais with friends in May 1998. She disappeared and was never seen again. Today's event is dedicated to the cause of missing women. If you have any information that might shed light on this 25-year-old mystery, please contact Lynda Bernal.'

Maria read it out loud, then looked at Digger. "I don't know about this. Do you think anyone might come forward after all this time?"

Digger's thoughts had been miles away but Maria's voice brought her back to the present and the reason they were going to the fundraising event.

"I don't know," she said. "Nancy told me there were four friends out there with Julie that day. The retired sheriff that Manny tracked down pretty much agreed with Nancy that the friends knew what happened to Julie but for some reason they kept silent. Two of those friends are dead and I haven't been able to reach the other two, but it's been twenty-five years. Maybe somebody is finally ready to talk."

Maria laid the flier in her lap. She stretched out a hand and rested it on Digger's thigh. "When we first met, I accused you of not being able to commit to something you believed in, of sitting on the fence. So, why are you so fixated on this? You barely knew Carmen."

At Maria's words, she felt a lump in her throat. Maria had made the accusation when Digger told her she couldn't advocate for her protest campaign because she was a reporter and had to be objective.

"I dunno. This just seems different."

She didn't want to tell Maria how much she kept thinking of Carmen and Nancy. Their dead faces brought flashbacks. She'd never seen her parents' bodies after the crash, but in recent days she'd dreamed of them again. In those dreams, her parents had the faces of Carmen and Nancy. She hadn't told Maria about the dreams and she wasn't sure why she needed to know what happened to them. It was a gut feeling, like needing to know why the driver who killed her parents never went to jail. If there was something to be uncovered, she couldn't let it rest until she uncovered it.

—➤

Lynda Bernal had arranged for the volunteers to park on the grounds of the private school. The fundraising walk would be on a popular public path that surrounded the school. When Digger and Maria arrived, Lynda and two other women were busy unloading supplies from the back of a van. As they drew close, they recognized one of the helpers as Alma, who had children at the school where Maria taught. Alma had also volunteered during Maria's political campaign.

"Oh my God, it's you!" Maria shrieked. She rushed to hug Alma. "You're always there for everyone."

A huge smile split Alma's face and her eyes sparkled. "Of course, I'm here. Lynda is related to my husband. She called me early this morning because a few of the people who promised to help let her down at the last minute."

Lynda, who had been unloading cases of bottled water from the back of a pickup, came over to their group and greeted Digger and Maria.

She wiped her hands on her faded red sweatshirt and looked at them with a slightly frazzled expression. "Thanks so much for coming. We need all the help we can get. Have you got the fliers you wanted to pass around? And Maria, since you are the state representative for our area, I wondered if you would say a few words to the participants before we start the walk?"

"Um, yes. I'd be happy to. We've got all the publicity material in the car. And we made a bigger poster we can put up somewhere so everyone can see it."

"Right," Lynda said. "Digger can you help Alma set up the table? Then I'll need you to sign people in and give them their numbers. I think we've got around fifty registered and more will probably show up." She paused, pulled a phone out of her pocket, and checked the time. "Okay, we've got about thirty minutes before people start arriving. Maria, I'll give you a quick rundown about our mission so you'll know what to say."

The next half hour was a flurry of activity as they set up for the event under Lynda's directions. They had just finished taping the poster to the front of the table when the first walkers showed up; a middle-aged woman dressed in a sky-blue sweatshirt with the message 'All who wander are not lost', and a younger woman, possibly her daughter, who looked as though she would rather be anywhere else on a Saturday morning.

Over the next fifteen minutes about fifty more people arrived.

They were mostly under forty, Hispanic or Native American women. Digger counted only seven men, husbands of the few Anglo women. Maria signed them in and handed each one a copy of the flier with the pictures of Julie Mondragon.

Once everyone was signed in, Lynda climbed on a chair and hoisted a megaphone to her mouth. "Thank you all for being here today!" she shouted, to quiet the crowd. "We are fortunate enough to have state representative Maria Ortiz joining us. She will say a few words about our mission. Your financial support is critical to our work."

Lynda climbed down, helped Maria onto the chair and handed her the megaphone. Maria took it and looked out confidently at her audience. Digger had seen Maria speak passionately at city council meetings and during her election campaign and knew she would do the same today. Maria was a woman who never sat on the fence. She embraced causes like most people breathed air. She began her speech and within seconds she had the crowd rapt despite the cold and the traffic sounds from the busy road.

"We are here today in honor of all the women who have gone missing. Some have been found murdered, some have never been found. Either way, the disappearance of each of these women has devastated the lives of their loved ones, family and friends. Those losses ripple out into their communities and affect their children and grandchildren. That is why they deserve justice.

"This wonderful woman, Lynda Bernal and her team of volunteers, have taken up their cause. They keep up the pressure on law enforcement agencies to take action to investigate. They raise money to assist families that are left without a mother or wife to care for children. And I am personally grateful that I met Lynda and found out about her work. As a state representative I will continue to advocate for her in Santa Fe. Thank you all for coming today!"

Digger moved from behind the sign-up table to mingle in the

crowd. She noticed the woman in the sky-blue sweatshirt holding the flier in both hands as she studied it. She looked to be early to mid-forties, about the same age as Carmen. Digger considered for a second, then, on a hunch, threaded her way between several people, to maneuver next to the woman.

"Did you know her?" Digger asked quietly, pointing at the flier.

The woman looked around in surprise, then back at Julie's face smiling in the photograph.

"No," she said, shaking her head. "But I've been there. My niece went missing a couple of years ago. She was on her way home from soccer practice and never made it. They found her body a month later near Salina, Kansas. We still don't know who took her. I don't have any faith in police anymore." Her mouth tightened in a grim line and there was rage in her eyes.

Digger knew that rage, the disillusionment of misplaced faith in a corrupt judicial system. She laid a hand on the woman's arm. "Let's hope that what we're doing here today will make a difference."

The woman's lips trembled. "Yeah," she said, roughly. "Lynda does great work. That's why I'm here with my daughter."

Lynda's voice sounded over the megaphone. "Okay everyone, the trail around the school is just over three miles. If you can make three circuits you win a prize donated by a local sports store. Here we go, ten, nine…" When she reached, "one," the walkers surged forward.

—➤—

Later, after the last walker had limped in and they'd loaded trash bags full of empty water bottles and paper plates into the back of the pickup, Lynda hugged them all and thanked them for their help.

Digger and Maria were about to follow Alma and the other

volunteers back to the parking lot, but Lynda called after them.

She walked up to Maria and grasped both her hands. "Thank you so much for your words today, Maria. And—if you meant what you said about advocating for us in Santa Fe, I would be so grateful."

Maria smiled. "I'd be honored."

Lynda turned to Digger. "And maybe you could write something about our group? Didn't you say you were working on something that related to Julie Mondragon?"

Digger nodded. "Carmen Lawlor. She was a friend of Julie's."

"Oh, I heard about that accident. Such a tragedy!" Lynda shook her head slowly. "She was one of our supporters."

"Oh really?" Digger shot a glance at Maria. "I interviewed Carmen's sister Elena. She told me Carmen and Julie were good friends in high school. Elena said Carmen never got over losing her. That's why we asked you to name the event for Julie. We thought there still might be someone out there who knows what happened to her. I'd like to write something more about their friendship. You'll let me know if anyone contacts you about Julie?"

"You have my word," Lynda said.

They helped Lynda close the tailgate of the pickup and watched her drive away. When they got home, they found Abuela in bed, still saying she felt tired.

"I'll be fine tomorrow, don't worry," she said, not sounding convincing. Maria fussed over her grandmother while Digger busied herself in the kitchen. She was consulting directions on a package of frozen Chinese vegetables when her phone rang.

Lynda!

"I just got a call." Lynda's voice was low and urgent. "This woman said she had information about Julie. She wants to meet you."

"Can you give me her number?"

"Sure. I should warn you. She sounded terrified."

CHAPTER 29

Danny Murphy raised the binoculars to his eyes and peered through the lenses. He could just make out three figures in the distance. They were moving among the chamisa bushes and cholla cactus. Behind them, the Jemez mountains loomed, almost purple against the deep blue of the afternoon sky. He handed the binoculars to Raposa. "Have a look and tell me what you think."

The other man took them, held them up to his face and adjusted the focus. Raposa said nothing for a while as he studied the landscape. Finally, he grunted and set the binoculars on the hood of the Jeep.

"If I had to guess, I'd say they look like some kind of surveyors. You think they're scoping out the site for the solar array."

"Mmm-hmm. That's exactly what I thought. These guys aren't wasting any time." Murphy picked up the binoculars, slid them into a case, and slung the strap over his shoulder. "I spotted some activity out there yesterday. That's why I wanted you to come have a look. We better get moving if we want to stop them."

Raposa zipped up the front of his fleece-lined jacket against the wind that kicked up flurries of dust around the construction site behind them. He'd been expecting to hear from Murphy about the solar deal, but not this soon. Everything seemed to be happening so quickly. He'd lost touch while he'd been inside. He used to be the one that called the shots but Murphy was now directing the show and he had to follow his lead if he was going to get what he wanted. He wasn't sure what it would look like but knew he wanted to see that Ortiz woman go down.

Murphy drove the Jeep over a quarter mile of packed gravel back to the network of paved streets where construction crews were putting in foundations for the first homes in the development. He glanced over at Raposa to gauge his reaction. They'd done a lot of deals together in the past and he felt bad when Raposa took the hit for the last one. Murphy thought of it as a misunderstanding, but the county people saw it as fraud. Still, he was glad it was Raposa, not him.

Glancing over at the man he wondered briefly if Raposa might try to find a way to get back at him. He dismissed the thought. Right now, he felt confident he was in the driving seat and it felt damn good.

"I found out that most of the solar array is going to be on state land but there's a corner of it that's inside the county. So, we go to the next county commission meeting and complain. I've got people I can bring to the meeting to back me up. Make as much noise as possible."

Raposa didn't answer and Murphy wondered if he was listening, or maybe the sight of this development, a project they had talked about working on together, upset him.

Finally, Raposa said, "I dunno, Danny, you think complaining to the county people is going to be enough to stop them?"

Murphy chuckled. "You missed out on the last election. Chris Lovington, the guy who was running for governor was caught up in a big scandal over a phony solar project. A lot of people in Santa Fe are still touchy about it. The current governor is more of an oil and gas guy if you get my drift, and one of the regulars at my golf club works for the industry group. I think he'd be interested in helping us out."

———➤———

Chris Lovington pulled his armchair closer to the fireplace, picked up the tiny glass and took a sip of Tawny port. He savored the rich sweet taste and the warmth of the port as it slid down his throat. The weather had abruptly turned cold with a sharp wind and flurries of snow. The skiers will be happy, he thought, along with pretty much everyone else in New Mexico. Temperatures had hit 100 degrees in the southern half of the state for nearly three weeks straight in July. Even Santa Fe felt unbearable in the middle of summer. The rains that normally brought relief, had been scarce and the danger of wildfires persisted well into the fall.

The prospect of snow raised Lovington's spirits too. The year since he lost the election had been tough. He'd been lucky to get another job with a government department. But it was frustrating to see the new governor derail many of the efforts his predecessor Jim Sheridan had put in place to boost the renewable energy sector. Lovington had promised Sheridan he would continue his work. Carmen Lawlor had been a lone bright spot in this discouraging political landscape. Her death had been another blow. Now, another young woman had emerged to carry on Carmen's legacy. The day he met Maria Ortiz and the solar company executives had revived his flagging spirits.

He was thinking about the meeting, gazing into the flames from the piñon logs in his fireplace when his phone rang.

"Hi Chris, I'm sorry to call you so late, but I thought you'd want to hear this."

Lovington recognized the voice of Ed Silva, one of his former staffers at the State Land Office. "Sure, what's up?"

"You know I'm working for the county now, in the assessor's office," Silva said.

Lovington had no idea the man was working for the county. For weeks after his election defeat, he wanted to hide. He'd deliberately avoided contact with his old colleagues. He was grateful for his faith, that alone had buoyed him through that awful time. But that was past and he needed to focus on what his caller was saying.

"I was at the county commission meeting tonight," Silva continued, "and there was a bunch of people who made public comments. They all complained about that solar array that's supposed to be going in near San Fermin Pueblo."

Lovington was alarmed. "You know anything about them?"

"The guy that started it was Danny Murphy. He was the first one to speak, the others were just following him." Silva paused. Then, as if a thought struck him, added, "Wasn't Murphy the guy that ran for the state legislature last year?"

"That's him," Lovington agreed. "He ran against Maria Ortiz. She won, but it was close. He demanded a recount but it didn't change the result. He was pretty sore about it."

"Yeah, I remember."

"What was Murphy complaining about?"

Lovington's mind was racing. He knew Murphy was also linked to the Arizona developer behind the solar scam that wrecked his bid to become governor. Now Murphy was coming out against a legitimate company that wanted to invest in a solar array in the same spot. What was his game this time?

"Well," Silva said, "he's got a fancy development going up right near there. Says it will spoil the views and might pose a danger to wildlife. He's questioning whether this solar company has got the right permits, wondering if they need rights of way. The rest of the people that spoke said the same kind of thing."

Lovington had heard the same bullshit complaints at hundreds of public meetings over the years. "How did the commissioners react?" he asked.

"Two of the five seemed to side with Murphy," Silva commented. "One of them mentioned there had been talk of exploring for oil or gas in that area a few years ago."

Lovington was incensed. "As if that would be preferable to a solar array! Okay Ed, thanks for calling."

"Sure. Oh, one more thing, I forgot. There was this guy sitting next to Murphy, he didn't speak publicly but I saw them huddled together before and after the meeting. One of my colleagues said it was Johnny Raposa. They said he was accused of embezzling money from the county for some development a few years ago. Know anything about him?"

Lovington wasn't familiar with Raposa's name or reputation but this additional information increased his anxiety. "Well, keep me posted if you hear anything more about this."

After he hung up, he sat wondering. Was this Murphy's payback because the solar scheme he'd invested in was exposed as a scam? Or was it his way of getting back at Maria because he lost the election?

He picked up his phone again and found a number. "Hi Maria," he said. "We've got a problem."

Chapter 30

Maria set down the phone, closed her eyes, and blew out a long breath. Then she sank onto the bed and buried her head in her hands.

Digger waited to hear the bad news. Finally, Maria looked up and said, "Murphy's at it again."

"How so?"

"That was Chris Lovington. He got a call tonight from a former staffer, letting him know that Murphy went to the county commission to complain about the solar project."

"What!! Last year he was ready to invest in solar. What's his beef now?"

"I don't know." She shook her head, sighing.

The next morning another problem presented itself. Abuela, normally the first one up, was not in the kitchen. Maria went to check on her and found the old lady complaining of fatigue.

"I'm worried it might be another heart complication," she remarked when she emerged from her grandmother's bedroom. "If she's sick I should probably stay home from work."

They'd had a fright a couple of years ago when she fell ill and was diagnosed with atrial fibrillation.

Digger shook her head. "Look, Abuela has been doing fine with the meds. She's probably just a bit overtired. Let's let her rest. Besides, Friday is your busiest day. Why don't you call Paul Marquez and tell him what you heard from Chris Lovington. Marquez has been in politics a long time. He's a lawyer and you trust him. He'll have some good ideas. I'll also talk to somebody at the county today and see what I can find out." She put her arms around Maria, squeezed her, and felt her relax.

Paul Marquez pressed his thumbs into his temples and let out a long groan. He had just had another of the wrenchingly painful discussions with his daughter, Joanna. He hadn't even finished his morning coffee when she called. Angry and aggressive, she still blamed him for the divorce. No amount of repeating that her mother left because she fell in love with a woman would convince Joanna that it was not all his fault. He hadn't heard from his ex-wife in weeks. She didn't answer his calls or respond to messages. He was loath to go through a lawyer. He was a lawyer, dammit!

His phone rang. "Hello?"

"Oh hi, Paul. Did I catch you at a bad time?"

"No," he lied. Actually, the sound of Maria's voice was balm to his shattered nerves.

"Chris Lovington called me last night," she said and related Lovington's news. "He said he's going to talk to the NovoSolar people, but I wanted to let you know about this as soon as possible."

As Marquez listened, he caught the anxiety in her tone and his moment of calm evaporated. He wondered if Murphy was acting on his own behalf or whether he was the front man for an opposition group. He thought of the recent conversation he'd had with Fred Carter at the Country Club. Carter hadn't spelled out any details, but he'd made it clear that the oil and gas producers he represented wanted to keep the governor focused on their interests. Carmen Lawlor had been a thorn in their side and Maria Ortiz's plan to continue her work was not welcome.

Maria, however, had her own theory. "You know Murphy ran against me last year," she said, "and he was furious when he lost. He keeps making posts on social media claiming he should have won. I think this could be another way he's trying to get back at me."

Marquez considered. She had a point. He'd seen failed political candidates launch smear campaigns before. People always complained at county commission meetings. Murphy's rant might go nowhere. But if he drew the attention of powerful voices in Santa Fe, it could delay the solar project indefinitely.

"Leave it with me, Maria. I'll make some calls and get back to you." He hoped he sounded confident even though he didn't feel it. He wanted to reassure her.

***

While Maria spoke to Marquez, Digger thought she'd look in on Abuela.

She knocked gently on the bedroom door and heard a faint, "Just a minute."

Digger waited anxiously, then opened the door a few inches and peeked inside. The old woman stood in front of the dresser, winding her long gray hair into a bun at the back of her head. She sensed Digger's presence, turned and nodded. "It's alright. I'm feeling a little better today."

Relief washed over her. Abuela would be eighty-two in a few weeks and she knew the clock was running down. One day they would lose her—but not yet, Digger's heart said, please not yet.

Abuela's presence in their lives was like an olive tree, ancient and enduring. She hugged the old woman and said, "Maria has to get off to school. I'll make the coffee. How about some eggs too?"

"Oh Cowgirl, you spoil me!" Abuela tutted, smiling.

When Digger arrived at the little house on Harvard that served as the paper's office, she was surprised to find the door locked. She tried Roscoe's number. No answer. She sent a message and stood staring at the screen of her phone, willing him to respond. A couple of joggers went by, then an overweight woman with an equally overweight dog. She pulled her scarf closer round her neck, warding off the bitter chill. There was a dusting of snow on the crest of the Sandias. Frost still glinted on the roofs of cars parked along the street.

Finally, her phone pinged a message from Roscoe: *Pipes burst last night. Toilet not working. Plumber coming at 11. I'm working from home till then. You can too.*

Great! Thought Digger, too bad he didn't let me know before I drove into town. I could have stayed with Abuela. She tapped a response: *OK. Got a tip about the solar project. Checking it out. See you later.*

That done, she tried the number Lynda had given her for the woman who said she had information about the Mondragon case. She'd tried it as soon as Lynda called her but no answer. Same again this morning. Lynda said the woman sounded scared, maybe she got cold feet. Hoping that wasn't the case she left another message. Next, she consulted her contacts and punched in the number of the county's public information officer, hoping he would remember her.

"Hi Rick, Elizabeth Doyle here."

"Oh, hello. It's been a while. Too bad about the *Courier* closing. I heard you were at that new paper, *The Searcher*. What's up?"

Fibbing, Digger said she'd missed the weekly commission meeting and asked if she could get access to the list of those who made public comment, and the video recording.

Rick Severin was silent for a moment. She hoped he wouldn't

make her file a public records request. If he did that it would take days before she could get her eyes on what she was looking for.

"Well, I guess you'd have seen it all if you were at the meeting. Can you come to my office at 9:30?"

She offered up a silent prayer of relief. "Thanks, Rick, see you soon."

By the time she reached the county building, snow had begun to fall. Light, wispy flakes drifted gently down, landing on the parking lot, melting immediately. Abuela would be glad, Digger thought. She often talked about how much it used to snow when she was a child and how dry it had become in recent years.

Rick Severin's office was on the second floor with west facing windows that overlooked the sprawling neighborhoods of Las Vistas. Her colleagues at the *Courier* used to joke about him, saying Severin had been the county spokesman since Moses was in diapers. He stood when she entered, towering over his desk. From his stooped shoulders, aluminum-gray hair and the deep lines on his forehead she guessed he probably had his pension secure and was coasting toward retirement.

He greeted her and offered a chair. They sat and he said nothing for a few seconds, regarding her from behind heavy-framed glasses that made him look owlish. Finally, he asked, "You wanted to see a list of those who made public comments. Are you looking for something specific?"

Digger gave him a quick account of the solar project and what she had heard about the complaints made at the commission meeting.

Severin nodded then picked up a sheet of paper. "I've got the list of those who spoke at the meeting. Here," he said, sliding the paper across the desk.

"May I take a picture of the names?"

"I'd prefer you just copy them down." His tone was quiet but firm.

She scanned through the list, noting Murphy and Raposa. There were some other names she recalled from when she was a reporter at the *Courier*—people who showed up regularly at meetings to complain about whatever was bugging them that week.

"How about the minutes of the meeting?"

Rick's eyebrows lifted briefly. "You could find them online."

She shrugged. She'd have a look later. "What about the video?"

He pursed his lips and regarded her with slight irritation. "You could see that online too."

Digger knew she was pushing it but she went ahead anyway. "I just want to hear the public comments about the solar project. I don't know if you remember, but Danny Murphy ran against Representative Ortiz last year and it was an ugly fight. I'd like to hear his actual words if possible and ask you a couple of questions."

He glanced at his watch. "Okay. I've just reviewed the video footage myself. You can use that computer over there to watch it. But I need to leave in about fifteen minutes. I have a dental appointment."

He led her to a desk on the other side of the room and tapped on the keyboard. When the screen flashed, he hit another key and started the video. "Use this to advance, that one will adjust the play speed. If you have headphones, you can plug them in there."

Digger sat and followed his instructions to advance the video to the point where she recognized the beginning of public comment. She waited while two people spoke, then Murphy stepped up to the lectern. He greeted the commissioners by name, then began his comments warning them that if the solar array was allowed to proceed the county stood to lose 'thousands of dollars' from all the 'high dollar' visitors that would come to his new resort. Digger had heard the same complaints dozens of times. It was his next words that caught her attention. "The state representative behind this project also plans to ban activities like enhanced drilling techniques, sometimes called fracking. Those activities are essential to oil and gas production here and bring valuable revenue to the state's education system. Is that what we want?"

It was a direct attack on Maria and a complete fabrication. She watched as Murphy returned to his seat and consulted with someone next to him whom she didn't recognize. She stopped the video.

"Rick, could you have a look at this please."

Severin rolled his chair over next to her. She pointed at the man beside Murphy.

"Do you know this guy?"

Severin peered at the image for a few seconds. "Hmm, I think that's Martin Granger, he's a lobbyist."

A lobbyist? Who was this guy? And why was he there with Murphy? Whatever it was, it couldn't be good for Maria.

CHAPTER 31

Heart pounding, Digger sprinted down the hallway and clattered down the stairs. In the foyer she flicked a glance at the digital clock, 10:25. Roscoe said the plumber couldn't come until eleven—no point in going to the office.

What to do first?

Her brain raced. She wanted to call Maria and tell her what Murphy had said, but Maria would be in a classroom, unavailable. Manny needed to know too. She punched his number, praying he would pick up.

He did.

"Hey, any way you could meet me?" She tried not to sound anxious, but he picked up on it.

"You okay?"

"Yeah. I just have a lot of stuff I want to share. Can you meet in about forty-five minutes at the usual spot?"

"Umm, yeah. I can swing it. See ya."

Her thoughts whirled as she sped toward Santa Fe. Maria had said Paul Marquez mentioned there'd been a lobbyist with the industry group he'd met at the resort. She hadn't been able to remember the lobbyist's name but she said the group represented oil and gas companies. Marquez had warned Maria they might oppose what she wanted to do.

Could the guy that was with Murphy at the meeting be the same guy Marquez met? If so, what did that mean?

            ➤

She arrived at the gas station cafe, ordered a couple of burritos and sat at a table near the window. Manny walked in a few minutes later. She waved, held up the paper-wrapped burritos and handed him one as he slid into the chair opposite. "Here, it's still warm. I figured you wouldn't have much time so I ordered for you. Cheese, bacon, pappas and green, right?"

"Thanks. I'm pretty hungry."

When he took off his jacket, she saw he was wearing a shabby sweatshirt. That struck her as odd. Manny was careful about his appearance and sweatshirts weren't his thing.

"You look a little rough," she commented. "Stressful morning, or did you have a bad night?"

A lock of hair slipped from his ponytail as he shook his head. "It's Lina. She wants to get back together."

"I thought she was the one who left you."

He exhaled, sounding frustrated. "She can't make up her mind. Part of her wants to be back on the rez with family. And part of her wants to be in Santa Fe."

"With you?"

He shrugged. "I'm not even sure about that."

Digger was tempted to pat his arm but she knew that would bother Manny more than reassure him. "I'm sorry, man. Girls who can't make up their mind can wear you out. I know. I dated a lot of them before I met Maria."

He gave a lop-sided grin. "Well, we didn't come here to talk about that. What gives?"

"There's a lot. Go ahead and start eating your burrito because you'll probably be done before I get to everything."

She told him what she'd learned talking to Carmen's sister Elena, and about the woman who had responded to the appeal for information at the fundraising event. Then she mentioned Danny Murphy's effort to stop the solar project.

At that, Manny paused, his half-eaten burrito mid-way to his mouth. "I don't get it. What does Danny Murphy and the solar project have to do with Carmen and Nancy and all this other stuff?"

Digger leaned on her elbows, keenly aware of the clattering sounds from the kitchen, the voice of the cashier, and truck engines outside. "Maybe nothing," she began. "It's like this. Maria has publicly announced she will continue Carmen's work. Carmen's stance on renewable energy made her pretty unpopular with some people. Murphy was already pissed because he lost the election to her. So now he's protesting the solar array, saying it threatens his luxury resort."

Manny waved a hand impatiently. "Yeah, I get all that but how does it tie back to what Nancy was saying, or how she ended up in the cathedral with a fentanyl overdose."

Digger looked down at her burrito still in its paper wrapping and now cold. When she looked up Manny was staring at her, eyebrows raised.

Seeing his skeptical expression, she wondered again if she was making connections where there weren't any. "I dunno. I hoped I'd find a connection from that drug bust. That maybe the dealer's uncle might be the Billy Switzer Nancy mentioned and he knew Carmen. But that went nowhere," she shrugged. "Still, I think there's another angle we should look at. Have you ever heard of a lobbyist called Martin Granger?"

Manny set down the remains of his burrito and leaned back

in his seat. "Hmm, name sounds familiar," he said slowly. "If that's the guy I'm thinking of, I saw him a few times at the legislature last session. He gets around."

Digger leaned closer. "He was at that meeting with Danny Murphy."

"Where are you going with this?"

The sharpness in his voice stunned her. The times they'd worked together they'd developed a bro-like camaraderie, joking and sparking ideas off each other. *What was eating him today?* "Remember there was an industry group that tried to get Carmen defeated at the last election?"

"Okay, so they don't like her stance on electric cars or whatever. What does this have to do with Maria's solar project?"

"Oh, come on! You said you saw him around the legislature last session. What if this lobbyist guy works for the group that went after Carmen?"

Manny shook his head, his face a stubborn mask. "Digg, I still don't see it. I think you're just pissed about this because you think Murphy or this guy might threaten your girlfriend's project."

"Wife!" she said, angrily. "Maria is my wife—and yes. If this Granger guy is hooked in with Danny Murphy, I think he could be bad news for her."

Manny shook his head. "I think you're going off on another wild goose chase."

Just then his phone pinged. He read the message, winced, then looked back at Digger. "I gotta go."

"But…"

He stood up, grabbed his jacket and turned toward the door. "Thanks for the burrito. I'll get back to you."

"What the fuck? Manny?"

Dumbfounded, she watched him leave and saw his orange Beetle speed out of the parking lot. What was eating him? They had worked on so much together. She thought they were on the same page with this. Was he really quitting now when they'd come so far?

Mumbling angrily to herself, she got in her car and headed back to Albuquerque. Halfway there, her phone rang.

Roscoe.

She let it go to voicemail. He was probably worked up over some minor crisis. With Roscoe there were always crises. She wondered if she'd made a mistake taking this job. Right now, there were no alternatives.

Chapter 32

Chris Lovington stood beside his car unwilling to move despite the chill morning air that pinched his cheeks. He was late to work, but he stood rooted to the spot. One minute he looked at the Wendell Chino office building's nondescript tan exterior, the next out at the snow-topped outline of the Sangre de Cristo mountains. Then he glanced up again at the solar panels that shaded the parking lot. Why didn't people understand that the future lay in solar and wind energy? The heat, the wildfires, the lack of rain. The signs were all there.

That's what his campaign to become governor was all about. He wasn't interested in power for himself. It was the chance to bring real change, something to benefit New Mexico and put off the worst effects of drought for a few more years. Instead, his dream foundered because he fell for someone's cynical plan to use a solar project to exact revenge for an old political rivalry—and Danny Murphy was part of that plan.

He had been shocked when Ed Silva called and told him how Murphy had shown up at the county commission meeting complaining about the new solar project. It was as if his past was coming back to haunt him. It was at times like this that he most missed his wife: raged against the aneurysm that had taken her. Then he rebuked himself, trying to remember his faith. He looked again at the distant mountains, recalling the words of a Psalm. 'I will lift up mine eyes unto the hills, from whence cometh my help.'

Sighing, he turned toward the building. After his humiliating election defeat, he felt lucky to have a job. He started toward the building and was almost at the door when his phone rang.

"Chris, this is Paul Marquez."

Lovington remembered Marquez from the meeting at the pueblo where they had shown the NovoSolar executives the solar site. He tried to recall other details. Oh yes, the man was a lawyer in Albuquerque and served on the House Economic and Commerce Committee.

"Morning, Paul. What can I do for you?"

Marquez said he had spoken with Maria Ortiz and wanted to meet with him urgently to talk about Murphy. "I can come to Santa Fe this morning if that helps, Chris."

Lovington thought for a minute then suggested a quiet bookstore near the center of town. "I can meet you there at noon. They have a cafe. We can get a sandwich or something."

Just before twelve, Lovington entered the bookstore cafe from the narrow street and peered down the long room with its book displays, wood-topped tables and array of comfy chairs. The warm aroma of coffee was welcome after his walk from the downtown parking lot. He spotted Marquez browsing at one of the book stands.

Lovington approached him. "Find anything interesting?"

"Lots of interesting titles, if only I had time to read."

Once armed with coffee and sandwiches, Lovington led them to the table farthest from the entrance. Watching the other man fold his long legs under the table, Lovington was reminded of an old friend who ran track at his high school in Clovis. Marquez's voice brought him back to the moment.

"Thanks for agreeing to meet me at such short notice, Chris," Marquez began. "I wanted to get your take on this guy Murphy. As I recall, Murphy was somehow involved with that solar scandal during your election campaign last year. Am I right?"

Lovington winced. He hated being reminded of that fiasco. How he'd been so trusting and naive that he ignored all the warning signs. He hoped he'd put all that behind him. Murphy's reappearance threatened his peace of mind.

He sighed. "You're right. Danny Murphy was an investor. I think he was the only real investor, everything else was a sham. The state was going to kick in some funding for the access road to the solar site, which, conveniently, went right by the entrance to his resort development. I think you get my drift." Lovington paused.

"So, he was going to get a big boost for a small investment. That didn't work out, so now he's opposing the new project." Marquez raised an eyebrow, questioningly. "Sour grapes, you think?"

Lovington sipped his coffee, savoring the bitter taste of the espresso. How to answer Marquez? After the call from Ed Silva, he checked into Murphy's background. What he found convinced him that Murphy was likely motivated by a grudge against Maria Ortiz.

"You could call it sour grapes. I'd say revenge," he acknowledged. "Murphy's a developer and he's out to make money. My guess is he was trying to get elected last year so he could get his hands on more state money for his pet projects. When he lost to Maria Ortiz, he was furious, and this is his way of getting back at her."

He waited for a response, but Marquez was staring at the table, twirling the coffee spoon in his long fingers. Lovington continued. "I also think Murphy's working with someone else on this. Do you remember there was a big fight in Las Vistas a couple of years ago? A group was protesting a new road to a subdivision because it would damage a historic chapel. The person leading that protest was Maria Ortiz and the subdivision developer was Murphy's business partner Johnny Raposa."

Marquez's face registered a glimmer of recognition. "Hmm. As I remember, that's when the press started looking into Raposa's other deals and found he owed the county several million. He ended up in jail, didn't he?"

Lovington nodded. "Exactly, and I'm betting Raposa blames it on Maria Ortiz."

Marquez continued to stare at his hands clasped around the mug containing his now-tepid coffee. The sandwich remained untouched on the table.

"What you say makes sense." He set down the coffee mug and looked up at Lovington. "But I believe there's more to it."

"What do you mean?"

"It's like this. The legislative session is two months away. During the last session, Maria publicly supported Carmen Lawlor's stance on renewable energy. Now she's announced she will carry on her work. That makes her a target."

"For whom?" Lovington had a good idea but wanted to hear what Marquez thought.

"Chris, you've been around New Mexico politics long enough to see how young ambitious people get crushed. Anyone who tries to make changes runs up against a steamroller of vested interests. They get ground down till they give up or lose an election."

Lovington met the lawyer's gaze. Yes, he knew how careers were destroyed. As a young man he'd worked on a campaign that wrecked a man's life and he'd lived with the guilt ever since. He wondered if Marquez had heard the stories. Was that why he'd made the remark? He said nothing and waited for the other man to go on.

A few seconds ticked by, then Marquez said, "Maria Ortiz reminds me of Carmen Lawlor. Four years ago, when Carmen arrived at the Roundhouse, she made it clear she wanted to change things. That upset a lot of people. Given time, they would have beaten her down like all the others—if she hadn't had that accident at the wind farm."

As Lovington heard the words it hit him. He stared at Marquez, mouth open, seeing the lawyer's eyes widen as he too grasped the possibility. They stared at each other for a moment. Then Lovington said quietly, "You think it wasn't an accident."

CHAPTER 33

It snowed again during her trip back to Albuquerque so it took longer than Digger had estimated. It was nearly two o'clock by the time she arrived at the little house on Harvard. She was reaching for the knob when the door flew open and Ginny stormed out nearly knocking her over.

"What the hell, Ginny?"

Ginny's face was a mask of fury, cheeks red, mascara smeared, lips twisted in a grimace.

"He fired me!" She spat the words as though Digger had done the firing. "Good luck keeping this shitty little rag going. I'm going back to Florida!" She swept past and stomped across the yard. Her long coat caught in the gate as she slammed it. "Godammit!" Snarling, she wrenched it free, ripping it in the process.

Digger closed her eyes, waiting for the sound of Ginny's footsteps to recede down the street. She took a deep breath to summon reserves of patience before venturing inside. Still reeling from Manny's desertion, she didn't need another Roscoe drama right now. However, instead of the tantrum she expected, she found her editor calmly typing at his computer. He barely looked up when she sat down in front of his desk.

"Okay, what gives? Ginny nearly flattened me on her way out. She said you fired her."

"Yup," he said, bushy eyebrows raised. Taking off his glasses, he began to clean them with exaggerated concentration as he said, "Ginny was supposed to be covering the school shooter trial this morning." From his high-pitched tone Digger knew he was inwardly seething. "But no," he went on. "I got this call from the 'Au Naturel Spa' saying she'd left her purse there after her massage appointment. They'd found her business card with the office number on it and thought she needed to know where it was."

A spa! That was rich, even for Ginny! The thought of her luxuriating on a massage table while she was supposed to be working made Digger laugh so hard that she had to make a quick trip to the toilet. Mercifully, it had been fixed. When she emerged, Roscoe was humming to himself. He looked up.

"I'm glad you find it so amusing," he said. "It also means you're it. I'm going to contact all the freelancers and put the word out, but in the meantime we're kind of up shit creek. So, can you go down to the courthouse and get me some kind of story."

Digger nodded. She'd have to catch up on the solar business later. She checked her phone, hoping for a message from Manny. Nothing. She tried Lynda Bernal's contact again, still no answer. She left another message, grabbed her backpack and headed downtown.

➤

It was long after dark when she drove back to Los Jardines. A quarter moon hung low in the sky, casting a pale silvery glow over the land. Lights gleamed from the homes dotted across the valley each side of the winding road up to the village. She found Abuela in the kitchen, peering into the oven, watched by Lady Antonia from her favorite perch on top of the pantry cupboard. A rich aroma of stewed meat and spices filled the air.

Digger dropped her backpack on the table and flopped onto the couch.

"Is Maria home yet?"

"Hola, Cowgirl," Abuela said, glancing over her shoulder. "Maria is in the studio."

"Bad day?"

Abuela nodded. Digger's heart sank. She dragged herself off the couch and headed out to the studio. Maria hadn't turned on the main light or the space heater. The tiny shed that served as Maria's studio was breathtakingly cold. Digger noticed that the landscape she had been working on for the community Christmas show was on the worktable. On the easel, where the painting had been, Maria was making a charcoal drawing. Digger had never seen her create anything like it. She had drawn a stark, surreal desert landscape. Dominating it, she had sketched the unmistakable image of a wind turbine and the distorted figure of a woman. Her windswept hair whipped around her as she stared, eyes wide at a giant blade that looked poised to cut her down.

Digger looked at it, unable to speak.

Maria, her eyes still on the drawing, said quietly, "I couldn't paint. I had to draw this. I've been seeing it in my dreams."

She turned to Digger, her face pale, expression bleak. Digger put an arm around her shoulders.

"Murphy is spreading lies about me again," she said, voice taut. "Someone emailed accusing me of trying to ruin the state's economy. Somebody else warned me to stop working on the fracking ban."

Alarmed, Digger sank to her knees, thinking of the video, Murphy's angry words at the commission meeting and the image of the man seated beside him. She told Maria what she'd seen. Then, trying to sound calm, she said, "It could be Murphy, or one of those groups that targeted Carmen. Remember, Paul Marquez told you people might try to stop you." She took hold of Maria's hands. "Hey, Love, I know you. You don't give up. You always fight for what you believe in. You'll get through this. I know you will." She leaned forward and kissed her.

They held each other for a long time in the dimly lit studio.

Finally, the chill forced them to return to the house. After dinner, they snuggled on the sofa while Abuela dozed in the over-stuffed armchair with Lady Antonia on her lap. A fire burned in the kiva-style fireplace that dominated the corner of the living room and the scent of piñon wood permeated the air. Digger closed her eyes, breathing the scent of Maria's hair, grateful they could retreat to this old adobe home with its walls that seemed to grow from the earth like a living thing. She wanted the moment to last.

Maria's voice woke her. "It's time for bed, mi amor."

Digger groaned. She didn't want to move. On the way to the bedroom, she checked her phone again. Still nothing from Manny or the mysterious woman who had called Lynda Bernal. She had started to wonder if it was a hoax and the caller was playing a sick prank.

Half an hour later, she had just turned out the bedside light when her phone rang. Wearily, she picked it up and peered at the screen. Manny. Abruptly, she sat up, answered, and mouthed, "I have to take this," at Maria.

"Hey? It's late, what's going on?"

He gave a long, tired-sounding, sigh. "Digg, I wanted to apologize for today. I heard what you said, and everything made sense. I think you're right about this Switzer guy. I just don't know how we can prove it. Last time I checked the so-called 'investigation' in Quay County was going nowhere."

"What about the second car? And what Jake saw on the video? Someone was there with Carmen at the wind farm that morning. And what about the OMI report?"

"Like I told you, the investigation is stalled. And even if the official OMI report confirms that Nancy OD'd on fentanyl, I don't know if that helps us."

Digger couldn't believe what she was hearing. She had never heard him sound so defeated. "Manny, we can't let this go. It's a big story. We have to look into this guy." She paused, then decided to go ahead and tell him about Murphy and the solar site protest, maybe it would spur him out of his slump. "Manny, I need your help. I don't know how much time I'm going to have. Roscoe fired Ginny today and I'm going to have to take up the slack. But I am not giving up. We can't."

A long silence.

Finally, he said, "I haven't told you why I ran out on you today."

Digger recalled the moment just before he left. "It was that message, wasn't it?"

"Yeah," he said, quietly. "It was from Lina. She told me she's pregnant."

"You're sure it's…?"

"I'll let you know." He ended the call.

Chapter 34

The next day, Saturday, dawned clear, bright and warmer. A thin layer of snow still blanketed the upper slopes but it had melted from the foothills. Digger rose, put on trail shoes, and headed out for a run leaving Maria and Abuela enjoying a second cup of coffee. The trail that passed close by the end of their street, wound southward, snaking between clumps of juniper and gnarly piñon. Despite the sun, a chill hung in the shaded areas and she increased her pace.

She kept thinking about Manny's news. When she told Maria she had sounded delighted, saying Manny would make a great dad. Her reaction gave Digger a niggling suspicion that Maria was envious, but she didn't want to say anything. Now was not the time. She knew it was selfish, but she resented the distraction brought by Lina's pregnancy. Right now, she wanted Manny to focus on helping her with the investigation.

Back at the house, she fixed herself a bowl of oatmeal while Maria went to her studio and Abuela left to visit her neighbors. With the house to herself, she could start the research on Billy Switzer. First, she scoured all the social media platforms; searching for Bill, Billy or William Switzer, but there were only a handful of hits that looked credible. Reluctantly, she decided to try Sylvia's husband again. Neal Logan had been pissed off when she'd called him before, but his advice had been, "Talk to that asshole Billy Switzer." Well, she would ask his help to do just that. Luckily, the man's number was still in her notes. She dialed and hoped he would answer.

"Hello? This is Neal."

"Hi, this is Elizabeth Doyle, we talked recently."

"I told you not to call me again."

"I know. I'm really sorry, but the last time we talked, you said I should track down Billy Switzer. I'm having trouble with that and I was hoping you could help me. I just need to know what he did after high school."

There was a long, angry sigh, then, finally, "Look, all I remember is he left town. I think he went to Colorado. He wasn't my favorite person. You could try calling Jody Trent, I met her at a reunion and she said she'd kept in touch with him."

"Can you give me a way I can contact Jody?" Digger pressed.

"Yeah. Gimme a minute."

She heard rustling, a dog barking, a TV in the background. At last, he was back and gave her a number.

"Thanks, I appreciate your help."

"Fine. But don't call me again, and I mean it!"

Digger got up, made herself another cup of coffee and peered out the window. The clear brightness of the day tempted her to stop work and go outside again. A short hike with Maria, maybe? Then she thought of how busy she would be during the workweek. With Ginny gone there would be no time. She turned back to her desk, picked up her phone and punched in the number for Jody Trent.

A woman's voice answered. "This is Jody. If you're calling about the futon, hon, it's already gone."

"No, I'm actually a reporter with *The Searcher*. I'm doing some research for a story about Carmen Lawlor. Neal Logan gave me your number, he said you might be able to help me with some background on Billy Switzer."

"Oh, I heard about poor Carmen. What a tragedy! Her and Bill were friends in our senior year."

"Neal said you kept in touch with Billy after high school," Digger prompted.

"Neal? I always liked Neal," Jody said. "So sad about his wife Sylvia. That was a shock to all of us. Anyway, he's right about Billy. We did stay in touch, at least for a few years. You know how it is, you get busy with kids and all. Anyway, after high school, Billy went to Colorado to study pharmacy. Then he worked for one of them big chains for a while. I forget the name. A few years later, somebody told me he was a drug rep. You know, one of those people that push pills to the pill pushers." Jody giggled at her own joke. "I can see how that work would suit him. He was always good at charming people."

"Do you know how I could get in touch with him?"

"Oh, I'm sorry, hon. After he and Margaret got divorced, I just lost touch. It was like he disappeared. His phone number didn't work no more. I even tried his work and they told me he quit. Listen, hon, I'm sorry I can't help you anymore. I've gotta go take something out of the oven."

Digger thanked Jody, hung up and studied her notes. Switzer's career path, from pharmacist to drug rep gave him the right knowledge to harm Sylvia and Nancy if he wanted to. If only she could find a way to contact him. Frustrated, she stood and walked to the window hoping for inspiration. Frost glistened on the surface of the adobe wall. Beyond it, sunlight gilded the twisted arms of the cholla cactus. She watched the light seep down the mountainside. Something Jody said tugged at her mind like a crumb stuck between a tooth. Then it struck her. What about Billy's ex-wife?

She rushed back to the table, grabbed her phone and called Jody again. "Hi, sorry to bother you, I was wondering…"

"Oh, it's you again."

"Yes, I just thought, would Billy's ex-wife know how to reach him? You didn't say whether you had talked to her. What about kids?"

"No, hon. They didn't have no kids and Margaret was no help. She never liked me much."

Margaret. Billy's wife was Margaret. Jody had said the name before but it didn't register. The property records showed Margaret Switzer as the owner of the drug bust house.

"Did they have a nephew?"

"I have no idea. I do have to go now, I've got people coming over for lunch." Jody ended the call.

Digger's heart raced. Maybe she was right all along. She was about to call Manny when the front door opened with a blast of cold air.

Maria rushed in, shivering. "Brrr! It's freezing in the studio. I couldn't stay out there any longer." She rubbed her hands and looked around. "Abuela still out?"

Digger nodded. "She's still over with José and Ana."

Maria glanced at the table where Digger's notes lay spread around her laptop. "Oh, mi Amor, you're always working!"

"Says she who never stops!" Digger said, laughing. The phone beside her laptop trilled. She picked it up and saw Manny's name.

"Hi," she said, cautiously.

"Hey, Digg. I was wondering if you and Maria would like to get together for lunch today. We could meet at that place in Bernalillo."

This was not at all what she was expecting.

"Uh, sure. We'd love to."

They agreed on a time and he ended the call without any further explanation. Digger set the phone down and looked at Maria, perplexed.

They took Digger's Subaru and parked on the main street a short distance from the restaurant. The Copper Kettle was famous for its carne adovada, and popular with families on weekends. As soon as they walked in, Digger caught the warm scent of grilled meat and green chile. Manny was just inside the entrance, smiling, the flat tweed cap on his head, his arm around Lina. Wrapped in a long quilted coat, her dark hair braided to show off silver-and-turquoise earrings, Lina beamed at them.

Whatever issues they'd had, Digger thought, they must have worked them out.

"Glad you could come," Manny said, in greeting. "You remember Lina?"

A server led the way through the crowded dining room to a table in a corner where the walls were hung with black-and-white prints of the old sawmill that had once been the heart of the town.

During the meal, Manny made no reference to the investigation, instead he joked with Digger about their days at the *Courier*. At times he brought Lina and Maria into the conversation as they shared anecdotes about their families and growing up in Crownpoint. Digger noticed the adoring way Lina's eyes rested on Manny. Maybe she really did want to be with him, if so, she was happy for Manny but she was impatient to talk with him away from Lina. She was bursting to tell him what she'd learned about Billy Switzer.

When they left the restaurant, the four of them lingered a moment on the sidewalk. Maria caught Digger's eye.

"Hey," Maria said, grinning at Lina. "I know this great little ice cream shop down the street. Let's go check it out."

Digger knew Maria was giving her an opening to talk to Manny and shot her a grateful look. Maria linked arms with Lina and Digger fell in step with Manny behind them. As they walked, Digger filled him in on what she'd heard from Jody Trent.

Manny listened without comment and when she finished, he

continued walking without saying anything for several seconds. Digger waited.

Finally, he half-halted and turned to her. "I think you're on the right track, but all the stuff about the nephew's drug arrest or his background in pharmacy, that could just be coincidental."

Digger stopped abruptly. "Come on! It makes sense!"

Manny looked at her, shrugged and called out to Lina. "Hey babe, order me a Rocky Road, two scoops, in a cone and save us seats."

"Mine's a salted caramel," Digger shouted, and when they were out of earshot, she turned back to Manny. "I guess you and Lina figured things out."

He gave her an enigmatic smile. "Yeah. You could say that."

He looked away abruptly and started walking again. She knew she would get nothing more from him about Lina or their relationship. In any case, it wasn't her business.

"So, what do you think we should do about Billy Switzer?"

He looked back at her, shaking his head. "I think we may be going down the wrong track on this whole thing."

"What?" Digger faced him, jaw open.

He halted, looked around at the street, then back at her. "Remember that letter you found in Carmen's backpack? I told you I'd run it by a doctor friend of mine. He finally got back to me this yesterday." Manny paused.

Digger's chest clenched. "Wow. Why didn't you call me before?"

"I know. I meant to but I was kinda busy. Lina and I had a lotta stuff to work out."

"Okay. Well, what did he say?"

"He said those kind of results would typically indicate a serious liver condition."

"How serious?"

"Probably cancer."

CHAPTER 35

The Las Vistas golf club sat on a gentle rise of ground overlooking the city's older neighborhoods. Paul Marquez parked his Lexus next to a line of golf carts and headed toward the sprawling tan stucco building that reminded him of the elementary school he had attended in the early 1970s. The air was fresh and crisp and the fairways and greens closest to the club house shimmered with frost in the morning sun. To the east, a slim layer of cloud lay draped like a scarf over the crest of the mountains.

Inside, the place smelled faintly of warmed-over coffee and bread. A muscular young man in a Kelly green fleece jacket with a club logo emerged from a side door and asked if he needed help.

"I'm supposed to be meeting Danny Murphy," Marquez said, glancing around.

"Oh, Mr. Murphy will be in the Zia Room, he and some of the staff meet there every morning. It's right down there on the left."

As he approached, the door opened and two young men in green golf shirts, carrying laptops, emerged. They left the door ajar but Marquez knocked anyway and waited until he heard a man's voice say, "Come in."

Marquez had never met Danny Murphy. Before his conversations with Maria and Chris Lovington, he knew the man only by his reputation as a developer, someone who had come to New Mexico from the Phoenix area looking to capitalize on cheaper land and an influx of sun-seeking retirees. He'd called Murphy after he talked with Lovington. When they spoke, he asked for a meeting to discuss what he carefully referred to as, "problems with the solar project." He half expected Murphy to be defensive, but he was upbeat and eagerly suggested they get together at his "club".

Marquez entered the Zia Room and found the developer and two other men seated at one end of a long table made of heavy-looking dark wood. One of the men was Martin Granger, he didn't recognize the other, a broad-shouldered guy with a beard.

Granger jumped out of his chair and strode over to shake Marquez's hand, beaming. "Great to see you again, Paul."

The sight of Granger at the meeting he'd requested with Murphy alarmed Marquez. The only reason he could think of for the lobbyist to be there was because he was helping Murphy in his effort to halt the solar project.

"Good to see you too, Martin," he said, hoping it sounded genuine.

Murphy stood and gestured to the other man. "Paul, this is my business partner Johnny Raposa."

Marquez's level of alarm rose. He looked away abruptly to avoid betraying his emotions. Everything he read about Raposa's legal troubles made him wonder how, or why, Murphy would consider having him as a 'business partner.'

"Can I offer you some coffee? Water? A Coke?" Murphy offered.

"Coffee would be fine, thanks. Cream, no sugar."

Murphy nodded, pulled out his phone, punched in a number and ordered the coffee. Then he said, "You wanted to talk about the 'solar project'? While we're waiting for the coffee, let me show you this." Murphy turned to a white board behind him tapped the laptop on the table and an aerial picture appeared. It showed a section of desert landscape crisscrossed with pale lines that indicated streets and a cluster of work sites.

"This is Mesa Vista, it's my dream. I've been planning this ever since I got to New Mexico. It is going to be an exclusive, resort-like, gated community with all kinds of amenities to bring in high net-worth people who are looking to move here from the West Coast. It is going to be terrific for Las Vistas, the county and New Mexico because it's going to put us on the map nationally."

Marquez listened, wondering how much of this Murphy actually believed. He'd heard the same speech dozens of times from lawmakers in Santa Fe, from developers in Albuquerque, even the Chamber of Commerce. And how many times did those projects materialize? He put the odds at about one in fifty.

Murphy tapped the laptop again and the picture zoomed out, revealing a larger expanse of desert. He pointed at a spot in the upper right-hand corner. "See this? This is where those people are planning to put that solar array. See how close it is to my resort?"

Marquez heard the indignation in Murphy's voice. He was about to comment when there was a knock at the door and a young woman with honey-colored blond hair entered carrying a tray with the coffee.

"Thanks, Cheryl. If Melissa calls, tell her I'm in a meeting, okay?"

Cheryl smiled at the two men and Murphy's gaze followed her to the door.

Marquez picked up the packet of powdered creamer—he'd have thought a fancy place like this could do better than that—tipped it into his coffee and stirred. "You know, Danny," he said, "we've got serious problems with drought and wildfires in this state and unless we make changes soon, those problems are only going to get worse. That's why we need more solar energy, that's why a group of legislators is working to draft measures that will enable New Mexico to take advantage of its natural resources in sun and wind to make that shift before it's too late."

Granger interrupted him. "Oh, come on, Paul," he said, smoothly. "Sure, we need the solar and wind stuff. But you know as well as I do that the state gets about half its revenue from oil and gas. Renewables aren't going to make up for that any time soon."

"As far as I'm concerned," Murphy interjected. "Solar and wind are fine, but I don't want anything going up next to my resort."

Marquez decided there was no point pulling punches. "I seem to remember you were willing to invest in that solar project slated for the same location last year. The one that turned out to be a total sham."

Murphy's face darkened and he shot a look at the other two men. "That was different," he snapped.

"How was it different?" asked Marquez, slipping into courtroom mode. "Was it because you stood to benefit from the state paying for the access road to the solar array?"

Murphy thumped a hand on the table. "That's nonsense. I realized that project was phony and I pulled out as soon as I could."

Marquez was feeling confident now that he had Murphy rattled. "Or is it different because Maria Ortiz is the one pushing the solar project this time? I heard you were pretty upset when she beat you at the last election."

There, he'd played the card. He sat back in his chair, studying their faces the way he would the members of a jury. He didn't care if they were mad at him. He wanted to protect Maria.

Murphy's face reddened. "Why are you suddenly so interested in this? Have you got a stake in this solar deal?"

Marquez scowled. "No. I've just been around long enough to realize that this state has a major problem with drought and climate change is making it worse. We need to take steps now."

Murphy's expression was skeptical. "That sounds like politics to me. So, since we're talking politics, I'm going to be upfront with you. I plan to run again because this county needs all the jobs and business it can get. We need the kind of revenue that oil and gas exploration can bring in. That's why I've asked Marty here to help me get support in Santa Fe."

The silence that followed his words lasted for several seconds.

Then Martin Granger spoke up. Holding a hand out in a conciliatory gesture, he said calmly, "Paul, believe me, this has nothing to do with Maria Ortiz. I'm sure she's a nice young woman with high ideals, but she's new to politics and she doesn't know how things work."

Marquez stared at him. It struck him suddenly that Granger spoke like one of those televangelist preachers; handsome face, voice soft and cajoling, blue eyes bright with sincerity.

Marquez leaned forward and said slowly, "Is that what you thought of Carmen Lawlor, too?"

Granger's gaze was steady as their eyes met, but Marquez thought he detected a frisson, like a ripple of movement under the still surface of a pond. Then Granger's mouth widened in a smile.

"Why I thought Carmen was a wonderful woman. I truly did. I even proposed a way that the industry group I represent could work with her. We were going to go public with the proposal at the press conference she arranged out at that wind farm. Unfortunately, I couldn't make it that day, stomach flu. And then there was that terrible accident." He paused, his face flushing. "So tragic."

Were those tears in his eyes? Marquez had heard enough. Whatever reasons Murphy gave for opposing the solar array, he was surer than ever that the real reason was Maria Ortiz.

He took a last sip of the tasteless coffee and carefully set down his cup. He rose, nodding at the three men. "Well, thanks for meeting with me, gentlemen. You made your position clear. I'll see myself out."

—⟶

After Marquez left the room, Murphy rounded on Granger. "What was that all about?" he said, sharply.

"Nothing," Granger replied, face now sullen.

Raposa, who had been silent throughout the meeting, now broke in. "We need to do something about her. Can you stop her, Marty?"

Granger nodded slowly. "It will be my pleasure."

Chapter 36

On the short drive home Maria was full of praise for Lina; how she'd overcome resistance from her family to go work in Santa Fe, how she had plans for what she and Manny could do. She even talked about them moving in together soon. Digger barely listened. Her mind was grappling with Manny's last comment. He was right, once Nancy had told her about the connection with the missing Julie Mondragon, she'd switched focus and all but forgotten about the telltale letter Maria found in Carmen's backpack.

According to Manny's doctor friend, the letter would have been seriously bad news for Carmen. But did that have anything to do with what happened to her at the wind farm?

She thought of Nancy's ghoulish pronouncement as she hovered over Carmen's inert body. "I guess we'll find out if she fell, jumped or was pushed."

Would a cancer diagnosis make her suicidal?

And why do it in such a public place?

And what about the second car?

She'd asked herself those questions a dozen times already. It didn't make sense. All the same, she found it deeply troubling. She had wanted to know Manny's thoughts but before she could ask him, Lina had called saying his ice cream was melting.

When they arrived home, they found Abuela busy stirring a large pot of soup under the watchful eyes of Lady Antonia.

"Ah, there you are," the old woman said anxiously as they came in. "I'm going to need your help with my neighbors. Ana fell and José and I could barely lift her. He's nearly eighty-six you know and his back isn't what it was. We managed to get her into a chair by the fireplace and she's comfortable. I said I'd make them some dinner, but they need someone to bring in firewood and take hay to the donkey."

"I'll do the firewood," Digger volunteered, shooting Maria a glance. "That donkey loves you."

"And I thought *you* were the cowgirl."

"Don't let the boots fool you."

They left Abuela stirring soup and crossed the narrow village street to José and Ana's house. Maria headed around back to the small barn, while Digger knocked at the front door. A man's shaky voice beckoned her in.

She had never been in the old couple's home before and she found herself in a dimly lit, low-ceilinged room. The only light came from two small windows filtered through the fleshy leaves of potted geraniums. It smelled of old dry wood and wool. A dresser in one corner was covered with framed black-and-white photos, a niche above the dresser held a statue of the Virgin of Guadalupe.

Ana was sitting in an old-fashioned armchair in front of the empty fireplace. Her husband, José, was tucking a blanket around her. Digger stepped closer and cleared her throat. He looked around and nodded at her.

Digger nodded back. "Abuela sent me. She said you need help getting firewood."

"Ah, Señora Ortiz, she's so kind," José said. "The wood's round the back. I'd get it myself but my back's..."

"It's okay, Señor José, It'll only take me a minute."

The barn was a corrugated iron structure tacked on to the

rear of the house. On one side a stall had been created from old pallets. She saw the donkey's ears and the yellow eyes of a goat peering at her over the stall. The animal smell hit her like a wave.

"What's with the goat?"

"Donkeys need company. They get lonely," Maria answered, as she tossed a bundle of hay into the stall.

Digger grinned at her. "I learn something new about you every day."

"Ha, ha!" Maria said and jerked her head, pointing to the firewood stacked against the wall opposite.

Digger loaded the basket and took it inside. Guided by José's instructions, she laid a fire and lit it to his satisfaction. Moments later, Abuela came in carrying the soup pot. She directed Digger and Maria to find bowls and utensils in the kitchen and lay out the meal on a trunk that served as a coffee table. They left the old couple eating in front of the fire and returned to Abuela's.

Later, as darkness fell and the three of them sat around the table eating the rest of the soup, Abuela set down her spoon and regarded them solemnly. Digger caught the expression on her face and shot Maria an inquiring glance. Maria gave an almost imperceptible shrug of her shoulders.

"M'ija, Cowgirl, I have something to tell you." Abuela's voice was low and hesitant. They waited.

"I've been thinking about this for some time," Abuela began, "but when I saw my old friend Ana today, it became clear to me." She paused, eyes downcast on the delta of veins on the back of each hand. When she raised her head, her eyes glistened with tears. "When I am gone, I want you girls to have this house."

Maria let out a stifled gasp. "But…"

Abuela held up a hand. "No. No buts. I am going to visit my lawyer next week and make the arrangements."

Maria jumped up, rushed from behind the table and hugged

her grandmother, her long dark hair cascading down and wrapping around them like a blanket.

They wept.

Digger watched, emotions churning. She should have seen it coming. Abuela adored Maria. She was the one who had offered her lesbian granddaughter a home when her parents told her she was no longer welcome. And when Digger had come into Maria's life, Abuela had opened her arms for her too.

Digger had grown to love Abuela and this little adobe house, she loved Los Jardines. But sometimes, just sometimes, she missed her own apartment and the intimacy she and Maria had shared when they first married. They had returned to live with Abuela because Maria wanted to run for a seat at the legislature and Los Jardines was within the district boundaries. Shortly after the election they had talked about moving out, but they all agreed they were happy with the situation. Now Abuela wanted to give them the house. Was Abuela hiding something from them?

Abuela looked radiant now as she suggested a toast and retrieved her treasured bottle of tequila from the kitchen. Maria's father had bought it during a vacation in Mexico some years back and Abuela brought it out on special occasions.

Later, when they were curled together in bed, Digger wanted to ask Maria if she was worried about her grandmother. She was formulating a question in her mind when Maria turned, and, leaning on her elbow, said, "What do you think about having children?"

Digger's stomach flipped. This was the second shock of the evening. Of course, she should have seen this coming too, she thought. The way Maria held her sister's baby, the way she lit up when she was around her young nieces, and the way she and Lina had bonded over the lunch outing today. All the clues were there. Still, she didn't know how to respond. She'd thought about children, she knew lesbian couples who had babies. But it was all in the abstract. Something that happened to other people. People who grew up with parents.

"Um," she said, faltering. "I… I don't know."

Maria put an arm around her. "It's okay. I can tell you're scared, but I think you'd make a wonderful mother. *We* would make wonderful mothers."

Chapter 37

They made love, slowly and tenderly, as if realizing again how much they needed each other, how much they had overcome to be together. Later, as she lay listening to the sound of Maria sleeping, still warm with the glow of her touch, Digger thought of Maria's words. "We'd make wonderful mothers."

Anxiety stirred in her gut. She'd lost her own mother so young that she couldn't remember what it felt like to have a mother, let alone imagine how to be one. For years she had comforted herself with a fantasy about what it would be like to have a mother, that person who would hug her at bedtime, the person she would call when the world fell apart. Then she met Maria. Watching the way Maria and her mother Consuela clawed at each other sabotaged that whole fantasy.

Yet Maria and Consuela had overcome the hurts of the past. They had found a way back to care for each other. It was possible. There was also Abuela; steady, constant, always welcoming, always loving. Abuela had offered them her home and now she wanted to make it permanent. Digger couldn't imagine Abuela not being with them, but the years did not lie. She would leave them someday. The thought of losing Abuela stirred up all those old feelings. Did you ever get over those losses? Did you heal, or did you just forget? Maybe not forget, but just not remember the pain of missing them so acutely?

Maria stirred in her sleep and Digger nestled closer. This was the woman she loved. Finding Maria had turned her world around. A rush of joy flooded through her. She could let go of the past. She could trust Maria. They could be good mothers.

When she woke, Maria was gone. A note lay propped on the bedside table.

NovoSolar emailed. They want to meet me after work today. Am going into school early. Love you. XX.

She stared at the note, disappointed, wishing Maria had roused her. After last night, there was so much she wanted to say. She checked the time on her phone. How long ago did Maria leave? Would she be at the school already? She tried calling but it went to voicemail.

Half an hour later, she was showered, dressed, and working on a bowl of instant oatmeal when her phone rang. She grabbed it, hoping it was Maria. It wasn't, but the number looked familiar. "Hello?"

"This is Donna. You've been trying to reach me."

She sat bolt upright. At last! She'd been trying to contact the woman for days. "Hi Donna, thanks for calling. I'm hoping you might be able to help me with a story I'm working on. It's about Carmen Lawlor and her friendship with Julie Mondragon."

There was a long pause and Digger was afraid Donna was going to cut her off.

Finally, she said, "What do you want to know?" Her voice was barely above a whisper.

"Sorry, I'm having trouble hearing you. Is there some place we could meet and talk?"

"When?"

"Is today possible?"

Another long pause, then, finally, "Okay, how about two

o'clock by the statue in front of the museum in the old part of town."

"Fine, I'll see you there." She would have preferred an indoor location but it had been hard enough to reach Donna, she didn't want to let the opportunity slip through her hands.

At ten minutes to two, she squeezed her car into a spot beside the park near the museum. It would be quicker, she decided, to cut across the park instead of walking along the street. The park was one of her favorite spots in summer. She and Maria spent afternoons lying on the grass there, listening to music. Now, in late fall, the trees were bare and the air rang with the angry sound of leaf blowers.

As she was about to cross the street heading toward the museum, she realized there were several statues. Which one did Donna mean?

She checked the time. Two minutes to go. The most obvious choice was a collection of bronze animals and people on horseback. A middle-aged couple who looked like tourists had stopped in front of it to take pictures. She waited, glancing around anxiously as minutes ticked by. She was about to walk over to the entrance of the museum when she caught sight of a woman hurrying in her direction. The woman wore a long faded blue jacket, a gray knit hat pulled down over her ears and dark glasses.

"Donna?"

The woman halted and glanced around nervously. "Are you...?"

"I'm Elizabeth Doyle, we spoke a little while ago."

More nervous glances, then she edged closer. "I know a place where we can talk. Follow me, but not too close."

She bent and pretended to pick something off the sidewalk, then turned around and walked off in the opposite direction. Digger gave her a ten-second head start, then followed, keeping her in sight as she continued through the landscaped garden in front of the museum and across a small parking lot. She saw Donna turn into an alley and hurried to reach the entrance. Passing under an arch, she found herself in a tiny courtyard flanked by shops selling custom photos, ceramics and yarn. Donna was ahead of her now, exiting the courtyard.

Digger quickened her step, but lost sight of her momentarily. When she emerged onto the street beyond the courtyard she looked left and right, frantically trying to spot the blue coat. She caught a glimpse of it disappearing amongst a jumble of tourists grouped outside a storefront. Keeping the coat in sight, she stepped out onto the street, jogging a short distance before jumping back onto the sidewalk to avoid oncoming cars.

At last, she saw Donna stop, as if waiting.

They made eye contact, then Donna ducked right and disappeared. Digger rushed forward, dodging between people on the sidewalk until she came to the corner where she'd last seen Donna vanish into an alleyway that led off the main street. The alley was dimly lit by the late-autumn sun and so narrow she could have touched the walls on each side without stretching her arms. Donna was somewhere up ahead. As she followed the twisting route, fear stirred in her gut. Was Donna for real? Or was this some kind of trap. She glanced around, tempted to turn back. She took a breath and told herself to calm down. She needed to talk to this woman.

After a few more steps, she turned a corner and suddenly found herself in a courtyard of adobe buildings. Ahead was a doorway and beside it a sign said 'Capilla de Nuestra Señora de Guadalupe.' Our Lady of Guadalupe, the patron saint of Mexico.

Digger stepped through the entrance and saw a brightly colored image of the Virgin surrounded by what looked like ribbed fins. There was a story behind it but she couldn't remember it. Venturing further inside, she found a chapel no bigger than Abuela's living room. The soft contours of the tan-colored adobe walls looked almost like the living hide of an animal. Ahead, taking up most of the wall, was a stained-glass window showing a ring of red circles surrounding a sphere of brilliant turquoise, with an orange sphere at the center.

"That's supposed to represent the sun," said a voice behind her. She jumped.

Donna was standing in a floor-to-ceiling niche, just inside the entrance. Despite the gloom inside the chapel, she was still wearing the knitted hat and sunglasses.

"Why do you want to know about Carmen and Julie?" Donna's tone wasn't exactly threatening, but it wasn't friendly either.

Digger's fear level edged up. For all she knew, Donna could have a gun or a knife concealed under her coat. They were alone in this hidden space. Would anyone hear if she called for help? She took a breath to calm herself. This was the chance she had been waiting for.

"Carmen Lawlor died a few weeks ago. I wrote a story about it and I got some unexpected responses. I'm following up on a tip I was given."

Digger expected a reaction but Donna merely nodded.

She decided to push. "A former classmate of Carmen's contacted me. She wanted me to know that Carmen and two other friends were with Julie the day she disappeared. She mentioned names. One of them was you."

"So?" This time there was a hint of defiance.

"The classmate said you all knew what happened to Julie."

Donna's breaths came louder. When she spoke, her voice was rough, almost angry. "That was twenty-five years ago. What does that have to do with Carmen now that she's gone."

"I believe it has everything to do with what happened to Carmen."

Digger knew she had no proof, only the words of Nancy and the retired sheriff Chuck Mathers.

Donna's reaction was swift and dramatic. She wheeled round, barged past Digger and strode to the end of the chapel. She halted in front of the stained-glass window. Her gulping breaths, loud and harsh, echoed in the gloom. Digger waited.

Donna's heart slammed against her chest and blood roared in her ears. She gritted her teeth and stared at the stained-glass orange sun blazing at the center of the window until she felt calm. She did this every time she came to the chapel. This was the one place she could feel safe, shut out the fears that plagued her sleepless nights. For so long she had managed to quell the fear, then she saw the sign at the fundraising walk. She kept asking herself why she called the number. And when she received a response, she ignored the messages. She didn't know why she finally called back. Now here she was, hearing the young reporter's questions, and she relived all those moments with the police. How long could you keep silent? Did Carmen talk? And was this young woman right to think that her death was connected? How long could you let your life be ruled by fear?

She turned, pulled off her sunglasses and faced the reporter. "If you want to know what happened that afternoon, you need to go to the Malpais. If we go there, I can tell you what I know, but it isn't everything."

Digger caught her breath. This was more than she'd hoped for. "Alright. When?"

"Saturday. I'll text you where to meet me."

She strode past, out the door, and was gone.

Chapter 38

Paul Marquez hurried down the hotel corridor scanning the names atop the doors, looking for the meeting room. Another harrowing call from his daughter had caught him as he was leaving the office and he'd spent nearly twenty minutes trying to calm her. Now he was late. He spotted the sign, knocked, and entered.

Maria was seated at the conference table, light glinting on her dark curtain of hair. She looked up as he came in and smiled.

"Ah, I'm so glad you could make it."

"Sorry, I'm late. Something came up." Marquez took an empty seat, glanced around the table and nodded to Chris Lovington and the NovoSolar representative, Jim Spencer.

Marquez had called Spencer to ask if he had heard about Murphy's complaint at the county commission meeting. He hadn't. When he heard Marquez's news, Spencer said he would arrange a meeting to discuss how to respond.

Once Marquez was seated, Spencer stood and leaned over, letting the tips of his long fingers rest on the table. "I requested this meeting today because I understand there is opposition to the solar facility my company is planning to build." He looked around the table as if waiting for comments. When no one spoke, he addressed Lovington. "Chris, I'd like to know just how serious this is. I know about the history of the other project you were involved with, but I thought we were cleared to proceed."

Everyone's eyes were on Lovington who looked as if he'd been caught naked in public. Marquez hadn't had a chance to tell him about his meeting at the golf club. It would have been better to have that conversation before talking to Spencer, but right now Lovington looked as though he needed to be rescued.

"Jim," Marquez said, "there is widespread support for your kind of project. I happen to know that the opposition you refer to came from a developer who has a personal grudge against Representative Ortiz. Mr. Lovington and I will go talk to the county people and I am sure we can resolve the problem. This kind of 'not-in-my-backyard' stuff is all too common I am afraid."

The look Lovington shot him was pure gratitude.

Spencer sat and turned to Maria. "What do you know about this developer?"

Maria frowned. "Paul is right," she said. "This man ran against me in the last election and lost. He's been claiming the election was unfair. So, yes, he has an axe to grind. But we need to focus on the bigger picture. The next legislative session is only two months away and projects like yours, Jim, help me convince more people that renewable energy sources are a viable alternative to the way we have been doing business in this state. Carmen Lawlor was my mentor and friend and I pledged to carry on her mission. She had been working on proposals that could radically change our economy and she was about to go public with them when she died. That's why this is important to me, to us all."

Maria's voice rose louder and higher as she spoke. Marquez's heart ached with admiration as he listened, watching the fierce passion in her eyes. She even looked like Carmen, with her face lit by the same fiery conviction. It reminded him why he had wanted to be in politics, the burning desire to serve, to bring about something better. He used to have that same passion. What had happened to him? Did he just become inured to the daily grind of morally sordid decisions, the veiled threats and the expected quid-pro-quo. He wished there were more people like Maria Ortiz, they were like young tree saplings, full of promise and needing so much protection. He needed to protect her.

Lovington spoke up then. "Jim, I can assure you that my department is behind this project. I talked with people in the governor's office a couple of days ago—you know he's not a big fan of wind and solar—but the feedback I got was that he saw this as a good opportunity. I think he's afraid of negative publicity because of the circumstances of Representative Lawlor's unfortunate accident at the wind farm."

"I see," Spencer said. "Well, you've done a lot to reassure me. I'll fill you in on what we've got planned for the next few weeks."

Marquez did his best over the next half hour to listen to the details Spencer laid out but his mind kept straying elsewhere. He wondered how much Maria had done to get other legislators on board with her work. She would need every vote she could muster if she hoped to get her proposals through the maze of committees before it made it to a final house vote. More than that, he worried what Murphy's plans were.

As they wound up the meeting, Marquez again assured Spencer that he and Lovington would talk to county officials to convince them that the solar project should move ahead. Maria thanked him and confirmed her ongoing support, then the three of them left the meeting room. As they walked down the hotel corridor Marquez felt a strong urge to lay a comforting hand on Maria's shoulder. At that moment, he was thankful for Lovington's presence. This was not the time to make a fool of himself with a woman who was only a few years older than his daughter.

"You were very brave in there," he said.

Maria stopped in the middle of the corridor and shook her head. "I just keep thinking about Carmen and how much she wanted to make a difference and then I... it was so awful what happened to her." Her voice caught.

Marquez shot a glance at Lovington who nodded back at him.

Maria looked from one to the other. "What? What are you thinking."

Lovington closed his eyes briefly as if he were steeling himself for what he was about to say. He took a large breath. "Paul and I think what happened at the wind farm was not an accident?"

Maria exhaled slowly as if her whole body were deflating. Then she rallied, shook her head. "I've wondered it myself a thousand times," she murmured. "My wife is a reporter and she's investigating rumors. I know Carmen had enemies, but I can't believe... Or maybe I just don't want to." She pressed her hands to her face. Finally, she straightened her shoulders and faced Marquez. "Why did you tell Jim Spencer that Danny Murphy is trying to stop the solar project because of a personal grudge against me? Have you talked to him?"

"Yes, I have. I'm sorry. I haven't had a chance to tell either of you yet. I met with Murphy and his so-called 'business partner' Johnny Raposa on Friday. I know you have a history with them, Maria..."

She interrupted, jabbing a finger in the air. "I will not let them stop me!"

Marquez thought fast. How could he calm her? Then he remembered the conversation he'd had with Fred Carter.

"I think there's a way to go around Murphy."

"How?"

"Murphy has engaged the lobbyist Martin Granger to help him. Granger also represents the oil and gas industry group I told you about a few weeks ago. The head of that group told me that Granger had pitched a plan to Carmen, something that would make it look like they were all in harmony. They were going to make a joint statement at the wind farm that day, but he couldn't make it and had to back out."

"What?" Maria frowned. "She never said anything about that to me, and there was nothing in the press release either."

"I'm just telling you what I heard. It might be worth contacting him. If you got Granger on your side, it would go a long way to getting the support you need at the next session and you wouldn't have to worry about interference from Danny Murphy."

CHAPTER 39

Manny Begay leaned against the hood of his car and shrugged. "You think she's blown us off?"

Donna's text had said to meet in a convenience store parking lot off the freeway just outside the city limits. Digger was grateful Manny had agreed to come along today. On one hand, she worried that bringing him might scare Donna off. But after the creepy meeting in the chapel, she wanted backup. She just wished he wasn't so edgy. Manny said everything with Lina was going well, but his body language and his attitude suggested otherwise.

"Donna said she'd be here at ten. Last time I met her she was on time."

"We'll give it five, then I'm outta here."

Moments later a sun-faded gray Honda Civic rolled slowly into the parking lot. Digger recognized the knitted hat and sunglasses. She waved and the Honda eased into a space a couple cars away from Manny's. Donna emerged, glanced around, then approached.

"Who's this?" she said, eyeing Manny suspiciously.

"This is Manny. We're working together on the story about Carmen. You can trust him."

Donna took off her sunglasses and ran her eyes over Manny, as if weighing Digger's words.

"Good, you're wearing boots. You'll need them." Donna's boots looked well worn. She looked around the parking lot again, then said, "Come on, we'll go in my car."

The inside of the old Honda smelled of ancient plastic, cigarette smoke and dog. Before Digger had clicked her seatbelt, Donna had backed sharply and peeled out of the parking lot. She accelerated onto the freeway and headed west.

"Where exactly are you taking us?" Digger asked.

"You'll see."

It was not reassuring. The place they were headed, the Malpais, was a vast area, 160 square miles of lava flows, caves and tunnels. Julie Mondragon wasn't the only person who had gone missing there. Digger glanced nervously over her shoulder at Manny in the back seat. His dark eyes met hers and he nodded. She nearly sighed aloud with relief. They were a team again.

Once they were on the road, Digger asked about the location where they were headed. Donna ignored her, she wouldn't even glance her way. Digger gave up and they made the trip in silence. Reaching the town of Grants, Donna turned south on a two-lane road that meandered through a landscape of straw-colored grass dotted with dark green clumps of juniper. In the distance she saw glimpses of the lava beds stretching like a dark shadow or a lake of black water.

Digger guessed they'd gone about fifteen miles when Donna slowed and swerved into a wide graveled spot off the road. A sign at the entrance to a dirt lane said, "Acoma-Zuni Trailhead." Donna drove a short distance past the sign, pulled into a shaded area with picnic tables, and stopped.

"This is it." She turned off the engine and they got out. She looked around and took a deep breath. "This was where we had the picnic."

Digger had read about the trails in the Malpais. According to the National Park Service website, this one was an ancient route traveled by the Acoma and Zuni peoples, 7.5 miles over jagged lava rocks that could lacerate shoes and skin. Hikers had to navigate their way by sighting a series of cairns.

"Come on, this way." Donna set off briskly toward the trail.

Digger and Manny shared a look then followed.

They hiked for several minutes through scrubland of pale grasses, cholla and juniper. Then, turning a corner it lay before them, an immense expanse of dark and twisted volcanic rock. No wonder the Spanish explorers had called it *malpais,* badlands. Digger's chest clenched. She was glad she had food, water and a pocketknife in her backpack. Especially the knife. She still wasn't sure she could trust Donna. Did she have an ulterior motive in luring them out here?

She stopped and faced the woman, hands on hips. "Alright, Donna, I think it's time you told us what happened that day?"

→

Donna sat on a rock and began to cry. Fear gripped her again as the images flooded her mind. The afternoon, the horror, the endless grilling by the police. The way she'd recited the statement over and over. "We were a bunch of dumb young kids. We just wanted to have fun."

It was time to tell someone. Fear had kept her silent all these years. It was time to speak out.

Now, sitting there, with her eyes closed, it was as if she traveled back in time. In her mind's eye, she was there again. The five of them in Billy's car. The old green Ford Explorer he got as a graduation present. It was mid-afternoon. Sylvia brought a six-pack of beer she'd snuck from her parents. They each drank one and then they hit the trail. She could feel the afternoon heat and hear the voices of the others. They were supposed to be friends. Underneath the surface lay a network of jealousy, lust, and resentment.

As they walked the trail, the sun beat on her head. Sweat seeped down from her armpits. Billy was ahead of her, his arm around Julie, and jealous Sylvia scowling at them. Carmen pretended not to notice. The heat radiated up from the rocks, the disoriented feeling as the beer took effect.

After walking only a short distance Sylvia complained she was hot.

"I'm too hot. I can't go any further. I need to stop," she whined.

So, they all sat under the shade of a big rock. Billy started stroking Julie's leg and then he pulled her up and guided her away. It almost looked like he was dragging her. Yes, that was it. when Julie looked back at the rest of them, she looked scared.

Sylvia just sniggered. "Billy's just hoping to get lucky."

She laughed too because she knew Billy had a reputation. That's when Carmen got mad and told them to shut up.

"Ha, ha! We know why you're jealous!" Sylvia taunted.

Carmen shot her a furious look and jumped to her feet.

That's when they heard Julie scream. "Leave me alone!"

They ran towards the sound, squeezing through a gap between the big rock and a gnarled tree stump. They saw them then, Julie with her shirt half off, Billy holding her by the hair. His face scarlet with rage as he shouted, "I love you, dammit!"

Julie smacked his cheek, screaming, "I don't love *you*. I love her."

Julie broke free and ran.

Carmen charged after her but Billy blocked her with an elbow, knocked her down, and shouted, "This is your fault you lesbo bitch."

Carmen tried to get up but Sylvia grabbed her. "Billy's right. This whole mess is your fault!"

Donna covered her eyes now as if to blot out the memories.

So much time had passed but the images were still fresh.

Carmen's face distraught.

Sylvia holding her.

Billy livid, yelling, "I'm going after her. Don't any of you follow me!"

They waited, maybe twenty minutes. It seemed like forever. When Billy came back, he said he couldn't find her.

Carmen went hysterical, screaming, "We have to look for her, We have to find her!"

They'd climbed over rocks, slipped through crevices, scraped their arms and legs, tore their clothing. They'd called until they were hoarse.

Nothing. No Julie.

Donna opened her eyes. There was no way she could go on. She clutched her arms around her, leaning forward over her knees, and groaned. The memories haunted her dreams. She rocked with the pain of it all. She asked herself for the millionth time why she did nothing. Instead of obeying Billy, she should have followed him. If she had, maybe the last twenty-five years would have been different.

Why didn't she stand up to Sylvia or help Carmen?

She just sat there, frozen and waited, weak and afraid. The fear was like a chronic disease, sometimes quiescent, but always lurking.

—

Digger glanced at Manny, then looked at Donna slumped over, arms wrapped around her knees, as if she were exhausted from retelling the experience.

"Why do you think Julie was never found?" Manny asked.

Donna looked up, face pale, lips trembling. "Billy took charge. He said whatever happened to her was our fault and we'd better all say she just wandered off."

Manny lost patience. "Come on, Donna! You brought us all the way out here to tell us that? We read the police reports."

Her face twisted in a grimace. "Billy was the kind of guy that could make anybody believe whatever he said. And we were young and stupid and we did believe him—at least at first."

"What do you think really happened to Julie?" Digger asked.

A long pause, then. "He killed her and hid the body."

"Why the hell didn't you tell the police? Why keep it a secret?"

Donna leapt up, eyes blazing, face contorted. "Once we'd told the police what happened, he threatened us, saying we had to stick to the story. That's when we realized he'd killed her. That's when I really got scared. Every so often he'd call so I knew he was watching. Then, a while ago, maybe four or five years—it was after Sylvia died—the calls stopped. I thought I was safe, until I heard about Carmen's accident."

Chapter 40

Donna stubbornly refused to answer questions from Digger or Manny on the drive back to the truck stop where they had met that morning. After a few minutes of trying the reporters gave up. Digger stared out the window at the desolate landscape thinking of Julie Mondragon.

Somewhere out there, among those twisted rocks, lay the remains of the girl she had seen in the high school yearbook, pretty and sparkling with life. A life unfinished, her family left with the agonizing hope of a miracle, that one day she would reappear. There had been no miracle and the parents were now dead and so were two of her friends.

Donna pulled into the truck stop parking lot and told them to get out. Her parting words were, "I've said all I'm going to say. Don't contact me again."

They had to jump aside as she sped away.

"Nice one! She nearly ran over my foot!"

Digger took his arm. "Let's go inside. I need some coffee."

They headed into the souvenir store cafeteria that served long haul truckers, tourists and the temporary inhabitants of a nearby RV park, bought coffee and found a table.

"Weird woman!" Digger remarked, shaking her head. "No

wonder she's fucked up. Keeping a secret like that must eat at you."

Manny looked skeptical. "Think about it, though. If she went to the police, she'd have to admit she'd been lying. That, and where's the proof? They never found Julie's body. Seven people have gone missing in the Malpais in the last twenty years. I looked it up."

Digger hated to admit he was right. It was plausible, but the terror she'd felt in Donna's presence was real. When she'd stood overlooking that morass of volcanic rock, like a turbulent black sea, she could easily imagine it. Billy angrily grabbing Julie, her pulling away. A push, a punch, that's all it would take to send her plunging onto a knife-sharp ridge of stone. The area was pockmarked with holes deep enough to swallow a body forever. No, she was not ready to give up.

"Do you think it's strange that she stopped hearing from Billy after Sylvia died?"

"Maybe he moved on with his life, or something happened to him."

"Exactly. Jody Trent said he got divorced and just disappeared." Digger rummaged in her backpack and pulled out a notebook. "I tracked down his ex-wife through the documents I got from the County Assessor and she agreed to meet with me tomorrow after work. Think you could come with me? I'm guessing she could fill us in on parts of this puzzle."

"Well, Lina…"

"Lina what?"

"She wants to look at an apartment," he said, sheepishly.

She could almost imagine him blushing. "That fast, huh? You know, Lina planted an idea in Maria's mind. She's talking about wanting a baby."

Manny raised his eyebrows, incredulous. "You guys?"

"What? I know women couples that have kids."

"Yeah, but?"

"I know, we would need a donor."

"Well, don't look at me."

Digger burst out laughing. "I'm sorry. You're a good friend, but that would just be so wrong! No offense."

"None taken." He smiled.

"Okay, go find your apartment."

➤

The next afternoon, Digger cruised slowly along the residential street, eyeing the numbers. The street was in an older Las Vistas neighborhood of small homes with large untidy front yards. Margaret Switzer's house stood out because it was neatly landscaped with decorative red lava rocks, clumps of red yucca, lavender, and cacti. On the front porch, a couple of iron chairs were leftovers from warmer weather.

A tortoiseshell cat curled in one of the chairs eyed Digger suspiciously as she approached the front door. She was surprised Margaret had suggested meeting at her home instead of a coffee shop or some other public place. As soon as she pressed the bell button, the cat hopped off the chair and began rubbing itself against her legs. Moments later the door opened and the cat darted inside.

Margaret Switzer was an imposingly tall woman, dressed in a long flowing brown garment that looked as though it had been handwoven. She wore her graying blond hair in pigtails that hung below her shoulders. Her face was free of makeup and had a fresh-scrubbed look.

"Elizabeth Doyle?"

Digger nodded.

"Well, come on in." She led the way into a small living room crammed with a dark leather sofa, two huge armchairs, all of which bore signs of repeated cat claw attacks.

On one side of the living room was a counter that divided the space from the kitchen. Digger immediately noticed the smell; something herbal? Floral? Whatever it was she found it almost overpowering. She hoped she could get this interview over quickly.

"Have a seat." Margaret gestured to two tall stools by the counter. "I've just made some of my peppermint and chamomile tea. Would you like some? It's great for anxiety and you look stressed."

Digger's heart sank. She was used to her grandmother's Irish tea, but herbal tea was not a favorite. She agreed reluctantly and Switzer bustled into the kitchen space and produced a pot and two mugs which she filled with a steaming liquid.

"Now," she said, settling herself on the other stool. "You wanted to talk about my ex-husband."

Digger had given brief details of her interest in Billy Switzer because of his friendship with Carmen Lawlor and the Mondragon case. She didn't mention Nancy, Donna or the visit to the Malpais.

Margaret sipped her tea thoughtfully. "Well, I guess I'll start at the beginning. We met when he was in pharmacy school in Colorado. He was doing a summer job at the drug store where I worked."

Pharmacy school. Digger's stomach flipped. Again she thought, someone who studied pharmacy would know all about drugs; legal or illegal. She had to clench her teeth to keep silent while Margaret continued the story of her romance.

She related how starstruck she'd been by Billy; his looks, his charm, his dreams. They'd married, moved back to New Mexico and settled in Las Vistas. "We'd been here a few months when I started hearing the rumors."

"About Julie Mondragon?"

Margaret nodded. "He always played it down. Said he didn't know anything. She just disappeared. After a while I started thinking he might be having an affair."

"What made you think that?"

"It was the phone calls. I'd sometimes overhear him talking to someone, sounded like it was a woman that he'd known for a long time. Sometimes he sounded like he was mad at them."

"Any idea who he was calling?"

Margaret shook her head. "When asked him about it, he'd always say it was nothing, or I was making a mountain out of a molehill. Then he'd get mad at me. Really mad. When I think about it now, I wonder if he is kind of bipolar."

Digger thought of Donna's description of Billy at the Malpais. Her paranoia.

"Did you ever meet Carmen, Donna, or Sylvia? According to the news reports they were with Billy and Julie the day she went missing."

"No. But I know he went to visit Sylvia. He told me she was sick and he wanted to see her for old time's sake. He went down to Las Cruces where she and her husband were living. Right after he came back, he got a call from Neal, saying she'd passed away. Billy was devastated. Cried all night. That did it for me. I accused him of having an affair with Sylvia. We had a huge argument. Next thing, I filed for divorce. He went with it. Just signed all the papers, packed up all his stuff, cleaned out half the bank account and left. He just disappeared out of my life."

Disappeared, the same word Jody Trent had used. "Do you have any pictures of him?" she asked, scanning the room for signs of family photos.

"No. What he didn't take, I got rid of."

"What about Facebook, something you might have posted a few years ago?"

Frowning, Margaret picked up her phone, tapped it, and started scrolling. Finally, she paused. "Here. It's something my nephew sent me." She held out the device for Digger to see.

The photo showed a youth and a man standing in front of a crowd of people, they wore running clothes, fuzzy pink wigs and had numbers on their chests. A sign behind them said, "5th Annual Run for the Cause."

"The man is your husband and the other one is your nephew? When was this taken?"

"Yeah, Tony. He and Billy were close. That was about five years ago."

Tony? Was that the young man she'd seen being arrested on Halloween? She resisted the temptation to ask about him. She was here to talk about Billy.

"You haven't heard from your ex-husband since he left?"

Margaret chuckled. "No, and I didn't try to find him. I wanted to completely change my life——and I did!" She rose from the stool, went into the kitchen and opened a cupboard. She pulled out a tray of tiny glass bottles and laid them one by one on the counter in front of Digger. "In fact, that's why I agreed to doing this interview here at my house. I'm now an aromatherapist and I represent this line of essential oils. Would you like to try some? They're wonderfully relaxing and you do look stressed."

Chapter 41

Half an hour later, and thirty dollars poorer, Digger escaped from Margaret Switzer's aromatherapy session, reeking of lavender and God knows what else. She did not feel relaxed. Instead, her mind buzzed from the conversation. Some of the details clashed. Margaret had described Billy as a charmer but also secretive and moody, possibly even bipolar. She made it clear she wanted no further contact. Was Margaret afraid of him? The word 'disappeared' bothered her. How did a person disappear? They could leave town, move to a different state, go to jail. But they usually left a trace.

Something niggled. Margaret had said, "I want to completely change my life." Then it struck her. Yes, you could change your life, but could you change into a different person? Had Billy changed his name and established a new identity?

On the way home she tried calling Manny, no answer, so she left a message. "Hope you found the place of your dreams. I had an interesting conversation with Billy's ex. Call me later."

Back at the house she found Maria bent over her laptop at the kitchen table, papers strewn all around her.

"Hi love, working?"

As she bent to kiss her Maria recoiled. "Ooh, what is that smell?"

Oh, oh. She'd driven with the window down hoping to disperse the reek of herbal oils but apparently it hadn't worked. "I, uh, had an unplanned aromatherapy session. It was that or lose the interview. I'll go shower."

Maria laughed. "No. It's not that bad. It's just so not you! I've been thinking a lot about what you found out at the Malpais. So, it was true, what the sister said about Carmen and Julie. That must have been who she was thinking of that night at Frankie's. So sad." Maria shook her head slowly.

Digger nodded, then filled her in on what she learned from Margaret Switzer.

Maria's eyes widened. "Now you think because Billy studied pharmacy, he could have given Nancy the drug that killed her?"

"Sometimes I think so, yes." Digger shrugged, closed her eyes. The thoughts kept whirling around. "But I don't know what happened to Billy so I'm stuck." She sighed. "Anyway, what are you up to?"

"Still working on draft proposals." Maria gestured at the papers spread across her desk.

She spent evening after evening on the phone with legislative colleagues, representatives from environmental groups, and energy experts as she prepared for the upcoming session. "We're looking at creating a framework that would reward companies for getting their electricity from renewable sources through a system of credits. At the same time, fossil fuel companies who pollute groundwater or flare methane into the atmosphere, would have to contribute to a fund to pay for the credits."

Maria delivered the speech as if she were speaking at a public meeting and Digger couldn't help admiring her tone of complete conviction. Maria was always all in.

"Maybe you ought to sell Danny Murphy on that idea. Subsidies for solar power at his new resort? He'd be all about that, don't you think?"

They both laughed. "Seriously," Maria said. "I reached out to the oil and gas group to see if we could find some common ground. I just had an email back. Sounds like they're willing to talk at least."

"Have you talked to Paul Marquez about this?"

"He was the one who gave me the idea."

A commotion outside the front door interrupted the conversation. Maria's grandmother bustled in carrying shopping bags, followed by Maria's sister Cristina and her daughter Anabela, similarly laden.

"Abuela, what's all this?"

"Dios mio, M'ija! Did you forget we were doing the shopping today for Thanksgiving?" Maria's hand flew to her mouth. "I'm so sorry. I was working."

Abuela huffed. "Working, always working. You too, Cowgirl!"

Cristina chuckled as she unloaded groceries onto the counter. "Abuela told me you two are making Thanksgiving dinner this year."

Digger shot a look at Maria. She'd thought Abuela was joking when she'd made the suggestion, but apparently not. Maria's wide eyes told her she was just as surprised. Before she could respond, Anabela's small voice piped from under the table where she was stroking the cat.

"Abuela told mommy she's gonna give you her house."

Maria looked aghast at her grandmother. "You told them?"

Digger knew Maria worried her sisters would be jealous or that her mother would think they had pressured Abuela into making the decision. Maria's relationship with her mother was delicate. But Abuela was a woman who followed her own star.

Now, Abuela drew herself up to her full five-foot-two inches and glared at Maria and Cristina. "This has been my house for fifty years. It's my decision who I leave it to. You just have to promise not to paint the door any other color. That *azul* is my favorite."

Digger had no desire to get mixed up in an Ortiz family drama so she tapped Maria's arm, whispered that she had to make a call, and escaped to the bedroom. She quickly opened her laptop and started a search. Ten minutes later, she had the information she needed but she would have to enlist Manny's help. She tried his number again. He picked up.

"Hey buddy, find the home of your dreams yet?"

"Nope," he groaned. "Anything she liked was way too expensive. She doesn't like my place either, that's why we went looking."

"Sorry man. This grown-up stuff is tough. You think you're ready to be a dad?"

"Let's not go there," he said.

Digger knew she'd touched a nerve. She switched gears and told him about her encounter with Margaret Switzer.

"Can you help me with something," she said. "Both Donna and Billy's ex-wife say he 'disappeared'. I think he might have changed his name. You need a court order to do that."

According to her research, if you lived in New Mexico and wanted to change your name, you had to apply to the district court in the county where you'd been living for at least six months. You had to provide a valid reason—situations like divorce, hating your given name or a desire for a life change, were okay—changing your name to escape debts or criminal proceedings, was not. Plus, the applicant had to publish the name change in a local newspaper.

"So, if Billy changed his name for his disappearing act, there would be a solid paper trail," she said. "Of course, he could have gone to a different county or state, but I'm guessing the residency requirement would make it quicker and easier for him to go to the district court in Albuquerque.

"Okay, so what do you need from me?"

"Any chance you could check court records for me? Since Roscoe fired Ginny, he's got me going flat out during the week. Right now, I can't afford to piss-off Roscoe, I need this job."

"Sure," he said after a brief hesitation. "I can squeeze it in, but where do you want to go with this? It's like you're obsessed."

Manny's attitude stunned her. He was always the guy who sunk his teeth in until he found what he wanted.

"Look," she said, trying to keep the disappointment out of her voice. "A girl went missing, three women are dead, and one is scared shitless. They all have links to Billy Switzer. I think he's still out there somewhere and he's dangerous."

Manny was silent for so long she thought he'd ended the call.

"Okay, Digg. I've just been going through a lot of stuff. I'll check court records and get back to you. You can count on me."

CHAPTER 42

Paul Marquez pulled his Lexus into the parking lot at the back of the Saddleback bar. The place was on one side of a courtyard of a former 1950s-era motel. Though refurbished, it kept the vintage turquoise neon sign out front that flashed an image of a cowboy whirling a lasso. Maria said she would meet him there but it seemed an odd choice. He wondered if she had arrived. It was just five o'clock and maybe too early for happy hour. There were only three other cars in the lot.

He entered and gazed around. Whoever refurbished the exterior, had skimped on the interior. A half-dozen picnic tables with wooden benches were scattered around the interior and the ceiling was like a city-map of exposed HVAC piping. It was nearly empty, but he spotted Maria at one of the tables close to the bar. He slid onto the bench seat opposite her and they shook hands.

"Hi Paul, thanks for coming at such short notice."

She wore a pale, wide-necked blouse that grazed the edge of her collar bones, showing off a fine gold chain. It reminded him of one he'd given his wife for her birthday. Stop, he told himself.

Looking up, he smiled at Maria and commented, "Odd place to meet. Must have been a long drive for you. Don't you teach in Las Vistas?"

"I do, but Martin suggested this place. It's different."

"Martin?" He felt uneasy.

"Martin Granger. You suggested I contact the oil and gas group, so I emailed them. He got back to me right away. Said he'd be happy to talk with me."

Recalling his conversation with Granger at Danny Murphy's golf club, he now regretted the advice he had given her. Too late. He noticed a figure in a long, belted coat, walking toward them. Granger.

He waved. "Paul! Good to see you! And you must be Maria?" He held out a hand to her, beaming. "Martin Granger. My friends call me, Marty."

He shed his coat and sat beside Maria. "This place is pretty cool, don't you think? I just discovered it last week."

A server came by and Marquez ordered beers for the three of them.

Granger turned his full attention to Maria. "So, I read the email where you outlined your research, and the concepts that you're crafting into a couple of bills you plan to introduce in the next legislative session. You're talking about big changes and from my perspective, Maria, a lot of that just isn't going to happen."

While he talked, Marquez noticed his face wore the same benign expression he had seen before. The way he made the negative sound like a hidden blessing was part car salesman, part evangelical preacher.

"Most of that research was done by Carmen Lawlor," Maria began. "She was a great friend and mentor to me. That's why I have dedicated myself to continuing her work. Her death was a great tragedy."

"Oh, yes, Maria. I completely agree with you. I admire your dedication. Carmen Lawlor was such a fine young woman. You even look like her. Has anyone ever told you that?"

Maria shook her head, laughing.

"No? I'm surprised." Granger turned to Marquez and nodded, smiling. "Well, anyway she did great work, didn't she Paul?"

Marquez had seen that same smile dozens of times in court. To him it was the visual equivalent of a corporate statement telling employees that cutting their health benefits was in their best interests. He merely nodded back. As soon as Granger was gone, he would warn Maria again.

"So, Maria." Granger's smile widened. "Maybe Paul told you, but I think there are ways the organization I represent can work with you. I talked to Carmen about it and we were going to do a joint presentation at the wind farm that day. Unfortunately, I got food poisoning the night before and I couldn't make it. And then... well, it was so awful. I felt terrible."

Maria frowned. "She never told me anything about that."

"Oh, I can understand how she wanted to keep it under wraps. We wanted to make a big splash. That's why I'm suggesting we could work together on this."

"Really? You'd be willing to do that?" Maria's eyes lit up.

"Yes. I know we can find common ground. We can work for the environment and the economy." Granger let that sink in, then he said, softly. "Maria, I know how much you cared for Carmen, I can see it in your eyes and I've thought of a way we can do this, and honor Carmen's memory."

"How?"

What was the man going to propose? Marquez's alarm level rose as he realized he'd made a huge mistake suggesting she contact him. If Granger was telling the truth about his proposal, why was he also working with Murphy against Maria? Marquez was convinced Granger was playing Maria now. What was his game?

"I think we could go out to the wind farm and make our joint announcement and dedicate it to Carmen. We could even put up a plaque at the site."

Maria was silent, she stared at the table, lips compressed as if trying to hold in her emotions. Finally, she looked up, eyes shiny, and said, "I like that idea."

Granger grabbed her hand. "Good. Believe me, this will bring Carmen the recognition you want for her." He turned to Marquez. "Don't you agree, Paul?"

Without waiting for an answer, he stood and put on his coat. "I'll email you with my proposals." He nodded at each of them and headed for the door.

As soon as Granger was out of earshot, Marquez pushed aside his untouched beer and leaned across the table. "Look, Maria, I have a bad feeling about this. I don't trust everything Martin was saying. Don't forget the organization he works for tried to defeat Carmen in the last election."

"But that's why you suggested I contact Marty. You said he had a plan for a way we could find common ground."

Marquez hoped she would understand his concerns. "I know you want to continue Carmen's work, make big changes. God knows we need them with the droughts and fires we're seeing. But sometimes you have to work incrementally. People don't like change. If you try to do everything at once, you'll get a backlash."

Maria leaned forward, elbows on the table, eyes blazing. "I thought you believed in what I'm doing! If I had done things 'incrementally' as you say, I would never have saved the Spanish Chapel, I would never have been elected. When I commit to something, I do not back down. I intend to honor Carmen's legacy!"

Marquez couldn't help but admire her tenacity, even as her stubbornness infuriated him. "You know Granger is working with Danny Murphy and that other guy, Raposa."

She recoiled. He decided to press his advantage. "I can help you. I've been in politics a long time and I know people. The oil and gas folks play the long game. Granger may have a good plan, but he's out for himself."

"I don't get it. One day you tell me that working him might be the best way to get around Danny Murphy, now you're telling me the opposite. As I said before, I am not going to back down." She stood, shrugged on her jacket and left.

Marquez watched her disappear through the exit door. How could he explain his change of mind about Granger. He thought it might be a way to get around Murphy, but watching the way he talked to Maria made him wary. He understood Maria's loyalty to Carmen, but returning to the wind farm? It was clear now that she didn't want to listen to him. He had to find another way to help her.

He fished his phone from his pocket and searched for articles about Carmen. Scanning through the hits he saw the name—the reporter she had introduced as her wife. He found an email address and typed, *Hello Elizabeth, could we meet? I'd like to talk about Carmen Lawlor. Best, Paul Marquez.* He left his phone number.

Chapter 43

The light glowing from Abuela's little adobe home was always a welcome sight on the dark side street that wound up from the main road. It had been a long, frustrating day, another Roscoe tantrum, an angry city councilor who demanded a correction on a freelancer's story, and her own grinding workload.

Abuela was in the kitchen when she walked in. Mingled aromas of frying meat and spices filled the air.

"Hola Cowgirl. You like chicken, no?"

"You bet."

"Bueno. I'm trying out a recipe from Maria's new cookbook."

Digger grinned to herself. Abuela's curiosity must have overcome her resistance to non-traditional cooking. "Great. Does this mean Maria and I are off the hook for making Thanksgiving dinner?"

Abuela turned around, peering at Digger over her glasses. "I might help you——just a little."

"I will be eternally grateful," she said, and hugged the old woman. Glancing around, she noted Maria's jacket hanging by the door. "Maria in the studio?"

"Si. She was in one of her moods when she came home."

Maria had been edgier than usual ever since Carmen's death. Digger took a breath, willed herself to forget how tired she was, and headed to the studio. She found Maria bent over her drawing board, charcoal in hand, swiftly sketching. Digger approached, leaned over her shoulder and saw the stark image of a wind turbine. As she watched, Maria's rapid strokes created a human form, a woman with long hair, hands outstretched, face upturned, triumphant.

"A different dream?" she asked, touching Maria's shoulder.

Maria set down the charcoal, took one of Digger's hands and kissed it. "In a way." She pushed back from the worktable and turned to face Digger. "I met Martin Granger today."

"What! The guy that's working with Murphy?"

"Yes. It was Paul Marquez's idea. He thought Granger might be able to help me."

"How so?"

"It may sound crazy, but there's a bigger picture." Maria stood and methodically began putting away her art supplies as she talked. "I know Martin is a lobbyist for that oil and gas organization that tried to defeat Carmen. Marquez told me that's probably why Danny Murphy wanted his help to stop the solar project. But he also told me that Granger had reached out to Carmen with a plan for a way they could work together. We've exchanged a few emails and I believe we can do it. He suggested a way we could announce it and honor Carmen. I'm really excited."

Digger listened with growing apprehension. Everything she knew about Murphy had taught her the man could not be trusted. She figured the same went for Granger. But she also knew that once Maria had set her mind to something, it was tough to dissuade her.

"What did Granger suggest?"

"He proposed we go out to the wind farm where we'll erect a

plaque in Carmen's honor— I've already ordered the plaque— and then we'll hold a press conference to announce our joint collaboration. We could do it next Wednesday. That's the day they have early dismissal from school. Since I want this to be like a memorial for Carmen, I don't want a crowd of media people there, but I'm hoping you and Manny can cover the event."

"Did you forget that's the day before Thanksgiving?"

Maria waved a hand dismissively. "We'll be back by early evening. Plenty of time to help Abuela cook."

Digger's fraying patience snapped. She had supported Maria through so much, but this latest plan rang all kinds of alarm bells. Time to speak. "You're not hearing me. Why would you go all the way out there to erect a plaque? You could put it somewhere in Santa Fe where people can see it. Secondly, are you sure you can trust this guy Granger and the oilfield people? That industry brings in millions to the state. They tried to defeat Carmen in the last election. They could crush you."

Maria shook her head. "Things are changing. You see it everywhere, more rules on emissions, more electric vehicles, more jobs in the renewable sector. If I can find a way to work with Granger's crowd we can move ahead together instead of fighting each other."

The thought of Maria returning to the wind farm where Carmen died sounded all wrong. What was Granger's real motive? A knot of frustration tightened in Digger's chest, wanting desperately to make Maria understand.

"You're not hearing what I'm saying," she said, angrily. "It's Granger's involvement you should be worried about. He's also working with Danny Murphy, and that means he could be bad news for you."

Maria ripped her sketch from the drawing pad, scrunched it into a ball and flung it at the floor. "Always the same! Why can't you believe in me! You're being just like Paul! One minute he recommends Granger, the next he warns me off. I *want* to go to the wind farm to honor Carmen. She was important to me."

Jealousy shot through Digger like a hot flame. "Just how important?"

Maria's eyes blazed. "I told you before, I did not sleep with her, if that's what you're asking."

Digger's heart banged hard in her chest. "Are we having a fight?" she asked.

The question hung in the air as if they were sliding toward a cliff edge.

"Yes, I think we are." Maria's voice was flat and cold.

Digger had had enough. She turned on her heel and made for the door. "If you want media coverage, you can call Manny and Roscoe yourself."

She slammed the door behind her, heart pounding and stomped into the house. She gathered a few things from the bedroom and headed out. As she crossed the living room, Abuela called out but she ignored it. Once outside she jumped into her car and sped down the narrow lane. She had no idea where she was going.

Ten minutes later, as she approached the freeway, she pulled over, stopped the car and checked her phone. No messages. She thought for a moment then called Lexi.

"Hey Digg…"

"You home tonight or at the bar?"

"Just got home. I've left Susan running the bar tonight."

"Can I come over?"

"Uh, sure. What's up? You sound terrible."

"Tell you when I get there."

Lexi and her wife, Susan, lived in an old farmhouse on the edge of the city. Motion-sensor lights flicked on when Digger's

Subaru crunched up the short gravel driveway. Moments later the front door opened, revealing Lexi's stout shape. Digger ran to her old friend and hugged her.

"We had a fight."

"Hey, hey, girlfriend, it's okay. Come on inside and let's talk about it."

Lexi guided Digger into the living room and pointed to a sofa where a large black Labrador was curled nose-to-tail. The dog eyed Digger with curiosity and thumped its tail.

"Have a seat. I'll go get us a beer," Lexi said.

Digger eased back on the cushions and stroked the dog's flank, listening to the faint sound of the Indigo Girls playing in the background.

Lexi returned, set the bottles on the coffee table and squeezed in beside her on the sofa. "So, what happened?"

Digger took a long drink and sighed. "I feel like we've been running in parallel tracks ever since Carmen died. It's like we're both obsessed with what happened to her, but in different ways. Maria is set on continuing her work. I'm trying to find out what happened to Carmen. What I know so far makes me scared for Maria but she won't listen."

"Oh, girlfriend," Lexi said, patting her arm, "I know you love her, but Maria doesn't like to be told what to do. Give her some space. You can stay here tonight if you want. You eat dinner yet?"

Digger shook her head.

"I'll go fix us some pizza." She heaved herself up and went to the kitchen.

Digger sat, looking at her phone, tempted to call Maria. Lexi's advice was to give her time. Maybe they both needed time. In an effort to distract herself she checked her email and found a message from Paul Marquez.

Digger stared at the message. She'd only met him once, at the solar project announcement. Why was he contacting her now? She thought about Maria's angry accusation, you're just like Paul!

She tapped in the number. It rang several times, no answer. She left a voicemail. "Hello Paul, this is Elizabeth Doyle. I saw your email. I will call you in the morning and arrange a time to meet."

Chapter 44

She woke early, back aching from a night on a rigid camp bed. Lexi had set it up for her in the cluttered room she used as her home office. She rose, dressed and packed her things. Lexi was already up and fixing coffee. Susan, who had come home after closing the bar, was still asleep.

"You gonna call her?" Lexi asked, handing Digger a mug.

"Think I'll wait a while."

Guilt weighed her down. She'd never walked out on Maria before. Was it jealousy or was it fear? You lose those precious to you and the fear of loss is always lurking.

Lexi gave her a knowing smile. "Just don't wait too long or she'll think you don't care."

The knot of shame in Digger's chest softened. Lexi was the solid friend she needed in moments of crisis. She would call Maria as soon as she got to work.

She didn't have to wait that long. Digger had just started her car when her phone pinged. Glancing at it she saw a message from Maria. "Preciosa, I'm so sorry. Mucho amor."

She tapped out her own apology, then added. *I'll call Roscoe and Manny*. The last part was an appeasement, she still hoped Maria would reject Granger's plan.

As soon as she walked into the office, Roscoe handed her a printout of his story lineup for the day. "I need you to go downtown and talk to some people at that homeless encampment. The mayor's office just issued a press release giving them till the end of the month to move. Get some good pictures."

A trip downtown would allow her to meet Marquez at his office. She called him and made the arrangement. Then she headed to the homeless encampment. The park was on the northern edge of a warehouse area. When she arrived, it was a hive of activity. Dozens of tents collapsed as men, women, children, and even pets, prepared to leave. Those she talked to had no idea where they would go to be safe on the city's unfriendly streets. The photos she took told a bleak story.

Half a mile away, Marquez's office was in one of the tallest downtown buildings. She rode the elevator to the top floor and spotted the sign on the door. "Marquez, Ferreira and Salazar." A receptionist in a neatly tailored yellow linen suit buzzed Marquez and he came out to meet her.

She had forgotten how tall he was, or how formal. His gray suit and dark hair smoothed back over his scalp reminded her of pictures of her great-grandfather. The brown eyes behind his glasses were kind. Smiling, he welcomed her into the office and offered her coffee.

After her experience in the homeless camp, she was grateful to accept his offer and sink into one of the leather-covered chairs.

He studied her for a few seconds, face somber, then said, "I wanted to meet with you because I am worried about your wife, Maria. She told me she's planning to go to the wind farm with Martin Granger, the oil industry lobbyist. I'm afraid that is my fault. I thought Granger might help her get around Danny

Murphy's opposition to the solar project. We had a meeting and that's when I became suspicious. It's not just his association with Murphy and that shady guy Raposa. I can't put my finger on it, but I think Granger has another agenda. It was the way he came on to her." Marquez met her look and quickly waved a hand. "I don't mean in a sexual way, but he was very charming and calculating. He saw how much Carmen meant to Maria and played on it. He planted a tempting idea and she went for it. I tried to warn her against it, against him, but she wouldn't listen. That's why I emailed you."

Digger exhaled slowly, releasing the tension knotted between her shoulder blades. It all made sense now. Maria's angry reaction, her accusation that Digger was behaving like Paul.

"I gather you've been investigating Carmen's death," he continued. "What can you tell me?"

She considered his question. How much should she say? Marquez had shown genuine concern for Maria, he'd supported her solar project. She decided she could trust him.

"Okay. Here's what I know so far," she said and gave him a summary: Nancy's theory about the links with the Mondragon case, Nancy's apparent overdose, Carmen's relationship with Julie, Donna and the visit to the Malpais.

Marquez listened without comment. His expression grave. When she finished, he nodded. "Some of that I read in the news stories. I also understand the Quay County Sheriff's people are investigating a tip that another person came to the wind farm with Carmen the morning she was found. Is that right?"

"Yes. A woman said she'd seen another vehicle there that morning, but she wasn't able to give any details about the make or model or license plate, so that hasn't gone very far."

Marquez nodded thoughtfully, then opened a drawer in his desk and pulled out a notebook. "I've been looking into Granger's background and found very little. He just showed up at the

Roundhouse a couple of years ago, but nobody I've talked to knows where he came from. I'd assumed he was from out of state, but I can't find anything. You do investigative reporting, don't you think that's odd?"

Yes, everything about Carmen's death was odd. Tracks that led nowhere, phantom figures that vanished, rumors. She shrugged but said nothing. Marquez then stood and walked over to the window that ran the length of the room. He stood back to her, gazing out at the view of the city and the mountains beyond. A thin strip of cloud lay draped along the crest, above it the sky was a brilliant blue. The room was so still Digger imagined she could hear the traffic ten floors below.

His voice broke the silence. "What do *you* think happened to Carmen?" He wheeled round, his dark eyes intense.

Digger swallowed. The thought had run through her head hundreds of times but she'd held it back. It was time to speak. "I think someone pushed her deliberately."

"Exactly," Marquez said. He walked over, took the chair beside her and leaned close. "What does Maria think?"

Digger had agonized over that question all night and now, as she talked to Marquez, the answer became obvious. "She knows but she won't admit it. She idolized Carmen. I think that's why going to the wind farm is so important to her. She needs closure. But—" Her voice caught. She swallowed, fighting to keep her emotions in check before continuing. "I may sound superstitious, but I worry about her safety, and going back to that place seems like tempting fate."

Marquez took her hands in his. "I think you're right. I advised her against going but she is determined. I will come to the wind farm with you."

Chapter 45

Digger slipped through the front door quietly, still wracked with guilt for walking out on Maria. Abuela was watching the Spanish-language news on Univision and didn't hear her. The cat, however, leaped down from the counter and rubbed herself around Digger's ankles. At the movement, Abuela turned, saw Digger, and rushed to hug her.

"Oh, my Cowgirl, you came back," she said, breaking into tears. "I was afraid you left us for good. Maria runs away when she gets mad, but you—never, never." The old woman clung to Digger, weeping

The sound of Abuela's sobs made the guilt infinitely more painful. She hadn't thought of the effect her anger would have on this woman who had always shown such kindness, welcoming her into her family, offering her own home. As she held Abuela, the old woman's frail body, felt light as a child's.

She heard Maria's car in the driveway. Kissing the top of Abuela's head, she released her and went to meet her wife. Maria saw her through the car window. Their eyes met, the window slid down and Maria leaned out to kiss her. "I'm so sorry, so sorry," she murmured

Abuela beamed as they came inside, arm in arm. "My girls."

They shared the meal of *calabacitas* with corn tortillas that Abuela prepared. The old woman winked at Digger as she piled food on her plate. "Guess I knew you'd show up. Always hungry, Cowgirl."

After Abuela had gone to bed, Digger eased in beside Maria on the sofa. A fire glowed in the wood-burning stove. Light from a small table lamp gleamed on Maria's dark hair. The silence between them felt safe. She had started to doze when she felt Maria shift beside her. She opened her eyes, sensing Maria had something to say. "What is it?" she asked.

"I had an email from Elena today. She wants to come to the wind farm."

In the turmoil of the past few days, she had forgotten about Carmen's sister. "How did Elena know about it? You only told me the night before last?"

"I posted something online about the plaque for Carmen," Maria began. "She told me she has her sister's ashes and she wants to take them there to scatter them where Carmen died."

Digger recalled her conversation with Elena in the restaurant, how bitter she was that she couldn't attend her sister's funeral. She was glad that Elena had somehow managed to get Carmen's ashes. If scattering them at the place where she met her end was Elena's way of finding peace, so be it.

"Well, since we're talking about the wind farm, I should tell you I met with Paul Marquez today."

"Really? What did he want?"

"Yes. He contacted me saying he wanted to talk about Carmen and what happened to her. He wants to come to the wind farm."

"So, he changed his mind?" Maria said, with a hint of

sarcasm. "He was mad at me when I suggested the trip. I'm glad he reconsidered."

Despite understanding Maria's motivation, Digger wished she too would reconsider and call off the trip. But she kept quiet. She had agreed to go to the wind farm with Maria—even clearing it with her editor—and she would not back down now. "Are you still planning to go on Wednesday?"

"Yes. Martin said he's got to go to Roswell the day before so he'll drive from there and meet us at the site. Elena has asked for the day off and she's driving down from Santa Fe. She can pick me up at school then we can all meet at Paul's office downtown and go from there. Did you contact Manny?"

"He's not sure if he can make it. There's a big trial coming up and he has to cover it."

Maria looked disappointed. "That's too bad."

Digger had a sudden thought. If Granger was a lobbyist, surely he would want to publicize his so-called plan. "What about Martin? Doesn't he have media contacts?"

"I told him I wanted this to be more of a private ceremony."

"Has he given you any details of what he plans to say?"

"He said he'd email me the proposal before Wednesday." She stood and started toward the bedroom. "I'm tired. Can we let this go now?"

Digger waited for a kiss, an invitation. None came. She guessed that the last question upset Maria because she didn't have an answer and she was embarrassed to be caught out. Wearily she rose and followed her wife. Here she was, home again, feeling the same chasm between them.

➤

Wednesday morning arrived cold and clear. She followed Maria to her car and hugged her before she set off for school. "See you at one outside Paul's office, okay?"

Digger tried to keep the anxiety out of her voice but Maria sensed it. "Of course. I'll message you when I leave my school. See you later." Maria gave her a quick kiss on the cheek and opened the car door but Digger pulled her back, wrapping her in a close embrace. "I'll be waiting for you."

Digger watched until her car disappeared down the narrow street.

As soon as she reached her office, Digger contacted Manny, still hoping he could make the trip. He couldn't. He was on his way to District Court when he answered her call. "What about that research you were doing? About the name change? Any luck?"

"It's been complicated. Can't explain now. I gotta go. If the hearing ends early, I may get more information this afternoon and I'll call you."

Later, as she put on her jacket ready to head to meet Marquez and the others, Roscoe glared at her. "You know, I need you here, not gone for half a day. We've done the Carmen Lawlor story to death—no pun intended—I don't see much of a news angle on this."

"Oh, come on, Roscoe. You've got a state representative that died in weird circumstances, another state rep who's carrying on her legacy. A grieving sister. The whole renewable energy thing. It's got potential."

He folded his arms across his chest and glowered. "You better send me something good!"

He was arguing with someone on the phone when she left. She bought a Spicy Italian sandwich from the Subway place down the street, stuffed it in her backpack, and headed downtown.

Fifteen minutes later she walked into Paul Marquez's law office.

They waited, growing more anxious as the minutes passed.

At twenty-past one, Digger's phone rang. When she answered, Elena sounded upset, "I got here and couldn't find Maria anywhere. I just picked up a message from her saying she got a ride with Martin Granger. Nobody told me there was a change of plan."

Digger's anxiety skyrocketed. "There wasn't. Maria told me he was in Roswell. He was supposed to meet us at the wind farm. Hang on, she's trying to call me now. I'll get back to you."

She picked up Maria's call. "What's going on? I've just had Elena on the line. She said you're with Martin Granger."

"Yes, sorry love. Martin arrived here at school saying the Roswell trip was cancelled. He offered to take me to the wind farm and that way we could have time to talk about our plans on the drive. There's a lot of stuff we need to go over so I thought it made sense. He said he'd already cleared it with Paul and asked him to let you and Elena know."

Digger gritted her teeth to stop herself from yelling at Maria. "Well," she said, tightly. "Paul never mentioned anything to me or Elena. Where are you now?"

"We're just east of Albuquerque," Maria answered, ignoring her rebuke. "See you there." She clicked off.

Digger stuffed the phone in her pocket, slumped into one of the leather chairs, and looked at Marquez. "Did Martin Granger call to let you know there'd been a change of plans?"

"No. I never heard from him. Is Maria on the way to the wind farm with him?" he said.

"Yup."

"Call Elena back and tell her to get here as fast as she can."

Chapter 46

They met Elena in the parking lot next to the Marquez's law firm's building. Elena's hair was swept back from her face giving her a severe expression. Under one arm she held what looked like a shoe box. Digger guessed it contained her sister's ashes.

After she introduced Elena to Marquez, they shook hands and climbed into his car.

He tapped in the destination on his navigation panel and looked at Digger who sat beside him in the front. "They've probably got about a half an hour head start on us. I'll do what I can to catch up." With that, he started the engine and drove swiftly through the downtown streets and out onto Interstate 40 eastbound.

Once they were outside the city and beyond the canyon pass through the mountains, Marquez floored it. Maneuvering into the fast lane, he eyed the speedometer hovering on ninety, then nudged it higher. He cursed himself again for suggesting Maria contact Granger.

All those weeks ago, when Fred Carter mentioned Granger's proposal to reach out to Carmen, he'd thought it was far-fetched. But he'd rationalized it. With all the concern about climate change, a public handshake with a renewable energy champion like Carmen Lawlor would look good for the oil and gas industry. It might even help them get their hands on a big chunk of new federal funding. Money was a great motivator.

He recalled the conversation; Carter had said Granger proposed to make a joint announcement with Carmen at the wind farm—but he never went there. Carter said Granger claimed he'd had stomach flu. But did he? Marquez stared ahead at the road cutting a straight line toward the horizon of the Eastern Plains and his stomach knotted.

Digger sat beside him, thinking anxiously about Maria. Why had she changed her mind so abruptly and why hadn't she told her about the change of plan? She glanced around at Elena sitting in the back seat with her arm around the box. "Are you okay?" she asked.

"I just want to know what happened to my sister," Elena said. Her eyes were dull, but her chin was taut, as though she were fighting to keep control.

We all want to know, thought Digger. And Maria had lost all sense of perspective. She pulled her phone out and tried Maria's number again. No answer. Why didn't she pick up?

The miles sped by punctuated by billboards advertising the gift shop at Clines Corners. Beyond that, miles of beige high desert dotted with dark clumps of juniper. No one said anything. Digger checked her phone for the umpteenth time. Still nothing. She turned to Marquez.

"Do you have Granger's number?"

Marquez shook his head.

"Shit." With every minute, every mile, her anxiety grew.

Who to call? Thoughts raced through her brain. Then, finally it came to her. Jake, the site supervisor. She could ask him to call when Maria and Granger arrived. Frantically she searched through her call log. A long list of numbers. Which one was his? She couldn't remember.

She pulled out her notebook and flipped through the pages. It must be somewhere. Manny had given it to her when he'd heard about the second car. Shit, where was it?

There. Finally.

She punched in the numbers and waited, heart thumping. Voicemail. Damn! By now she was ready to scream with frustration. She texted. *Jake, it's Elizabeth Doyle, call me back. URGENT!*

They passed Santa Rosa and turned off the interstate onto Highway 84 toward Fort Sumner. Marquez braked sharply to slow his speed on the two-lane road.

They immediately got stuck behind a slow-moving truck. Digger inwardly cursed at the delay. A few minutes later Jake called and Digger quickly explained the situation.

"They're on their way here, now?" Jake sounded confused.

She tapped speaker mode so Marquez could hear him.

"I don't understand," he said. "I got an email saying y'all weren't coming till tomorrow."

"Who sent the email?" she asked.

"The guy working with Representative Ortiz, Martin something. He said there'd been a last-minute change of plan. Right now, I'm on my way to Tucumcari. I got a message that I had to go make a statement at the sheriff's office."

Marquez shot a glance at Digger and shook his head. "Jake," he said. "Can you hear me? This is Representative Paul Marquez, I'm a lawyer. I think you ought to check with the sheriff's office to see if that message was genuine."

"Really?"

"Yes," Marquez said. "What you said doesn't sound like normal procedure to me. Can you call them and get back to us?"

"Okay. Will do." He clicked off.

Elena leaned forward from the back seat. "What's going on? Who's this guy Jake?"

"He's the supervisor at the wind farm," Digger said.

She waited for Marquez to say something, but his eyes remained locked on the road. Ahead she saw a dark band of cloud. Rain? She hoped it wasn't a storm. The minutes and miles ticked by. Finally, she couldn't stand the waiting.

"What the hell do you think is going on with Jake?" she demanded.

Marquez slid a glance at her, his face grim. "Something's off. First the email changing the day, then the phony-sounding message from the sheriff's office. Someone didn't want him to be there this afternoon, and I'm guessing it was Granger."

She'd suspected this, but hearing Marquez say it aloud was like a punch on a bruise. She remembered the conversation she'd had with Jake when he'd told her about the rancher woman's story and the security video. Jake said he would have been at the wind farm the morning of Carmen's press conference, but he got to work late because he had a message to pick up supplies in Fort Sumner. And there were no supplies waiting for him there that day.

She turned to Elena again. "Remember at the restaurant you told me your sister had been edgy lately. Did she tell you about some health tests she'd had?"

Elena shook her head, eyes wide with alarm. "No. Why?"

Digger debated with herself. Should she tell Elena? If the test results she'd seen were as serious as Manny's friend indicated, why hadn't Carmen told her sister? Maybe there was another reason Carmen was worried. "Did Carmen mention hearing from Billy Switzer in the weeks before she died?"

"If she did, she probably wouldn't have told me. That was a part of her life she never liked to talk about."

Digger let it go. A sign up ahead said it was five miles to Fort Sumner. She tried Jake again. It rang and rang. She was about to give up when he answered.

"You guys were right. I called the sheriff's office and nobody there knew anything about me coming in to make a statement. What the hell is going on?"

"I think Representative Ortiz may be in danger. How soon can you get to your office at the site?"

"I've just left Tucumcari. Maybe forty minutes."

Damn. She'd hoped he was closer. Maria and Granger would probably get there before he arrived. She ended the call and looked at Marquez. "How soon can we make it?"

"The GPS says it's about half an hour from Fort Sumner. These roads aren't the greatest."

Digger pounded her fists on her thighs, thinking about Maria. She had never been more worried. Why had she been jealous? Maria was passionate about her work and fearless. Her need to honor Carmen was no different from all the other causes she plunged into; except that this time it was dangerous.

The rain hit as they left the little town of Fort Sumner behind. Big, fat drops that smacked against the windshield. Ahead, the sky loomed lawyer-suit gray and threatening. She saw the line of wind turbines straggling along the ridge top. A tiny wave of relief washed over her. Then her phone rang. It was Manny.

"Hi, I just got out of court."

"What is it?" In the turbulence of the last few hours, Digger had completely forgotten that Manny promised to call.

"Billy Switzer. You asked me to check if he'd changed his name. It was more complicated than I thought. I finally found it in District Court in Roswell…"

Digger didn't want to hear explanations. "Just tell me. Did Billy change his name?"

"Yup. Billy Switzer is Martin Granger."

Chapter 47

Billy Switzer slid a glance at his passenger. He could tell she was scared. He liked that, the little thrill of control it gave him was a turn-on. She even looked like Carmen. They could almost be sisters. He hadn't expected it to feel this good—or be this easy. She must have *really* liked Carmen. Was it in *that* way? He wondered. The thought of her with Carmen ignited a flicker of jealousy. He glanced at her again and he knew she felt his eyes on her but she wouldn't look at him.

"So, you're doing all this for Carmen?" he asked, hoping for some response.

She nodded, nothing else.

"Carmen and me, we went way back. High school."

Her shoulders moved, a swift intake of breath. Still, she wouldn't look. Damn, she might be gullible but she was tough. He kept on anyway, this was going to be fun.

"I asked her out on a date but she turned me down. I couldn't believe it. No girl ever turned me down. So, I thought I'd get to her through Julie." He paused. "You've heard of Julie Mondragon? Or maybe you've been living in a cave all your life."

The sarcasm worked.

"Of course, I've heard of her," Maria snapped.

"I heard rumors about them," he said. "Carmen and Julie. People at school were starting to say nasty stuff. So, I followed Julie home one day and asked her out, said it would stop people talking."

Poor Julie. He could tell she wasn't into him. The stiff kisses, the way she pulled her hand away when he made her stroke him, while he thought about Carmen. Whose idea was it to go on the picnic? Sylvia. He suspected Sylvia suggested it hoping she'd have a chance with him. She flattered herself.

No, the day worked out quite differently. That was the turning point, the first time he felt that thrill. The moment he dragged Julie away from the others and grabbed her shirt. That's when she told him the truth.

"I only dated you because of the gossip at school. When we go to college, Carmen said we can be together."

Anger surged inside him when she ran away. He charged after her, panting as they dodged the jagged rocks. Then the moment he smacked her and she stumbled, falling at the edge of a ledge.

Twenty-five years later he could still see her face, tear-streaked, desperate.

Still defiant she whispered, "I love Carmen."

Her body fell, bouncing down and down into the dark deep crevice, and the silence.

Maria's voice brought him back to the present.

"You killed Julie!" Maria looked at him with horror and disgust.

"I slapped her and she fell."

He told the others she ran away and when they couldn't find her, he told them they should stick to the story. "If you don't we'll all be in the shit. Unless you want to go to jail you better say nothing."

"And they believed you?"

"I can always get people to believe me." Billy shrugged. "It worked fine till Sylvia got religion and said she had to confess. I wasn't going to have that, so I paid her a visit." He chuckled. "Being a pharmacist gives you some special skills. Poor Sylvia. She had a heart attack. Even her own husband didn't suspect."

Maria said nothing but Billy didn't care. He was on a roll now. He kept talking over the hum of the engine. "After Sylvia, I figured I better lie low. Margaret and I got divorced and I went to Roswell. Got a job as a delivery van driver for a while. Then I changed my name and started working as a pharmacy rep. That led to the lobbying gig."

When he started visiting the Roundhouse he wondered if he'd run into Carmen. Would she recognize him with his dyed hair and beard?

She did.

He remembered the exact instant when they came face to face in the lobby. At that moment he wanted her the same way he had when he was eighteen.

"Hello Carmen," he'd said, smiling.

She didn't smile back. Dark eyes hostile, she'd leaned in close and hissed, "It's time I told the truth about you."

He'd smiled and said, "Oh, I don't think that would do your political career any good, do you?"

A few weeks later, when there was a committee meeting about a new renewable energy rule, he'd seen his opportunity. He pitched the idea to Fred Carter and he'd loved it.

"So, it was your idea to make the big announcement at the wind farm?" Maria asked, incredulous.

"No. She was already planning that. I just told her I could get the oil and gas guys on board with some of her environmental ideas if she would keep quiet. If not, they would fight her every step of the way. She pretty much had to agree."

"Why didn't she tell anybody? That would have been big news?"

"I advised against it and she got that. She knew those good 'ole boys were already dead set against her and she didn't want any trouble from them."

Switzer slowed to take the freeway exit to Fort Sumner. Not long now. He'd made sure Jake, the supervisor, wouldn't be at the wind farm office. All good so far.

"Did you kill Carmen too?" Maria asked, voice raw.

Anger or emotion? He couldn't tell.

"That wasn't my intention. I just wanted to keep her quiet about Julie."

Carmen had agreed to his last-minute suggestion to drive out early and practice their speeches before the media people arrived. He followed her in his own car and parked behind the supervisor's building so he could be out of sight if anyone happened to be watching. Carmen parked in front of the building.

"I guess he's running late," she remarked, as she walked past, noticing that the supervisor's office was empty.

"Let's go up there where we'll be holding the event," Billy suggested, pointing toward the wind turbines.

She even agreed to climb up the maintenance ladder. But that was where she stopped agreeing. "Billy," she said, face grim. "I can't keep silent any longer."

He'd gripped her arms. "You can't tell anyone! It will ruin us."

"You can't threaten me anymore. I've got pancreatic cancer. I've got nothing to lose. So— yes, I'm going public. I owe it to Julie."

"You can't do that!" he shouted.

It seemed that time stopped and he was looking into Julie's eyes as she lay on the rocky ledge. Did he push her or did she fall? He was never sure, just as he wasn't sure now as he watched Carmen's body plummet, landing head-first on the packed earth.

CHAPTER 48

Rain drummed down and Marquez struggled to steer as the gravel road turned to mush. As soon as he pulled to a halt outside the supervisor's office, Digger had the door open and a foot on the ground, her heart thumping hard against her ribs.

"Maria!" she screamed, over and over again.

They must be here somewhere. Her eyes raked the scene. There, hidden behind the supervisor's office stood a black SUV. It was empty. Digger guessed Granger was taking Maria up to the wind turbines.

"Come on!" she yelled over her shoulder. She started toward the ridge where the wind turbines loomed, the great blades—each as long as a jetliner's wingspan—sweeping rhythmically round and round. A dark blanket of clouds obscured the sky. Her feet sank into the soggy gravel. Behind her, Marquez and Elena struggled to keep up.

"Maria!" she shouted again, but her voice was like a droplet hitting a rushing stream. The whoosh of the wind turbines was all around them, reverberating through her chest. It beat louder as she climbed. Rain soaked the hood of her jacket and dripped down her forehead, half blinding her. The incline grew steeper, her feet slipped and twice she nearly fell. Her breath tore raggedly through her chest as she pushed herself. Near the top, she thought she heard a voice.

"Maria!" she shouted.

Then she saw them. Granger's back was to her, one arm wrapped around Maria, the other gripping her hair. He was dragging her. They were twenty yards away, nearly at the base of the first wind turbine. Fury surged through her and she sprinted forward, covering the ground between them in seconds. The roar of the wind turbine blades masked the sound of her footsteps. She grabbed his shirt, wrenching with every ounce of strength. The fabric ripped as she yanked to pull him away from Maria.

Granger tripped, but recovered quickly, whipping around he smacked Digger's face with his elbow. She reeled back, staggering. As he turned, he loosened his grip on Maria. She tore herself away and stumbled, half falling.

"Run!" Digger gasped, then lunged at Granger's chest. She head-butted him, connecting with his shoulder and knocking him off balance. His hands gripped her hair, and pain seared through her scalp. Granger shoved her down and moved to kick her but she rolled aside, scrambled to her feet, and looked around wildly, hoping to see Marquez.

The lawyer appeared at the top of the ridge.

"Help!" she screamed.

Marquez charged toward Granger. The lawyer was still yards away when Granger landed a kick that sent Digger reeling again. Granger blocked Marquez's attempt to tackle him. He smacked Elena with one arm as he passed and she fell to her knees.

Panting, Digger pushed herself off the ground and stood wobbling dizzily. "Where's Maria?"

"I'm here."

Digger caught sight of her, leaning against the tower. She hobbled over and flung arms around her.

"You've got to stop him!" Maria sobbed.

Digger shouted at Marquez but he was already sprinting after Granger. Seconds later they disappeared down the slope. Maria and Elena helped Digger hobble to the edge of the ridge where they saw Marquez chasing Granger toward the cars.

Granger had a twenty-yard head start. He reached his car, jumped in, and backed around the building, spewing gravel behind him. The car sped toward the gate and out onto the country road.

From her viewpoint atop the ridge, Digger spotted a farm road that intersected with the main route to the wind farm. She could see the roof of a truck as it moved slowly toward the intersection. Granger's SUV smashed into the truck just as it emerged from the side road. The roar of the wind turbines muffled the sound, but the impact demolished the car. Even from that distance it was clear that Granger wouldn't be walking away.

They clambered down the slope and joined Marquez to gape at the scene. A field of metal and glass debris surrounded the crash area. Half the front end of the SUV lay crumpled like a soda can beneath the immense bumper of the cattle truck. Steam rose from the mangled mass of steel that had housed the engine. The smell of burning rubber filled the air. Digger closed her eyes. Flashback to her parents' crash. She fought off the nausea and wrapped her arm tighter around Maria.

Another car appeared. It stopped abruptly about fifty feet from the crash site. The door opened and Jake leapt out, surveyed the scene, recognized Digger and Maria and ran toward them.

"What the hell happened here?"

"Watch out! It might catch fire," Marquez shouted.

They waited, then cautiously approached. The crash buckled the driver's door of the SUV and Martin Granger lay, body folded backward, his head nearly touching the earth. His eyes stared blankly at the cloud-filled sky, blond beard dark with blood. He was very dead.

Just then, the door of the truck opened and the driver tumbled out. He staggered to his feet and stared at Granger's body.

"Never saw him coming."

"I'm calling 911." Jake made the call and then pointed to his office building. "Y'all better come inside. Get some coffee and tell me what the hell's going on."

→

While they waited in Jake's spartan office for the sheriff and an ambulance, Maria told her story. Shaking slightly at times as she spoke. She described the moment when she got a call from the school receptionist that someone had arrived to pick her up. Puzzled she went out and found Martin Granger waiting for her. He told her his Roswell trip was canceled and offered to take her to the wind farm. He said he'd already cleared it with Marquez and asked him to let Elena and Digger know about the change.

"The way he said it made sense," Maria said. "Even when you called me a little while later saying Elena was worried, I just thought there'd been a miscommunication. It never occurred to me that he was lying."

She said they had stopped at the Clines Corners Travel Center to get gas. Granger went into the gift shop and returned with a package. He got into the car, then handed it to Maria, asking her if she could put it in the trunk for him. Maria said she'd thought it strange but did as he asked.

"I left my purse lying on the seat. I think that's when he took my phone." Maria said she didn't notice until sometime later when she heard the hum of a silenced phone, looked in her purse and saw it wasn't there.

When she asked Granger, he just said, "You won't be needing it. Oh, and by the way, my real name is Billy Switzer."

"That's when I got scared," Maria said.

She paused and the room was silent save for the distant

whoosh of the wind turbines. Her head dropped, she rubbed at her eyes and groaned. After a moment she took a breath and continued.

"He told me the whole story. How he killed all those women; first Julie, then Sylvia and Carmen to keep them quiet. And when he saw Manny's article, he guessed Nancy had leaked the story. That's when he drugged her."

The sheriff's deputy, the same stern broad-shouldered young man who had responded to Carmen's accident, listened impassively. When she paused, he waited a few seconds then prompted. "What happened after you and Mr. Granger, 'er Switzer, got here?"

Maria exhaled a long ragged breath, then raised her head to look at the deputy. "He told me I had to agree to drop my environmental work and announce that I was resigning from the legislature," she said. "When I refused, he pulled me out of the car and grabbed my hair. He dragged me up the hill toward the towers. That's when the others got here and stopped him."

They heard the sound of the ambulance arriving outside. The deputy nodded at them and made for the door. "Wait here, I'll have to get a statement from each of you. I gotta talk to the truck driver and get the crash details."

Moments after he left Digger's phone rang. Roscoe. "Hey Digg, I'm waiting here with my tongue hanging out. You promised you'd get me something. I don't see anything online yet."

Digger closed her eyes and counted to ten. "We've got kind of a situation here, Roscoe. Give me thirty minutes. It'll be good."

CHAPTER 49

Marquez stared westward toward the setting sun. The rain had stopped and the evening light made everything look two-dimensional in its sharpness. Guilt weighed on him. He felt responsible for what had happened that day. In trying to help Maria he had caused harm.

He glanced in the rearview mirror. Elena and Maria were slumped against each other, alternately weeping or staring blindly out the window. Beside him, Digger's fingers tapped rapidly on the laptop keyboard. Why wasn't she back there comforting her wife, he'd asked.

"People need to know this, Paul."

He shut up and focused on the road again. His stomach twisted at the thought that if they'd arrived ten minutes later Maria could be dead and it would have been his fault. If he hadn't suggested Granger's plan none of this would have happened. Or maybe it needed to happen so Julie Mondragon's family could finally mourn her. So, Elena could know what happened to her sister. The box containing Carmen's ashes still sat in the seat beside her. When the deputies were finished with them and they could leave the wind farm, he asked her about the ashes.

Elena stared back at the spot where her sister died and Maria had so nearly met her end. She shook her head. "I can't leave them here. This place is evil."

He drove them to Albuquerque. As they stood in the parking lot beside his office he asked the question again.

Elena looked at the box she held. "I think Carmen would want to be with Julie." She looked up and met Digger's eyes. "Can you take me to the Malpais and show me where they had the picnic?"

"Of course."

Elena cradled the box in her arms as if she were holding a baby. "Thank you," she whispered. "That way my sister can be at peace."

➤

Digger called Abuela on their way back to Los Jardines and filled her in on everything that had happened.

The old woman was waiting for them when they arrived home. She rushed to the gate and flung her arms around Maria. "Oh, m'ija, m'ija," she moaned over and over again. They clung to each other, Abuela rubbing Maria's back as if she were a small child.

Without thinking, Digger went to the kitchen and began to make tea. That was Grandma Betty's recipe in times of distress. That's what Irish people did, she used to say. Never mind that she'd been in America for forty years.

Later, when they'd settled Abuela, they collapsed into bed exhausted. Aching with tension and fatigue, Digger burrowed close to Maria. Relief swept over her as she felt the warmth from her body. She had been so afraid of losing her. Losing this refuge, this life raft in a world of uncertainty.

"Thank you," Maria murmured. She rolled over and they kissed.

Digger had held in the question all the way back from the wind farm but she couldn't keep silent anymore. "Why, why did you agree to go there?"

A long sigh. "I kept thinking about Carmen—her dedication.

The more Paul warned me, the more I wanted to show I could stand up to them. When Martin, I mean, Billy told me he and Carmen had planned to make the announcement together in October, I thought I could take her place." She paused. "And for Elena, I thought it might give her closure."

Digger still needed to know more. "Paul told me he thought Danny Murphy hired Granger to scare you off. Why do you think he told you about Julie and the others?"

Maria rolled over and laid her face on Digger's chest. "I don't know. It was like he went into this other zone. He just started talking. He killed all those women and got away with it. It was like a game to him, some sick thrill."

Digger squeezed her eyes shut, forcing away the images of Billy dragging Maria and smoke rising from the crashed vehicles. She wondered if Billy simply needed to talk. If you live with a dark secret long enough, does it finally corrode your heart?

"I'm sorry. I let you down," Maria said softly and kissed her,

She felt the tears wet on Maria's cheeks. Wrapping her arms tightly around Maria, she whispered, "You always stand up for what you believe in. I know it puts you in danger. I want to protect you. I want us to get old together—and I do want us to be mothers."

Her heart fluttered as she said the words. Being a parent would be stepping into the unknown. But after the terrifying moments at the wind farm, when life hung in the balance, she knew she didn't want to lose the chance of that experience with Maria.

CHAPTER 50

"Lobbyist dies after revealing links to cold case"
FORT SUMNER-*Lobbyist Martin Granger died Wednesday in a collision with a farm vehicle near the Eastern New Mexico Wind Farm.*

In the hours before he died in a car crash in Eastern New Mexico, Granger revealed he killed Julie Mondragon, the teenager who disappeared in 1998 during a picnic with friends in the Malpais.

The incident happened near Fort Sumner close to the wind farm where Granger and State Representative Maria Ortiz planned to announce a novel cooperation agreement between fossil fuel interests and environmental groups.

Ortiz told the Quay County Sheriff's deputy who responded to the crash scene that Granger drove her to the site. During the trip, she said, Granger told her he had changed his name from Billy Switzer and he had killed his high school girlfriend Julie Mondragon, and State Rep. Carmen Lawlor.

Mondragon disappeared in 1998 during a picnic in the Malpais with Switzer, Lawlor, and two other friends. At the time, Switzer and the others told police she "just wandered off". Despite extensive searches, Mondragon was never found.

Lawlor died in October after a fall from a wind turbine ladder at the same wind farm, where she had planned to make a similar announcement. After Lawlor's death, Ortiz pledged to continue her colleague's renewable energy mission. She said she wanted to make the announcement at the wind farm to honor Lawlor's memory.

Ortiz told Quay County sheriff's deputy she intended to ride to the wind farm with Lawlor's sister. Granger told her plans had changed and said he would drive her to the site. During the trip, she said, he told her about his previous life as Billy Switzer. Hearing the story of how he killed the other women, Ortiz said she became afraid Granger would try to harm her when they arrived at the wind farm.

"Luckily help arrived just in time, or I believe I would be dead like the others," Ortiz said.

It was still early when Digger went out for a run to clear her head from the strain of the past forty-eight hours. The sun peeked over the Sandia crest setting the upper slopes aglow. Frost sparkled on the twisted arms of the cholla cactus.

Stillness.

Not even the sound of a bird, only her feet crunching on the gravel path.

She ran for a few minutes, found a rock, and sat on it. From there, she could see west over the tawny expanse of mesa and the blue outline of the Jemez range. Below her, nestled in a fold of land, was the cluster of houses on Abuela's street. A home that would one day belong to her and Maria. Where one day they could raise children.

When she returned, she found Abuela busy in the kitchen, watched by Lady Antonia from her perch on the back of the sofa. Digger chuckled. "I knew you couldn't resist cooking on Thanksgiving."

The old lady batted a hand at her as if she were swatting a

fly. "I have to make sure everything is done right. Maria said she was making something 'vegetarian.'" She scoffed. "What kind of person eats only vegetables?"

Thanksgiving in the Casa de Abuela was always a family affair; with Maria's parents, sisters, and their husbands and children. This year, Maria had invited Elena, Manny, and Lina to join them. Lina had decided to become vegetarian during her pregnancy.

By afternoon, the aroma of roasting turkey filled the house. Elena was the first guest to arrive. When Digger answered the door, she stepped shyly into the small living room and smiled.

"This reminds me of my parent's home. Thank you for including me today. Carmen and I always spent Thanksgiving together."

They were still in the doorway when a car horn signaled the arrival of Maria's parents. Her father Humberto's voice boomed across the tiny front yard.

"Hola a todos!"

Consuela, Maria's mother, elegant as always in a white silk blouse and navy blue skirt, sidled into the living room. She sniffed the air and nodded approvingly. Hugs all around.

Within half an hour, the rest of the family arrived and the little house resounded with voices and laughter. Digger was handing drinks to her in-laws when she heard the bell on the outside gate. Manny appeared with Lina dressed in a Navajo traditional-style flowing skirt, velvet top, and turquoise necklace. Digger rushed to greet them.

"You look wonderful! Thank you for coming."

Lina smiled. "Thank you for inviting us. It is an honor."

Manny fist-bumped Digger's shoulder. "Great story today. AP picked it up and it's gone national."

"No shit! I bet Roscoe is over the moon!"

Digger's editor sent stories from *The Searcher* to the Associated Press daily but they rarely made national news. "I couldn't have done it without you, buddy," she said, looking up at Manny with a smile.

He grinned back. "You were the one that kept on plugging away at it. Give yourself some credit. You know TV is going to want to interview you too."

Digger shook her head. "Not today. We need time to recover. On Thanksgiving, I only want to be with family."

Abuela came out of the house to call them in for the meal. She had changed from her cooking clothes and wore her lone dress, a floral print creation she found at a thrift store.

Eyeing Lina, she nodded approvingly and said, "Maria has made something special for you, mama."

They had nearly finished the meal when Abuela pinged a spoon against her glass, calling for silence. "I invited you all here today because Maria and her wife have some special news to share."

Stunned silence around the table. Blushing, Digger slid a glance at Maria. When did Maria tell her grandmother? They hadn't agreed on how they would make a public announcement, let alone how they would follow through on their plan. Too late now.

Maria took a long breath, looked at everyone, and said, "Digger and I have decided we want to have a baby.

Later, after everyone had gone home. Digger went out into the moonlit yard and made a phone call. "Donna," she said, "If you haven't seen the news already, Billy Switzer died yesterday in a car crash. I wanted you to know."

There was a long pause, then a faint voice. "Now I don't have to be afraid anymore. Thank you Digger."

The End

About the Author

Rosalie Rayburn is a former journalist and author of the Digger Doyle Mysteries. Her first, *The Power of Rain,* won a National Federation of Press Women Award. The sequel, *The Sunshine Solution,* won first place in a SouthWest Writers contest. She has written for newspapers in Ireland, Norway, and the U.S., covering local politics in New Mexico for nearly a decade. Since retiring, she has walked the Camino de Santiago in Spain and now divides her time between Portugal and New Mexico.

Dear Reader:

I hope you have enjoyed Digger and Maria's story in *Windswept.* Please take a minute to write a review on Amazon and Goodreads.

Be sure to follow me on Facebook and my website, RosalieRayburn.com.